Accidental Twins

A Silver Fox Dad's Best Friend Romance

Unintentionally Yours

Mia Mara

Caught in the heat of one reckless night, I couldn't resist him.
He's my dad's best friend, a single dad nearly twice my age.
But I'm supposed to find him a wife - not carry his twins.

I'm a professional matchmaker for New York's elite.
But my own love life? A total disaster.

I go on a blind date, for research, expecting to meet a stranger.
But instead, I'm locking eyes with Adrian Stone - my dad's best friend.
The silver fox billionaire I've fantasized about for years.

We both pretend not to know each other, but that one night leaves my body trembling and my world shaken.

Now my dad is forcing me to find Adrian the perfect wife... while I'm hiding I'm pregnant with his twins.

How do I focus on finding him a match when the only woman I want him to choose... is me?

Chapter 1

Ava

I knew deep down that it probably wasn't healthy to present as someone I wasn't. But the thrill of channeling the woman I wished I could be instead of the stuffy, affluent daughter of one of New York City's most successful businessmen was too hard to pass up.

Plus, I didn't want Dad to know what I was up to.

"So, *Lily*," Emily snorted, her fingers tapping against the rings dotting my hand from the other side of the table. The cafe around us buzzed with life—locals, tourists, students from Parson's, and families filled the space almost entirely, all with their own agendas and their own plans for the day. "Can you explain how, exactly, pretending to be someone you're not will help you find love?"

"Please don't call me *Lily*," I sighed. The white knit cardigan that covered my arms and tied beneath my breasts suddenly felt far too warm, and the gray and green multi-patterned skirt that reached to just beyond my knees did little to help. "I'm not doing this to find love, Em. It gives me a few hours to escape the world as *Ava* and if I can tell myself that it's for market research, that's all the better."

Emily's tongue clicked. Her blonde hair swayed side to side in its ponytail as her head shook, a knowing grin spreading across her pink-painted lips. If she was trying to fool anyone into believing she wasn't wearing make-up while she was dressed head to toe in Lululemon and looking like she was seconds from sprinting through Central Park, then she was sorely mistaken. The faint green eyeshadow that coated her lids and made her sparkling brown eyes pop was enough on its own to make anyone pause.

"What?" I pressed, meeting her playful gaze as she sipped at her chocolate-dusted cappuccino.

"*Market research,*" she snickered. "If you wanted to escape the world and leave Ava behind for a little while, you know you're more than welcome to hang out at my apartment. I don't understand why you feel the need to go out and meet random men if you're supposedly *not* looking for love."

Lifting the carafe of black, hand-brewed filter coffee, I poured more of its contents into the small cup and raised it to my lips to hide the expression on my face.

I could tell myself I wasn't trying to find love. I could scream it from the rooftops, could tell it to anyone who would listen on the street—in NYC, anything goes—but there was always going to be a part of myself that wished that maybe, on one of these stupid little dates where I gave myself a few hours to be who I wanted to be instead of who my father wanted me to be, that I'd find someone who saw through my fake persona of *Lily* and could discern the things that made me special.

But it had been a pipe dream so far, and so for now, it was just an excuse to be who I wished I could be, even if it was only for a few hours.

"You've gone all quiet."

"Sorry," I sighed, ripping off the Band-Aid and forcing myself back into the moment. "It's market research. It's a nonsense date that will net me information, and that's *it*."

Her pink lips quirked up at the side. "So no sex?"

"No sex."

"That's a shame," she snickered. "You could really use some..."

"And even if I *was* hoping for something real out of this," I interjected, holding her gaze over the lip of my mug, "we both know damn well my father would never let me have it. So let me pretend, or so help me God, you will end up in the Hudson River."

———

Six foot four.

Forty-five—clear from the dusting of gray that only served to emphasize the darkness of his black hair.

Sharp, blue eyes.

A jawline that could cut glass.

A crisp white shirt, leather jacket, and dark denim jeans.

Through the turning glass of the revolving door, I could see him standing in the lobby, his gaze flitting between the platinum watch around his wrist and the people entering through the doors. The description he'd given me of himself was accurate enough that I wondered how many times he'd described his looks to a woman online, but that thought was interrupted fairly quickly by a wave of nostalgia that hit me like a freight train as I readjusted the little knot I'd tied my cardigan into.

I hadn't been nervous about one of these in a long time, and for just a second, I found myself hesitating as I stood there outside the modern art museum. But I then pushed on.

He was easily one of the most attractive men I'd ever seen, even if there was an air of familiarity about him. I almost wished I'd met him on the street or through work or any other avenue than this—any other situation than one where I had lied about who I was and what I did for a job. Maybe, just maybe, I could have let myself go on a *real* date for once that wasn't clouded by fake identities and wishful thinking.

As I pushed my way through the revolving door, and the scent of cedarwood and fruit invaded my senses, I couldn't help but pause.

John, he'd said his name was. But as his intensely blue eyes drifted to mine, a different name came to mind. The likelihood of the man across the lobby being the same man my father had been friends with almost my entire life was small, but not small enough that I wrote it off. This was New York, after all.

I hadn't seen that man in at least ten years. And whoever this was, whoever John claimed to be, bore a striking resemblance to my father's friend—if not for a few extra gray hairs and deeper crow's feet by his eyes. I couldn't say if it was just the time that had passed and the stupid teenage crush that had lingered into adulthood that burned an image of his face into my mind. I couldn't be sure if my impression was tainted by John and his likeness. I couldn't be sure if this feeling was born out of the memory of his cologne and the similarities between them, or if I was staring down a man who could very easily ruin my decision to move to New York City.

If Dad knew what I was doing tonight, my time here and my business would be shut down by the time the sun was up.

But this man...whoever he was—he didn't know me. Even if by some weird happenstance of fate it *was* him, I'd changed a lot since I was fifteen. I doubted he'd even recognize me. I was long past the black hair dye and heavy foundation that had hidden my freckles. These were forgotten, along with my obsessions over Jane Austen and Charlotte Brontë and my flowing, mostly black wardrobe.

And if it wasn't him, all the better. For a couple of hours, I could pretend that the man I'd had the most wildly inappropriate teenage crush on had somehow found his way back to me and was giving me a shot. I could let myself fall a little bit more into the escapism that being *Lily* gave me.

I could leave *Ava* outside.

Chapter 2

Adrian

I spotted her the moment she appeared through the revolving glass doors.

A flash of long, auburn hair, hanging down over one shoulder in waves, caught my eye. Lily had warned me to watch for it—she'd said it was her most prominent feature, but with every clicking step she took in my direction, everything else about her seemed to *shine*.

The freckles that dotted her barely tanned complexion, the green of her eyes that looked almost as though sunlight were reflecting off dew-dampened moss, the flow of her patterned skirt and the white cardigan that stopped just beneath the swell of her breasts—all of it, every bit, was so vastly different from what I'd normally look for in a woman. It gave me pause, if only for just a moment, and luckily for me, she seemed in no rush to get across the room.

Even though her eyes were glued to me, wide as fucking saucers.

I wasn't necessarily unaccustomed to the occasional glance or longing stare from passersby, but something about *her*, something about the glimmer in her eye as she stepped up to me, her mouth moving, but the sound of the crowd drowning her out, was different.

Maybe it was how she was dressed so differently from every other woman I'd dated. Maybe it was how she was twenty years my junior and so obvious that she was going to look up to me. Maybe it was the one auburn brow raising and not a single wrinkle under her eyes. Maybe it was the almost ethereal way she moved, her twitching hands smoothing out the lines in her skirt and playing with the bell-like edges of her white knitted cardigan.

"Are you...deaf?"

Her *voice*. It hit my ears and stirred something, but I couldn't quite figure out why. "Sorry," I laughed, letting my gaze take her in entirely, top to bottom and back to top. "I didn't catch what you said."

Her cheeks reddened. "I asked if you were John," she said. She took a step back, nearly bumping into an older man with binoculars around his neck, and just briefly, her white teeth caught on her cherry-red lips. "I have the wrong person, I'm so sorry."

In a flash, she turned, her long lifting lifting and settling down her back. Somehow, I'd already messed up and spent far too much time ogling her than actually *listening*, and her calling me by my fake name just hadn't registered. It didn't snag my attention like a name was meant to.

Before she could take another step away from me, I reached out to her instinctually, one hand closing around the smallest part of her wrist. Her head whipped around again.

"You don't have the wrong person," I grinned, hoping it was enough of an apology so we didn't have to keep dancing back and forth. "You caught me off guard, is all. You must be Lily."

She blinked at me, her head tilting to the side like a confused puppy. "So you *are* John."

Yes. But no. It still didn't feel right, and I felt bad for lying to her, but I'd stick to the deception. "And you're Lily," I answered. A lie by omission was easier for me.

Her lips tugged up at the edges, and she stuffed her smile down, but not before I could see it. "Thank fuck for that," she chuckled. She took a step toward me, and I let my hand slip from her wrist, the sensation of her skin touching mine fading and leaving me tingling. "Thought I'd just royally embarrassed myself in front of a stranger."

Slotting myself in beside her, I motioned toward the hall on the right-hand side. The slow trickle of foot traffic headed in that direction, and rather than trying to go against the grain as I normally would if I were on my own, I didn't want to be weaving between patrons as I tried to speak to her. "I am technically a stranger, Lily."

"Nah," she laughed. "I've spoken to you at least...twice?"

"Twice," I nodded.

"Not a stranger, then." Her hand reached for a pamphlet in a plastic container hanging on the wall, and a flash of plain, white-tipped fingernails caught my eye. The polish didn't seem to clash with the rest of her outfit—not when everything else was so carefree. Those nails looked more like what I'd seen the women in my office block wear, and I couldn't seem to take my eyes off her hands as she flipped through the pamphlet. "Oh my god, they're showing Ai Weiwei's work this month. How did I miss this?"

Ai Weiwei. She knew who that was. Fuck, that was attractive. "Lucky for you, I bought us tickets to both the museum *and* the exhibition, so..."

I slipped the printed ticket the front desk had given me

out of my jacket pocket and held it out to her. Her head whipped in my direction, those wildly green eyes flitting between mine and the slip of paper in my hand, and for a split second, that motion felt like a wave of memories flooding into the back of my mind. A smile spread across her lips as she plucked it from my fingers.

"I'm not going to lie, I wasn't sure if you'd be excited for it," I chuckled. "You said you were into contemporary. Ai Weiwei isn't only that."

A single brow raised at me as we entered the main foyer. Massive glass panels above let in the cloudy sunlight, painting the marble floor and white walls in little dancing rainbows and soft lighting. People milled about around us, the gentle echoes of their footsteps bouncing through the bright space, but all I could do was look at *her*.

What *was* it about her? She was gorgeous, of course, but my God, it was like I'd been knocked off my game.

"And you said you were into photography, but Ai Weiwei isn't that either," she grinned.

I snorted. "I'm sorry, but *Dropping A Han Dynasty Urn* absolutely counts as photography."

"Okay, and *Ye Haiyan's Belongings* absolutely counts as contemporary art," she smirked. She spun on a dime, flitting in front of me and walking backward toward the exhibition room on her right as if she knew this space like the back of her hand. "And I'd argue that *your* example leans contemporary, too."

I followed her, enraptured by her knowledge of the subject and how little of a show it was. After the two conversations we'd had on that website and the letdowns I'd had before, I'd assumed, wrongfully, that the woman who turned up today would be somewhat interested in art, but mostly interested in sleeping with me. This one, though

—*Lily*—felt oddly like a reunion with an old friend. There was ease and comfort between us that I hadn't expected.

And she was *smart*.

"Contemporary?" I smirked, watching as she walked, slipping through the crowd easily. She maneuvered herself toward the gift shop that stood in the middle of the room to swerve around an older woman, nearly knocking a book off its display, but missing it by a millimeter. It didn't even seem to register for her. "Fine. You can say that. But you can't say that *A Study of Perspective* isn't photographic art."

Her nose scrunched, and shit, there it was again—that pang of familiarity. "The ones where he's giving the middle finger to different landmarks?"

"*National* landmarks," I corrected.

She shrugged. "They're okay, I guess."

"Not a fan of *fingers*, Lily?"

Her cheeks heated as her mouth opened for a retort, but a person walking far too quickly passed beside her. She shifted her weight onto one foot, her hip jutting out to the side to create some space, but she wasn't quite quick enough.

Bodies collided, and she spun, shifting her far more to her left than she had expected.

"Watch out—" I started, but nope, it was already happening. Too late to stop it. Not even my reaching out to her could have helped it, even if I'd managed to grab her.

She slammed into the little display at the gift shop.

A Greek-style column, about waist high, swayed back and forth as she desperately tried to grab for it. Atop it, little replica figurines depicting a scene from what I could only assume was the first Olympic Games started to wobble, and I dashed to her side, steadying them before they could crash to the ground.

But something warm brushed against my hand as the last one slotted back into place. She'd reached for it, too, and for the briefest of seconds, her fingers ran across the tops of mine.

Her face had gone a striking shade of red by the time we'd both retreated.

Only a handful of people turned to look at her, but the woman behind the cash register eyed her harshly, her gaze narrowing as Lily took a step away from the sculptures. "Anything broken?" she called.

"No," I called back. "Sorry!"

"Oh my God," Lily breathed, her fingertips resting against her lips as her gaze switched rapidly between me and the replica artwork she'd nearly ruined. "Why didn't you warn me?"

I blinked at her. "I didn't see her coming."

"I..." She shook her head, her cheeks somehow deepening one more shade of red. "Imagine if that was a real sculpture, John. I could've ruined something priceless."

John. Ugh. Why had I gone with that name? It sounded so wrong, so incorrect. No matter how many times I'd used it, it never hit my ears just right, and something about the way she said it just made my spine stiffen. It wasn't what I wanted her to call me.

———

The freeness with which she offered me information as we moved from exhibit to exhibit was fascinating.

She was an aspiring art teacher and a recent graduate

with her master's in contemporary art theory, along with being a freelance artist on the side. She'd recently moved to Manhattan and was sharing an apartment with her friend, and casual dates were her way of meeting more people and learning the area well. I didn't question how many times she'd been to this museum in particular on dates, but she seemed to know it inside and out, and the moment she told me that her favorite spot for coffee was SUITED, I had to stop for a moment to think.

I knew that cafe. I'd been a handful of times for lunch or on my way to work. My assistant often grabbed coffee from them.

They were in the financial district. As far as I knew, it was their only location, and although I could see an aspiring art teacher who had just moved to the city passing through the financial district once or twice, I couldn't imagine it would be her regular spot. But the way she spoke about it made it seem like she visited it almost daily.

"What about you?" she asked, her head whipping around with a grin so wide I could see the tops of her upper teeth and the thinnest line of her gums. Behind her, Ai Weiwei held the Han Dynasty urn in the first of the three images, poised and ready to drop.

But I caught it.

Not the urn, of course. But it hit me, staggeringly, as she smiled at me like that—why I'd felt those waves of nostalgia and familiarity around her, why it had been easy to talk to her, why it seemed less like a blind date with a stranger and more like reconnecting with an old friend.

Shit.

I wasn't the only one lying about who I was. At least I didn't have to feel as bad about filling her head with the idea of John. He was an idealistic version of myself where I wasn't the owner of an international events planning company, but instead a travel photographer with different tourism companies in my portfolio. I now saw that the face across from me was Ava Riley's, although she no longer had braces or dyed black hair. She'd grown up in the last ten years, so much so that I hadn't even noticed who she was at first.

But I should have known. I should have considered the possibility of running into her at some point. David, her father, had said she'd recently moved to Manhattan, and although I hadn't had the chance to visit his office as of yet, I was surprised I hadn't seen Ava walking around the financial district. From what I'd heard, she'd set up an office for whatever business she was starting in some of the spare, unused offices on David's floor.

"John?" she asked, blinking at me as if I was the one who had gone insane here. Maybe I had. Maybe we both had.

Fuck. I didn't know what to say to her. One minute ago, she had been someone else, someone I didn't know, someone I could freely admit to being wildly attracted to. But now...shit, she was my best friend's daughter. I'd met her when she was *ten.*

But she wasn't ten anymore, and she wasn't fifteen anymore, either.

"Sorry," I said, clearing my throat with a bit of fake laughter. I let my gaze move to the photo of the man behind her, his fingers just barely holding onto the urn. "I missed what you said."

She turned to look at the photograph before looking back at me. "Were you *that* into the picture of him?"

I shrugged. "It's an amazing work to see in person."

She watched me, her eyes practically burning a hole

through my head, and I couldn't tell if the little crease forming between her brows was from curiosity and attraction, or if she'd somehow made the connection, too. Surely, she must have—I barely looked any different than I had ten years ago in comparison to her massive transformation. I'd gone from thirty-five to forty-five, and yes, I'd gotten a few more grays and maybe a handful of extra laugh lines, but *she* had become a full-fledged woman.

A woman that I'd spent the last hour ogling and imagining how many different ways I could fuck her.

I, at least, had a solid reason for hiding behind the persona of John. It kept me away from the women who threw themselves at me solely for my money, and it allowed me to find casual partners that I might not be able to cling to as Adrian. That, and I didn't want to worry about having to disclose my son to anyone I was seeing.

Even if it crossed the lines I'd drawn out so clearly with him.

No lying. It was our one major rule, and every time I did this, every time I left the house to go meet someone, that's exactly what I spent my entire evening doing.

"Can I be honest for a second?" she asked, taking a single step toward me. Her hand came to rest on the length of my forearm with just barely enough weight to feel it over my jacket. Her cheeks warmed again, bringing those freckles I hadn't fully noticed ten years ago right back to the surface. *She has to know.* "I do these occasionally. Blind dates, or whatever. But I think this might be the most exciting one I've ever had."

If she'd said that moments ago, it would have been game over for me. Even now, it almost was. I couldn't deny that I was intensely attracted to both her body and her brain.

The cost of exploring what I felt would be her father potentially murdering me at the golf course next Saturday.

I let out a breathy chuckle as we started moving again, her wistful little movements as she found her stride alongside me feeling far too electrifying. Maybe she didn't know. She would eventually, of course, but could I get away with it until we bumped into each other at the next charity event or party of her father's?

Maybe.

"I can honestly, wholeheartedly agree."

———————

The sun had dipped well below the horizon as we finally emerged from the closing museum. We were among the last to be shooed out, partly because we were so engrossed in a conversation about whether contemporary photography counts as photographic art or contemporary art, that we'd barely had a moment to notice the time, and partly because I just didn't want it to end.

Her hand slipped into mine on the bustling sidewalk beside Central Park. Taxis honked, nightlife roared, and the sounds of the city bled into my mind, influencing me, convincing me that it didn't have to end just yet. Sure, I was meant to be walking her to the nearest subway stop, but we could go *anywhere*.

"Lily," I said. My feet stopped in their tracks, drawing a hasty "*asshole*" from the man who was walking behind me, and before she'd even heard me, she felt the tug on her hand.

She spun around. "Yeah?"

The lights from the overhead streetlamp and the head-lights passing by reflected in her eyes, and for a moment, she wasn't Ava. She was Lily, the mysterious New York newbie who loved art and frequented a cafe on the other side of Manhattan from where she should be spending her time. She wasn't the high-up socialite with a father who was my best friend.

And I could act on that.

I pulled on her hand, dragging her to me, closing the distance.

I let my free hand rest against her cheek, let it erase the little bit of chill on her skin from the late autumn air. I could feel the blossoming warmth across her face as she realized what I was doing.

I pressed my lips to hers, and Goddammit, I'd thrown myself into the deep end.

She melted into me. Her mouth parted, and in an instant, she let me in, and although I hadn't been able to pick up a distinct scent from her in the crowds, the *taste* of her mouth was unexpectedly calming in the sea of chaos.

The moment her tongue dragged across mine, some-thing shifted for her though. I could feel it in the way her fingers loosened in mine, in the way she brought her hand around the back of my neck, in the way she stepped back-ward but pulled me with her out of the middle of the side-walk. She met resistance, and as I dropped her hand to cup her waist instead, I felt the roughness of tree bark scratch against the backside of my knuckles.

Goddammit, I wanted more.

My brain ran in circles as she kissed me, cycling through idea after idea. I couldn't bring her home, not when she could easily run into an image of her father on the wall, not when my son was sleeping on the other side of my penthouse. I could take her to a hotel, but that seemed almost dirty, and even though I had all the money I could ever ask for, I would struggle to find somewhere good enough last minute in Manhattan.

I was running out of options as her lips reluctantly broke from mine, and I said the only thing I could think of.

"I have a boat," I breathed. I wasn't even sure if she could hear me over the sounds around us.

"A boat?"

"It's docked down at North Cove," I said, pulling back just enough to look into her eyes. They flitted anxiously back and forth between mine, and for a moment, I wondered if she really had no idea who I was. "Let me take you out."

"I..." Her teeth dragged across her lower lip just like they had in the lobby of the museum earlier, and for a second, I was right back there, not knowing who she was or what she could do to me. I could live in that a little longer. "Okay."

Chapter 3

Ava

I spent every second of the taxi ride letting lie after lie slip out from between my teeth about my time studying contemporary art at college while wracking my brain to figure out how I was going to avoid him for the rest of my life.

Or maybe I could just dye my hair black again, since that seemed to make such a massive difference.

But as his hand reached out for me from where he stood on the deck of his sailboat, I couldn't help but feel a massive pang of relief that he hadn't realized yet. The likelihood of tonight ending the moment he knew who I was weighed on my mind, and I would lie as much as I needed to in order to keep that from happening.

I took his hand and stepped off the dock, the far too large sailboat rocking just an inch from the inertia. He steadied me before I even had a chance to potentially lose my footing, and for a second, I almost told him that he didn't need help, that I had spent enough time on sail-boats growing up—even this one—and didn't need assistance.

18

But that could raise questions, so I accepted the assistance.

"One drink," I smirked, lifting a single digit between us as I stepped down off the edge of the boat and onto the main deck. "That's it. Nothing else."

The corners of his mouth twitched upward into a smirk and for the smallest of seconds, I let myself take this in, take it all in, as he stepped down to meet me. It was never truly dark in Manhattan, but the clear, black sky behind him mixed with the glittering lights of the city's skyline on his left lit him up almost like a dream, a dream I was sure I'd had hundreds of times in my life. Adrian—or *John*—had littered my thoughts for years, and now here he was in the flesh, likely not believing my insistence on one drink.

It was almost hard to believe that I wasn't dreaming again.

Adrian's tongue dragged across his upper teeth as he chuckled breathily through his nose. "One drink," he parroted. He slipped his hand into mine and dragged me toward the interior of the boat, right where I knew the kitchen and bar were positioned. "And what drink would that be?"

The polished oak door swung open, and he flipped a switch, illuminating the large space in a warm, soft glow. "What do you have?"

He didn't bother dropping my hand. Instead, he pulled me with him as he slipped behind the bar, marble countertops lining either side of us with a wall of alcohol and under-counter fridges to our right. "Everything," he said, releasing my hand in exchange for wrapping it around my midsection. For the briefest of seconds, our chests touched, his warmth seeping into me through his pressed shirt—but then I was lifting, up, up, up, until my rear slid onto the marble countertop. His hips slotted between my open thighs, his jeans catching and pulling just slightly at my skirt. It tugged the waistband just a little lower on my hips, exposing just an inch more of my midriff. "It just depends on what you want from me, *Lily.*"

The bar lights twinkled in the blue of his eyes as he leaned a little closer. Each little line in his skin reminded me that this wasn't just any man who was coming on to me. This was Adrian, dressed up as some strange, different version of himself who went by *John.* This was my father's friend. This was someone I was convinced I would never have the chance to go on a date with, let alone touch, and as I slid my fingers gently across the curve of his jaw and felt each little prickle of his five o'clock shadow, I couldn't help myself.

I'd wanted this for so long with him. Fuck my rules when it came to dates—this was different.

I pressed my lips to his. Taking that plunge *myself* instead of letting him do it felt like I was giving in to something I shouldn't. But this wasn't like how it had been up near Central Park. This wasn't confined and restrained because of the public nature of it.

He wanted more, and it was blindingly obvious here in the privacy of his sailboat.

He kissed me hungrily and greedily, his mouth devouring me as if I were a meal and he hadn't eaten in years. His hand, far larger than mine and so fucking warm, trailed along the top of my thigh over the patterned fabric of my skirt. His other wrapped around the back of my neck, holding me in place and keeping me from retreating from the invasion of him.

But I didn't *want* to retreat.

I wasn't sure exactly how far he would go. Memories of

him hit me the more his cologne demanded my attention, and although I hadn't heard much about him since my parents had divorced and my father left Boston for the shimmering lights of New York City, I had vague recollections of attending an engagement party for Adrian when I was fifteen, just a few months before I'd last seen him. *How many levels of bad is this?*

His hand trailed lower, over the curve of my knee and down around my calf, slipping under the lower hem of my skirt and meeting bare flesh. He gave me an inch of space as he pulled his lips from mine and half-lidded eyes met mine too close to focus on. "If you're truly just here for a drink," he said, his fingers tightening on the back of my neck, "you're doing an awful job of ordering one."

"It's hard to order *anything* when my mouth is preoccupied," I teased. "But I'll take whatever is nicest."

His digits traveled up the back of my leg, pulling the fabric up with it as it pooled on top of his jacketed arm. Slightly swollen lips pulled back into a far too cheeky of a grin, and for the briefest of seconds, his fingers brushed against the inside of my thigh, sending a wave of electricity through me. *Higher,* I wanted to say, but they disappeared as quickly as they'd come, and soon his hand was leaving me entirely and lifting up a bottle of red wine that must have been stored beneath where I was sitting. "*This* is the best bottle I have on the ship."

I almost wanted to scream at him for teasing me just to get to a bottle of wine, but I took it in my grasp and turned it to look at the label. A hand-drawn design of some kind of estate house took up the majority of it, and beneath that, in faded letters, were the words *CHÂTEAU LAFITE ROTH-SCHILD, 2009.*

I knew enough about wine from my father's obsession

with it to know that this was fucking expensive, and it was meant to be aged.

"Do you really want to waste opening a *Lafite* for one glass?" I asked, turning the bottle over in my hands.

"Let's be honest for one second," he laughed, plucking it from my grasp. He reached between my legs again, and my heart rate nearly doubled as he brushed against my inner thigh. Just like he had thirty seconds ago, he retreated, pulling out a multi-faceted corkscrew. "You're not just staying for one drink."

He cut away the top of the wrapping before I could protest and shoved the spiral into the top of the cork, twisting it down until it had almost entirely disappeared.

"Pass me two glasses, would you?" he asked. "They're just behind your head."

The moment his hand flexed, gripping the screw and leveraging it out, I gave up what little fight I had left in me. No going back now.

I spun around, reaching for the thin stemmed glasses with wide tops. Dad used to shout at me for grabbing the small ones whenever he had red wine, and for once, his training paid off. I passed them to Adrian—or *John*—and he carefully poured out two servings worth before handing me one back.

I stared at it for longer than I intended to, watching as it moved in the glass and painted the sides a clear, dark maroon. He watched me closely, his eyes lingering with far too much weight, and every second under that stare felt like a hurricane brewing far too close for comfort.

"Come on, pretty girl," he mocked, clinking his glass against mine. "Even if it's one glass, you have to at least try it."

I wasn't entirely sure how to tell him that I couldn't give

two shits about the wine and just wanted him to take me back to the bedroom I *knew* existed on this godforsaken sailboat, but I obliged, letting the heat of him calling me *pretty girl* settle in between my thighs as I lifted the glass to my lips.

Fuck, it was good.

"There you go," he said. He slipped between my thighs again, sliding his free hand around my waist and settling it on the small of my back. He pulled, and my rear moved along the slick surface, bringing my parted legs directly against his waist. Heat swarmed over my face, and I knew damn well it wasn't from the one sip of alcohol I had taken.

"You shouldn't have opened this one." I swallowed past the lump in my throat and sipped at it again, my mouth salivating from the tannins.

He shrugged. "I've got twenty more at home."

Twenty more. It didn't surprise me in the slightest, but I wasn't supposed to think he was as wealthy as he actually was—not as *John*, at least, and not as *Lily*. Lily knew him as a decently well-off travel expert and photographer, not the multi-millionaire head of a global events planning company. But Lily also wouldn't know how expensive this wine was, and I wasn't sure how exactly to respond in order to fit with the narrative we were both presenting.

"Besides," he started, offering me a little smirk as he set his glass down and brought himself closer, his lips hovering against the shell of my ear, "I find it hard to believe that you'd willingly sit in a taxi for twenty minutes just to have one single drink with me."

An electric current shot down my spine from the heat of his breath. Instinctually, my hand reached for him, landing solidly on the warmth of his shirt between the folds of his jacket, and his answering breathy chuckle only added to the sensation from my ear.

"So tell me, *Lily*," he rasped. His hand found the bare skin of my knee again, and within an instant, he was lifting the fabric of my skirt further, dragging it up my thigh, his thumb caressing the sensitive flesh. "What exactly would you like me to do with you?"

The heat in my cheeks flared further. *What the fuck am I supposed to say to that?* Did he expect me to just be as forward as possible and ask him to bend me over the counter?

"You've been talking all night and you choose *now* to lose your voice?" he laughed.

I swallowed again, forcing words to the front of my mouth and out from behind the vice of my teeth. I already knew the answer, but I asked anyway. "Do you have a bed on this thing?"

He pulled back from my ear, but his face hovered near the side of my face, his eyes locked on me. His hand moved just a little higher up on my thigh, just a couple of inches from dangerous territory. "I do."

I clutched the fabric of his shirt and downed the last of the small glass of wine for an added bit of courage. "Then that's what I want."

His mouth shifted as he sucked at his teeth, his head moving further from me until he stood at his full height. With one hand, he lifted the opened bottle and poured me another serving, topping himself up in the process.

What...the fuck?

"How old are you, Lily?" he asked. It was so nonchalant, so absurdly irrelevant, that it left me dumbfounded for a second.

"Twenty-five," I said. It wasn't a lie. I'd had it right there on my dating profile. He knew this, just as much as I knew his listed age of forty-five wasn't a lie either.

The hand on my thigh moved an inch higher, and dear God, he must have felt the heat coming off of me. Another inch and he'd be exactly where I was growing desperate for him to be. "So, you're old enough to make better decisions than this."

I swallowed. "So are you."

He chuckled as he wrapped his fingers around the stem of the glass I was holding, lifting it closer to my lips. His other hand kept steady on my inner thigh, his thumb brushing back and forth by the most sensitive parts of me. "You're not wrong."

I took a sip of the wine, letting it sit in my mouth for a moment and sink into my taste buds before swallowing. "Are you saying we shouldn't—"

"I'm saying that we're probably both walking into a mistake," he laughed.

I noticed the sensation of his thumb lifting the hemline of my underwear before I'd even realized he'd moved his hand again. He brushed against the slick skin between my thighs, and his lips parted instantly. I knew damn well he could feel what had been building there, but he still kept himself from touching *exactly* where I was growing desperate.

"But I don't think you care. And neither do I."

He pushed the glass to my lips again, and the moment the wine touched my tongue, a single knuckle dragged across the bundle of nerves that was aching to be touched. I struggled to swallow through the little sound that croaked from me, and before I knew what was truly happening, he was on me.

He stole the glass and set it to the side, his mouth

meeting mine in a fucking frenzy, the lingering tastes of wine mixing between us. All of his fingers on the hand between my thighs slipped beneath the thin fabric of my underwear and between the folds of the far too slick skin, and oh my *God*, Adrian was touching me, putting pressure just where I wanted, taking away the ache and leaving only pleasure in its wake.

His free hand grabbed for the knot in my knit cardigan just beneath my breasts, and a second later it was undone, both sides splaying out and leaving me bare-chested.

He didn't waste another moment on my mouth.

"Drink your fucking wine," he ordered, grabbing it for me once again as his lips left mine. Hastily, I took it, and as I shakily lifted the glass to my lips, he descended on my breast instead.

Warm and wet and soft, he dragged his tongue across my hardened nipple before gently sinking his teeth into the delicate, sensitive skin. It took everything in me not to gasp his real name, and instead, I buried the sound in the wine.

Rigidity pressed against my inner thigh as he made more room for his hand. Too many times in my life, I'd imagined what was beneath his jeans, filled in the gaps from what I hadn't been able to see at pool parties or the rare, occasional times he'd used our hot tub back home, and it was almost maddening that I had a chance to see all of him now.

I didn't want to wait.

I downed the rest of my glass and set it to the side, far enough out of reach that I didn't need to worry about knocking over two glasses rather than one. I couldn't reach much from the angle he had me at, leaning back onto the bar top—but I could grab for his jacket with one hand while holding onto his hair with the other, could push it off of his shoulders, could show him what I wanted.

I didn't realize the error in that, though. He removed his fingers entirely as he fully shrugged it off, leaving me needy and without stimulation on my clit. Adrian—or *John*—took that moment to slip out of his shirt as well, and pulled his mouth from mine.

For a horrifying second, I could consider how I must look. One elbow was holding me up on the marble counter-top, and I looked almost like a fucking meal had been laid out with my exposed chest and my legs spread, a load of fabric from my skirt bunching up around my hips. I'd done this so many times in my life, but this was different, this was something I'd wanted for *years*, and the reality of that was beginning to hit.

It hit especially hard as he stood there between my thighs, his hair a mess and his bare, sculpted upper body practically heaving as he, too, observed me.

I reached for the zipper at the side of my skirt and his hand halted me.

"Bedroom," he said, his tone making it sound more like an order than a statement.

———

I couldn't breathe.

With my bare body laid out on the plush white sheets, Adrian towered over me in nothing but his boxers, every ripple of muscle tight. From the bulk in his arms to his built-out pecs and abs, he'd clearly taken up working out in the time since I'd last seen him. He'd always been attractive, but his chest certainly hadn't looked like that when he had been relaxing in our hot tub, and I couldn't *stop* staring.

But neither could he.

"Christ," he hissed, his fingertips playing with the elastic band of his boxers. His cock was obvious beneath them, straining against the fabric for dear life, and even with it covered, I could tell that I was doomed. "You look like a goddamn painting."

I...had never been told that before.

Something about his words lit more than just my skin on fire. He was connecting with me on a level no one had ever seemed to care about—even if I was playing the role of Lily and not Ava, it was still a version of myself that I didn't dare to allow to breathe. I *wished* I could be Lily, and the readiness with which he was willing to engage with her on art and the silly little things I had said made my chest ache.

You look like a goddamn painting.

That was something that would stick in my brain and never fucking leave.

"Thank you," I breathed.

His hand dipped beneath the waistband, pulling it down, down, down—

Oh my god, I wasn't just doomed. I was *dead*.

His length sprung from his boxers, his hand wrapped around the base, and yet again, I couldn't *breathe*. Not only was he far longer than I expected, but the girth was almost wide enough that his thumb only barely met his fingers. His cock was just as tanned as the rest of him, and the veins that sprang along the sides and underneath were so prominent I thought they might burst. The tip, glistening and pink, fucking *dripped*.

"Roll over," he ordered. "Let me see all of you."

I almost didn't want to, almost wanted to stay and just watch him touch himself. But I followed his instructions.

Hands grabbed my hips before they could meet the mattress.

His fingers dug into my skin harshly as he pulled me back toward the edge, forcing me to my knees with my upper half down in the sheets. I sucked in air as his fingers slipped along my exposed pussy, trailing over the bundle of nerves over and over, as his other hand kneaded the soft flesh of my rear.

"Oh my God," I whimpered, and as if in response to it, pleasure bloomed at my core as he slid two fingers inside of me with ease.

"*Fuck*, love, you're tight."

A moan escaped me as another finger entered.

"And so goddamn wet," he added, his voice like fucking butter as the weight from his knee pushed down on the mattress. "You're dripping."

I lifted myself enough to look down between my parted knees, and sure enough, he was absolutely correct. Heat warmed my cheeks and I buried my face in the sheets again. "Sorry."

"Don't you *dare* apologize for that," he laughed, gripping the flesh of my ass so hard I was sure he'd leave bruises.

A slight, minor burst of pain hit me as his pinky slipped in with the rest, dipping so deep into me that his knuckles brushed against the bottom of my clit. Within a second the pain turned to pleasure, and I just wanted *more*, needed it so badly I could beg.

But before I even needed to, he retreated, leaving me aching and empty and needy.

"Put those hands to good use," he said. His grip on my rear relented as his hand slid along my spine, up and along the back of my neck. He grabbed it like he had before, his thumb and middle finger sinking in beneath my ears, and held me in place. "Touch yourself. It'll help."

Warm and soft, the tip of his cock pressed against my entrance.

Shit. He was right.

Moving frantically before he could push in, I slipped my right hand beneath me and along my stomach, cresting that ridge and finding my clit. It throbbed as he slowly sank an inch, flesh against flesh, little dots of pain sprouting as he stretched me. It blended into the ecstasy as I moved my fingers, the sensation nearly overwhelming, and for a moment my head swam as he gave me time to adjust to just an *inch* of him.

"That's it, pretty girl. Open up for me."

Another inch, and I wasn't sure if I was going to die and go to hell or heaven. But I wanted to find out.

"*Fuck* yes, just...relax," he rasped, his free hand coming to rest on the curve of my waist. Slowly, achingly, he pulled me back toward him instead of pushing forward, and every inch he sank made my pulse pound and my mind go blank.

Adrian was inside of me.

Filling me.

Destroying me.

I'd never escape those fucking dreams again.

"Good fucking girl," he said, his voice so low it was nearly a growl as he sunk in as far as my body could take him. "You okay?"

I swallowed as I forced myself to breathe. I couldn't think of a time when I'd ever felt so goddamn full in my entire life—not even with toys. "I think I've died and gone to heaven, John." *Good job. Right name.*

I could *feel* his laugh inside of me. "Not yet, you haven't."

I feared he might have been right.

Slowly, achingly, brain-scramblingly, he pulled himself back, sliding along my insides and hitting every spot I could ever hope for. But then he was pushing back in, unrelentingly and carefree, and *that* was enough to send me spiraling.

I couldn't even focus on moving my fingers. It was *everything*.

"God, you fit me perfectly," he hissed, his fingers tightening along the back of my neck. "Come here."

His cock moved inside of me, but I could barely process the sensation of the front of my body being lifted up, my back arched, head tilting back to rest against his chest. He hit a new angle like this, and *that* filled my vision with little bright lights, stealing my breath until I could remember to breathe again.

One of his hands replaced my stagnant one, and holy *shit*, he was right, this wasn't death, not yet. I reached up for his neck to steady myself, sounds I wasn't even positive were coming from my throat filling the room, but they *sounded* like me, and matched every strum of his fingers against my clit.

I couldn't even bring myself to meet his thrusts halfway. I was limp and useless, just a toy to be thrown around and manipulated however he wanted, and for once, I wanted nothing but that. Already, I was rapidly approaching orgasm, and if I wasn't already incapacitated, I couldn't imagine being much more useful than I already was.

But then his other hand moved.

The one that held me around the back of my neck slipped forward, his arm coming to rest across my chest, and his fingers gripped my throat from the front side. "Yes, yes, yes, please," I moaned, the first coherent thought I'd had being one I'd never wanted to voice. I reinforced his position with my free hand over his wrist.

"You like that?" he laughed, the sound far too deep and menacing.

His thrusts turned rougher the moment I nodded my head.

"*Goddammit*, you fucking do," he cursed. "You're squeezing me like a vice."

His thumb and middle finger dug in on either side of my neck as his palm sat flush against my windpipe, just like I'd done to myself time and time again in the comfort of my bedroom, pausing the blood flow. I didn't dare say a word, not when the only one running through my mind was his fucking name.

"Tap my hand when you want me to stop," he grunted.

Second by second, I hurtled toward the edge, his fingers at my clit keeping their pace. Just as I reached it, the sides of my vision darkened, and I frantically tapped my fingers against his hand.

He released immediately, and I did too.

The head rush hit me as pleasure set fire to my veins, sending me crashing and falling over the edge, shaking, twitching, *dying,* and coming back to fucking life. He pulled me through it, *fucked* me through it, and at the exact moment his fingers touching the most sensitive part of me turned from pleasure to torture, he removed them.

How he knew my signals better than I did was a mystery to me.

"Good fucking girl," he praised, his voice soft as his movements became choppy, rushed, and desperate. He held me around the waist and the neck, with not an ounce of pressure again on my throat but enough to keep me locked in position. "So good, so...*shit*, so good for me."

I looked up at him as his head tipped back, a groan filling the air as he broke, his digits twitching around my throat. His chest heaved as his hips slowed, warmth filling me from the inside, and with every leisurely thrust he gave, I could feel him leaking from me, could feel the warmth of him on my thighs.

I held onto the back of his neck, kept my back arched, and held myself in position as he slowly came to. I didn't dare move until his hold began to loosen.

He began to retreat, and to my absolute surprise, I spluttered a plea for him to stay inside. I didn't want to give it up yet. I couldn't remember a time that I'd ever asked someone to *not* get out after sex, but I knew that once he was gone, I wouldn't feel it again. Knew that the end of it meant that we'd likely go to sleep, knew that would mean the end of our encounter, knew that would mean the end of my time with Adrian.

I didn't want it to end. I'd spent so long dreaming about it, wishing for it, praying for it—and I'd had it. He'd given it to me. But every beginning has an ending, and as much as I desperately didn't want this to be it, he couldn't give me forever.

Not when I wasn't even *Ava*.

Chapter 4

Adrian

The sky had only barely begun to lighten to a dark blue when I stirred awake at my usual time.

Jersey City's streetlights were still lit across the Hudson and provided the only light through the long window at the back of the bedroom. Ava—or *Lily*—slept soundlessly beside me as I slowly hauled myself up until my back could lean against the headboard.

Opening the little drawer on the bedside table, I pulled out my spare reading glasses and put them on before reaching for my phone.

A handful of work emails littered my home screen, along with one text from my son's nanny. *Lucas is in bed. Assuming you're out for the night.*

A pang of guilt hit me. The good thing about having a live-in nanny for my eight-year-old was that I didn't need to worry about someone being there if I wasn't, but I still hadn't *been* there. He knew I'd been on a date last night due to our no-lying policy, but I really didn't want him questioning if I was there when he woke up. I'd never stayed out all night before, unless it was for work reasons, and *those* he understood. But this? I couldn't imagine trying to explain it to him.

I still had at least an hour and a half, but I needed to get going fairly soon.

And that meant the true ending of whatever the hell this was.

Gently, I moved the strands of auburn hair that had fallen from her bun out of her face, dragging my fingers along her skin. *Why did it have to be her?*

If she was anyone else, anyone other than David's daughter, I might have genuinely considered seeing her again. That wasn't something I did, but whatever the fuck last night was seemed worth the trouble that repeating the interaction would normally bring. But not when that trouble was *David.*

Her eyes fluttered open in the darkness, and there was that pang of guilt this time, but it wasn't for leaving my son overnight.

"Is it morning?" she mumbled, her arm reaching across my hips and practically hugging my thighs.

"It's just after five," I sighed.

"Why are you up?" Her eyes opened, and she turned her head to look up at me sleepily in the darkness, a little smile pulling her lips up. "You look cute in glasses."

I chuckled. "I've got a meeting at seven," I lied, dragging my thumb across her cheek, back and forth. "I need to leave soon so I can go home and change."

Her smile faded almost instantly as she lifted herself up onto one elbow. My hand fell from her as the blankets pooled around her waist, her bare upper body looking fucking sinful in the low light. I had half a mind to take her again right now—my concealed morning wood would have certainly come in useful for the first time in years if I had. But I didn't want to risk turning up after Lucas woke, and I cursed my body's clock for not running slightly earlier.

"If it's any consolation, I don't particularly want to go," I offered.

Her hand hesitated before reaching out to me, hooking around the very edge of my jaw and under my ear, pulling me down toward her. "Then stay," Ava whispered. "Tell them you're sick."

I let my hand drift to her waist and wrap around it, stopping her pull in its tracks as I lifted her up to me instead. She practically crawled into my lap beneath the sheets, her completely bare form slotting against mine so easily as she settled in astride me. "Fuck," I groaned as she pressed her warmth against the underside of my straining cock.

Her lips found mine in the low light. She kissed me slowly, exhaustedly, as if it took everything in her to be awake at this hour, and I just wanted to stay, wanted to stay like this even if it amounted to nothing, wanted to stay like this with her body on mine, wanted to talk to her for hours upon hours and forget that anything existed outside of this godforsaken room.

I wanted to take her again. But I couldn't, and this had to be the end.

"You are a *temptation*," I rasped, pulling my lips from hers and tightening my hold around her waist.

She giggled softly, her mouth moving to my jaw, my neck, my collarbones. "Is it working?"

I pressed a single kiss against the top of her head. "I'm so sorry, but no."

Dejected and defeated, she leaned back, putting a bit of space between us even as her hips stayed in place. I could feel the dampness of her pooling against the underside of my length, and *fuck*, I just wanted to be inside of her again. "You genuinely have to go?"

I slipped my glasses off and deposited them back into the little drawer. "I do."

She pressed her lips together as the reality began to dawn on her. For a moment, I hoped she knew who I was, hoped she understood that this was the inevitable end to what we had done. I hoped she didn't have lingering hope. But then she spoke, and the gears in my head suddenly stopped. "Do you want my number?"

What?

I had known there was a minuscule chance that I was wrong about who she was up until the moment I'd seen the back of her right arm last night. Even in the low light, the small port wine stain birthmark across the skin was evident and solidified every suspicion I'd had. I'd seen it a handful of times back in Boston. The possibility of her not knowing who I was seemed even more implausible. I looked almost exactly the same as I had back then. Had she genuinely forgotten what I looked like?

I picked my phone back up from my nightstand and unlocked it, hiding the lock screen's image of Lucas from her, before passing it across the short distance between us. "Yeah," I said.

I watched in confusion as she stared unmoving at the phone for a few seconds before glancing at me, typing in a number, and saving it as *Lily*.

"What time is it?" I asked, but just as the words left my lips, she turned off the screen. On instinct, she hit the button again to answer my question—but Lucas's grinning face in front of the Statue of Liberty filled the screen, and if I tried to reach for the phone, my attempt to conceal my concern would be glaringly obvious. *Fuck.*

She stared at the phone.

"Lily?" I swallowed.

"It's almost six."

She blinked too quickly as she passed it back to me, her eyes averted to the pillows and sheets beside her. Slowly, she removed herself from my lap, shifting until she sat cross legged on the comforter.

The heaviness hung in the air as I slowly slipped from the sheets, grabbed my boxers, and pulled them on. I couldn't hide the erection, not as the sky was slowly beginning to lighten along with the room. "I can call you a cab," I offered. "Or you're welcome to go back to sleep and go home later."

Her eyes met mine. "You're not worried I'll steal something?"

I pursed my lips. "No, I'm not. Unless you know how to sail."

She shook her head. "I'd probably just crash and sink and drown."

I couldn't stop the snort that left my nose despite the tension in the air. "Then I'm definitely not worried. Take as much booze as you want."

Her lips twitched in the corners, but a smile didn't sprout like I thought it would.

I leaned across the bed, half out of guilt and half because I just wanted to touch her again, and cupped her cheek. "I'll call," I lied. But the next words were far too true. "I genuinely had an incredible time with you."

Her teeth scraped against her lower lip, but she reached up and kissed me gently but far too quickly. I didn't want to assume that she knew that I was lying, but it felt like it, and I couldn't shake the feeling that as much as both of us needed this to be the end, it somehow wouldn't be.

We couldn't avoid each other forever.

———

The absurdity of having to sit in a cab for twenty minutes just to end up roughly where I'd started last night wasn't lost on me. But as I stepped out of the elevator into my private entry area and unlocked the door to my penthouse, the morning light was only just beginning to crest over the horizon, painting the main foyer and mostly gray living room in sharp oranges and pinks. Lucas would be up any minute, if he wasn't already.

I tried to walk as quietly as I could as I crossed the expanse of the house, listening intently for any signs of stirring as I went up the stairs to the second floor. Lucas's room was silent as I passed it, and that meant I had enough time to make it to my room, change into pajamas, and get back to him before he woke naturally or his alarm went off.

But even as I went about my motions, I couldn't stop thinking about Ava.

I couldn't remember the last time I'd connected with someone so easily, even if it was over something so common-place as art. I avoided finding meaningful connections when it came to dating, and walking into new relationships without trying hadn't been an issue since I'd reentered the dating pool last year. However, it felt almost as if I hadn't just walked into this situation but instead *run*, and as I tried to turn back, a mile-long brick wall had been erected between me and where I'd come from.

Maybe it was because I already knew her. Maybe it was because she was off-limits.

Maybe I was just going fucking insane.

No matter what it was, she was living in my brain now, filling up every empty space. I kept getting flashes of her laughing at the museum, the way her face had gone bright red when she'd nearly knocked over the cheap figurines, the way she'd looked sprawled out on my fucking bed back on the sailboat.

I hadn't even gotten to taste her.

Idiot.

Slipping from my bedroom in an oversized shirt and plaid pajama bottoms, I walked barefoot down the hall back to Lucas's room. I shooed the memory from my mind of how fucking beautiful Ava looked when her eyes had gone wide as my hand had locked around her throat and gently pushed the door open.

Lucas slept peacefully in his bed, his scruffy black hair a mess on his pillows. The moment I shut the door behind me, though, he stirred, rolled over away from the door, and pulled his blankets up over his head.

"Rise and shine," I chuckled, hitting the button beside the light switch. The black-out-blinds on his window slowly began to retreat, letting in the soft morning light and filling the space with life as he groaned. "If you get up, I'll make bacon."

The blankets slowly retreated as he lifted his head, just his squinted eyes poking out over the sheets. "Bacon?" Lucas asked, blinking the sleep away.

"Bacon."

In a flash, he threw the sheets off, revealing his mismatched dinosaur pajamas and getting up off the mattress.

I chuckled as I crossed the space, tucking him into my side. "That was easier than I expected."

He shrugged. "Maybe you should bribe me with bacon more often."

———

I wasn't sure if it was the lack of sleep or the stress of my day at work, but as I sat at my desk in my office on the forty-fourth floor and watched the sun creep toward the horizon, I couldn't help but stare at the number Ava had put in my phone under the name *Lily*.

She had to have known. Unless she'd somehow suffered a terrible accident and lost her memory without her father mentioning it, I couldn't imagine a scenario where she didn't realize who I was.

Why the fuck had she given me her number?

Some absurd part of me wanted to believe it was because she knew and didn't care. But I knew better than that—knew she would have been just as concerned about her father's reaction as I was.

The memory of burying myself inside of her as she relaxed around my cock took hold of me, and fuck it, so did my curiosity.

I tapped the little icon of a phone next to her number and brought my cell to my ear.

It didn't even ring.

The number you have dialed is not in use.

Beep. Beep. Beep.

Well, that made an upsetting amount of sense.

41

I deleted the contact and put my things away as I prepped myself for going roughly thirty floors up to the comfort of my home. It was for the best, realistically—I didn't need to be getting myself into situations like this, not when I had Lucas to worry about. I had to be cagey when it came to seeing other people, and last night had easily been my biggest slip-up in that regard.

I could stuff the memories down. I could bury her in my mind and never dig her out. I'd done it before with far more troublesome baggage, and I could do it again.

Chapter 5

Ava

The clinking of glasses and scraping of plates was grating on me as I sat across from Dad at one of the nicest steakhouses in the city. Even tucked away in our private corner, the sounds didn't stop, and I was far too aware of *everything,* from the painfully boring professional attire I wore, to the way the soles of my feet ached in my heels.

And a part of me couldn't stop checking over Dad's shoulder in case Adrian appeared out of thin air. My anxiety about running into him had been on high alert for almost two days now.

"Should have your office up and running by Thursday," Dad said around a mouthful of food, his short beard shifting with every movement of his jaw as he chewed. His bald head was so ridiculously polished that it reflected the overhead lights as he bowed for another bite. "So you can start moving stuff in if you'd like."

"Oh, cool." I checked over his shoulder again while he was far too distracted with his food to notice.

"Any hires yet?"

"Dad, I barely have *clients* yet. I don't really need to make hires until I've got a little too much work for myself." I smoothed out my napkin over my plain black slacks, debating whether or not to ask the waitress for a spare one to shove in the neckline of my shirt to protect the loose, white fabric from my soup, but I decided against it.

"Who have you spoken to so far?"

I shrugged. "A handful of people in your office."

His stare turned on me, his brows narrowing. "You've only spoken to people within SkyLine?"

I chewed on the inside of my cheek. SkyLine Exchange wasn't exactly a hub of people looking for elite match-making services, but it was at least a *starting* point. He didn't have to look so goddamn disappointed. "For now. I've got a couple of clients."

He shook his head. "Management or ground team? I know damn well there isn't anyone on the board that's single."

I sighed and picked up my spoon, my clam chowder getting colder by the minute. "Ground team."

"Nope, no, absolutely not," Dad snapped. "Drop them as clients. You need far more important people if you want this to work."

"I have to *find* them first," I explained. "My website isn't exactly popular yet, and all I'm going off is word of mouth."

"Your website..." He cut himself off as he shoved another bite of wagyu between his teeth, either deciding that whatever he was going to say was too harsh or too pointless. "We've got a charity ball coming up one week from tomorrow. Come to that and work the room. I'm sure you can get enough clients there to fit the bill and to warrant hiring a few people."

The idea of attending a *charity* event run by one of the

greediest businesses in Manhattan sounded like it would practically drain the last bit of hope for humanity I had left in me, but with Dad, it was easier to shut up and agree than try to fight it. He was a much more intense person than Mom, and as much as I loved the city, I almost regretted leaving her in Boston and coming to live here.

Especially when I now had the added worry of running into Adrian on my mind.

"Okay," I agreed, finally letting myself have a spoonful of my chowder. But the thoughts of Adrian swirled menacingly in my head. They were there nearly every second that my mind was unoccupied. I fluctuated wildly between worrying I'd see him, and remembering how his large hand had felt around my throat, and it was difficult to keep the thoughts from bubbling up to the surface.

Dad hadn't even mentioned him since I'd moved two months ago, and a wild thought crossed my mind—*what if they had had a falling out?*

"Have you spoken to Adrian at all lately?" I asked, hoping my tone was nonchalant enough not to raise suspicion.

"Adrian Stone?" he asked, one brow raising.

I nodded as I ate another spoonful of soup.

"Yesterday. Why?"

Shit. There went any hope that I didn't need to worry about them still being friends. "I just realized that I've been here for two months now, and I don't think I've heard you speak about him once."

He shrugged. "You and I haven't spoken much since you've been so busy," he explained. "I'm sure you'll see him around."

He took another bite of food, and for a moment, I genuinely believed I was in the clear. But then his brows were raising, and he met my gaze with the same green eyes I had, his fork jutting out at me as something worked itself out in his head.

"You should add him as a client," he said, and a fucking boulder dropped into my stomach.

"What?"

"Mhm. He said he's been dating a bit recently."

I stared at my father as his idea slowly sunk in. Why did he have to be such a hard man to say no to? "I...Isn't he, uh, married? Didn't we go to his engagement party like ten years ago?"

His fork moved as he shook his head. "His wife died a couple of years ago," he explained through his mouthful of food, and oh *God*, I didn't want the rest of my clam chowder. I felt like I was going to be sick. Dad must have noticed. "Nah, don't feel too bad. Jan was awful. She gave him Lucas, but that's the only positive. She was cheating on him before she died, and he had no idea until the police confirmed there were *two* people in the car that night."

My mind went fucking blank.

I didn't know how to respond to that like a normal human being. I'd slept with him, felt a goddamn connection with him, only to learn from my *dad* that his wife had died two years ago after having an affair. I'd told myself when the thought had cropped up as he touched me that maybe he'd gotten a divorce, or maybe they were separated—but *dead* hadn't crossed my mind once.

Swallowing through the sudden dryness in my mouth, I asked the only thing I could think of. "Who's Lucas?"

"His son," Dad clarified. "Forgot you wouldn't really know about him. He's eight, I think."

So that was the kid I'd seen on the lock screen of his phone. The puzzle pieces were fitting into place.

"I'll set up a meeting with him," Dad continued as if none of this was a bomb that had dropped and exploded inside of my brain.

"I don't think that's a good—"

"Ava, sweetheart. He's one of the top single men in New York, he'd be the perfect fuckin' client," he explained, stabbing a soft piece of meat with his fork. "I'll talk to him and put it in your diary."

Oh my *God*. I wanted to jump out of the goddamn window.

"How's your love life, anyway?" he added, just to twist the knife a little further.

"It's shit," I breathed.

He popped the bit of steak into his mouth and pointed his fork at me again. "I'll see if anyone I know has got a son around your age. Need to get you off the market before some creep swoops in wanting your inheritance."

No. No, no, no, I didn't want that, didn't want more of my father's meddling in my life. Especially not when all I could think of was Adrian, not when he plagued my dreams, not when I'd just found out about his wife's death and his son, not when I couldn't stop imagining his hands between my thighs and all over my fucking body. "Dad, please—"

He waved his fork to shut me up, gesturing toward my chowder. "Eat your soup, kiddo. It's getting cold."

Chapter 6

Adrian

David Riley stared me down with the same green eyes his daughter had from across the table at one of New York's finest steakhouses, a pristinely cooked wagyu steak in front of him.

I felt like a monster.

"This steak just keeps getting better," David said, slicing off a cut of it as his knife scraped against the polished china. "Had the same one earlier for lunch."

"Dave, you can't just keep eating steak and drinking whiskey for every meal."

"I damn sure can," he laughed. It wasn't the same, but I could hear a reflection of Ava's laughter in his, and for a second, the grave I'd dug for her in my mind became loose dirt. "How's the planning for the kids-without-lungs ball going?"

"Kids-without-lungs?" I snorted, covering my mouth with my napkin. "Do you mean the Childhood Interstitial Lung Disease charity?"

"Yeah," he said, his brows knitting as he sipped at his glass of whiskey.

I stared down my glass of Riesling, wondering just how much of it I'd need to consume to get through this fucking dinner. "They have lungs, David," I said, forcing a laugh. "You can't be born without lungs."

"Well, I don't know," he shrugged. "Either way, how's planning?"

I shook off the absurdity of the conversation and tried to do the same with the guilt that was eating me alive for sleeping with his fucking daughter, but it didn't quite work. I'd figure out a way to get through life without that ever coming up. "It's good. Everything's on schedule."

"You're coming, right?" he added, one brow raising.

I sliced off a section of lobster tail and popped it in my mouth. "Maybe. I'll probably be there for a bit to make sure it all kicks off without a hitch."

"Good, good. We've got some good stocks lined up for the bidding already, but need to go through what else we can offer—"

My phone lit up on the table, vibrating so much that the phone itself began to move along the polished wood. "Shit," I said, grabbing for it. "One second, it's Lucas' school."

David nodded as I slipped from my chair, grabbing my phone in one quick sweep before rounding the corner toward the restrooms. It was only slightly quieter, but I had nowhere else to go unless I wanted to ride on an elevator, and I didn't want to risk that when it could be an emergency.

"Hello?"

"Hello, this is Katarina calling from Midtown Preparatory. Can I speak to Mr. Stone?" The crackling voice through the phone told me that at least one of us had a poor signal, and I moved a little closer to the window in case it was me.

"Speaking."

"Great. Hi, Mr. Stone," Katarina said, and her voice sounded a little clearer. "I'm just calling because Lucas' basketball practice has been cut short due to the coach having a family emergency come up, so Lucas will need to be collected as soon as possible."

Shit. "Is there no other after-school activity he can join in on?"

"No, sir, not tonight, unfortunately."

"Fuck. Okay, I'll sort it. Tell him to hold tight."

I hung up before they could insist that I magically teleport to the school right that minute. The temptation to stab myself in the eye with a steak knife as a waiter passed with a tray of dirty dishes almost overwhelmed me.

I reopened my contacts and pulled up Lucas' nanny's number, calling her immediately.

"Hello, Mr. Stone," she answered, the phone not even getting to the second ring before she picked up.

"Hi, Grace," I sighed. "Any chance you could grab Lucas from basketball practice?"

"Was I not scheduled to do that already? I could have sworn you asked me—"

"No, no, I mean *now*. They've ended early and there's nothing else he can jump in on," I clarified. "Sorry, I'm a bit all over the place."

"Oh! Sure, I can head down there. No problem," she said. "I'll just grab dinner for him while we're out if that's okay."

"Always is, Grace. You don't have to ask to put money on the credit card," I explained for what had to be the hundredth time. My patience was waning. "Thank you."

"Of course. Have a nice evening!"

I hung up the call and pressed my forehead to the glass

of the window, needing a quick second to recalibrate and cool down. It was such a minor thing, and I knew that— knew it far too well. But it was times like this that I fucking hated being the only parent.

"Everything okay?" David asked through another mouthful of steak as I slipped back into my chair.

"Lucas' practice ended early," I explained. "They wanted me to pick him up."

"Ah, got Grace to do it?"

I nodded. "Yeah. I just wish I could put her on the call list sometimes so I didn't have to always be the one that deals with this shit," I grumbled, turning my phone face down on the table and stabbing my lobster with my fork. "Sometimes I wish Jan had just fucking divorced me so that Lucas still had another parent that could handle things when I'm busy. It's like every goddamn day they call me with something new, and it's never actually to do with Lucas, but to do with teachers or *practice* or scheduling conflicts, and I just don't have the capacity, you know?"

"So what you're saying is your son needs a mother," David offered, and I shot him a look.

"What I'm saying is that in an ideal world, I could marry someone that I didn't need to *love*, because fuck that. I'm not doing that shit again. And then I could add her to the call list, and she could handle half of the calls," I explained, eyeing him warily as he swirled his whiskey in its glass.

"You know," he started, and I could have sworn I could physically see the gears turning in his head, "my kid, Ava, you remember her?"

Absolutely not. No. Nope. Do not bring her into this, for the love of God, please. "Yeah, of course," I said, keeping my voice as level as I could manage.

51

"She's starting up a company. Elite Matchmaking, or something she called it. I think it's got a catchier name than that," he said. *Oh, thank god*, I could breathe again. "She just moved to town a couple of months ago, so it's all in the beginning phases right now, but I'll set you up for a meeting with her. Apparently, she's like some fuckin' guru when it comes to this shit, except, shockingly, for herself. Maybe she can find you someone."

And my breath was lost again. A meeting with Ava was my worst fucking nightmare right now. "Dave, I don't think—"

"Hey," he interrupted, pointing his steak knife directly at me. "Unless you want to marry that nanny of yours, it's worth a shot. I mean, how many dates have you been on in the last year? Twenty? Thirty? And none of them have stuck."

The idea of marrying Lucas' nearly sixty-five-year-old nanny wasn't exactly appealing to me, especially when the possibility of her needing retirement soon was on the cards. "I appreciate the offer, genuinely," I lied, shoving a piece of lobster in my too-dry mouth and swallowing. "I just don't know if Ava would be of much use when I don't want a *relationship*. I just want convenience."

His stare turned harder, and I knew that look. That was his *do it or I'll make your life a living hell* look. For a split second, I felt bad for Ava having to deal with that look her entire life, but then remembered that I was the one on the receiving end this time—and I was the one going to have either come clean that I'd recognized her well before I'd slept with her, or play pretend that I had no idea.

I was fucked either way.

"You got any meetings tomorrow?" he asked.

"No," I answered, and it was far too late that I realized

he *wasn't* changing the topic of discussion. He was checking my fucking availability to meet with his daughter. "David, please."

"This is good for you," he insisted. "It's worth a shot. And it would really help Ava out with gettin' her business off the ground."

I watched in horror as he took his phone out, lifting it to his ear as he chewed on his piece of steak.

"Ava, kiddo, great news," he said, and I could actually feel my last bite of lobster rising in my esophagus. "Adrian's gonna meet you tomorrow. How's eleven work for 'ya?"

For a split second, I wished I could hear what was being said on the other end of that phone call.

"No, no, he's thrilled!" David insisted, winking at me. "I can book you two in for a reservation at that Japanese place across from SkyLine since your office isn't ready yet."

He scooped up a bit of his baked potato with his fork and shoved it into his mouth.

"Honestly, kiddo, it'll be great. Don't worry about it," he continued, and *fuck*, I felt bad for her. She had to be panicking as much as I was. "Nah, eleven's the only time that works."

"David—"

He held up his fork to shush me. If it wasn't for all the good times I'd shared with this man, I would have called our friendship off there and then. "Great! There you go, Aves, gotcha a client. Ain't that hard."

Chapter 7

Ava

"**I**'m fucked. I'm so royally, horribly fucked." I couldn't stop bouncing my legs or chewing the inside of my cheek, couldn't focus and bring myself to calm down, and the incessant tapping of my feet on the sticky plastic floor of the taxi only made the cycle worse. We were three blocks away from the Japanese restaurant, and even though Emily had agreed to join me for support as my assistant, I knew this wouldn't end well.

"You'll be okay," Em cooed, tapping the binder in my lap. "Just follow this and don't go off script. Get the answers to your questions and then just let me do all of the communication from there."

I'd caught her up on everything that had happened. Much to my dismay, she'd taunted me for sleeping with him so easily. But I still didn't feel like she understood the gravity of this. The woman he thought he'd slept with, the woman who had begged him to stay that morning for just a little more time with him, the woman who had given him a fake number even when she offered it up—that wasn't *Lily*. And that realization was minutes away from taking hold.

I didn't even want to imagine how he'd react, let alone witness it.

"He's going to hate me," I said. I pushed the hair out of my face as we passed the Charging Bull statue, traffic finally letting up and letting us down one final block of Broadway. "He's going to fucking hate me and never want to see me again."

Emily's brows knitted as she turned to me, her blonde ponytail flying. "Isn't that what you want, though? For him to never see you again?"

The cab pulled over to the side of the road and the man clicked the button on his machine, but fuck, I wasn't ready to get out. We still had at least fifty feet to walk, but even being this close and knowing he could walk down the street alongside me was enough to put me on high alert. "I don't know what I want, Em."

Dad had given me his number in case I needed to contact Adrian before the meeting. I'd stared at it almost all night in my apartment, tempted to call and tell him in advance so that he wouldn't be surprised and caught off guard in a public location. But telling him privately meant he could react how he wanted, and although there wasn't a single part of me that expected violence, I was pretty sure he wouldn't yell at me in a restaurant.

"That'll be sixty-two eighty."

I swallowed down the bile creeping up my throat and tapped my phone against the card reader on the back of the driver's seat, waiting for the audible beep. "Thank you," I said, sliding the door open and invading the warm taxi with the chill of the October air. I tightened my suit jacket around my shoulders and waited for Em to step out, checking around me for any sign of Adrian.

But it was one minute to eleven, and the likelihood of

him already being there waiting for me hung heavily on my shoulders.

"Regardless of how this goes, you will be okay," Em assured me as she started walking toward the restaurant. "We'll figure it out."

But it didn't *feel* like it would be okay. It felt like it would all go to shit in the palm of my hand. The night I'd had that I'd never wanted to end might end up so horribly, disgustingly soiled that I would never be able to think about it again. "Okay," I choked.

Em walked in front of me, her hand locked in mine as she dragged me. Her all-white pantsuit complimented my black one, and without evening meaning to, we'd picked the exact same button-up to wear beneath—a light gray shirt we'd purchased together two years ago during college. We were like the grown-up version of when people dress their twin toddlers in matching-but-not-matching clothing.

Wait.

Before I could get the idea out of my mouth, the restaurant came into view, and I nearly ran. Right there in the window, with his back turned to my side of the street, Adrian sat at a table, his phone in hand. I could just barely see his profile in the glass, and oh my God, I couldn't do this, couldn't destroy that night, couldn't deal with the consequences of my actions—

"Ava," Em complained, tugging on my unmoving hand. "Come on."

"I can't," I said. "I can't. He's right there."

"You *can*." Her head turned to look in the window. "Oh shit, he is hot."

As if on fucking cue, his head turned in our direction, and before he could manage to make eye contact, I practically dove into the little space beside me between a cafe and an office building, lifting the binder to shield my face.

Emily moved to the space between me and the sidewalk, her lips forming a hard line as she looked at me, brown eyes boring a hole into my skull. "You can't keep running from him. He'll ask more questions if you don't show up, and your dad will hear about it."

Fuck it. It's worth a shot. "He hasn't seen me in ten years," I explained. "Hasn't seen *Ava*, I mean. The last time he saw me as Ava, I had jet-black hair and thick-as-shit eyeliner. I'd look different now. I *do* look different now."

One slicked-down brow rose. "I don't understand."

"You go," I insisted, the idea taking shape in my mind and flowing from my mouth without a second thought. Her eyes widened in response. "Be Ava. He'll probably be a little surprised, but I don't think he'll question it. Just greet him like you would if you saw one of your parents' friends that you haven't seen in years."

"You want me to pretend to be you?" she asked, and I nodded. "Ava, that's insane. You'd just be delaying the inevitable."

"Not if I change my entire look by the next time I have to see him."

"Oh my *God*. What if he brings it up to your father? Mentions how different you look?"

"I *do* look different. As long as he doesn't go into specifics with him, I doubt my dad will probe him further on that," I explained. I pushed the binder into her arms before she could protest. "Every question is in here. The whole fucking script is. Just follow it."

"*Av—*"

"Please," I begged. "*Please.* I'll go to Louis Vuitton right fucking now and get you that little bag you said you wanted in exchange for your help."

Her mouth popped open but shut just as fast, her head whipping toward the restaurant and back to me. "The OnTheGo?"

I nodded. "Yeah. Black, right?"

She shifted side to side on her feet, weighing up my offer. "Why do you have to fucking tempt me?"

"Because my dad has too much money and I have nothing to spend it on but silly stuff," I said, feeling her imminent *yes* and the relief it brought. "And because I'm desperate."

She groaned as she took a step back, nearly slamming into a man in the most boring suit I'd ever seen. "Fine," she said. "Meet by the bull in one hour."

———

Emily stood on the edge of the corner by the bull, just off to the side of the crowd of people desperate to take their photograph touching its bronze testicles.

With her arms folded across her chest and the binder tucked beneath them, she looked around anxiously as I approached, the carrier bag from Louis Vuitton clutched in my grasp. It didn't fill me with the extra reassurance I was hoping for, but all I could do as I stood on the other side of the street waiting for the pedestrian crossing to activate, was pray that maybe she was just nervous about Adrian being in the same area and potentially seeing me.

The light turned green, and I crossed with the crowd, making a beeline directly for her.

"How was it?" I asked, passing her the bag in exchange for my binder. I flipped it open, glancing at all the little notes she'd made as she started to speak.

"It went fine," she said, but there was tension in her voice. "He called me Ava and answered all of the questions. He was really nice."

I looked up at her over the edge of the binder, clutching the sharp edge as a tourist bus with an open top drove past us, kicking up the cold air and battering the both of us. "You're not telling me something."

She hadn't even opened her bag yet. And that look on her face, the worry in her voice, whatever it was, it was fucking obvious—something had gone terribly wrong, and once again, bile burned at my esophagus.

Her lips pressed together as she pushed the little tendrils of blonde curls out of her face. "When I went to leave," she started, her eyes shifting from me to the people around us, "he stopped me. He said, and I quote, 'tell Ava that I know who she is, and I don't like these games'."

Chapter 8

Adrian

The ballroom at Cipriani was completely packed to the brim with men and women and everything in between, in expensive attire. Golds, blacks, and maroon seemed to be the most popular choices. I assumed it had more to do with the logo for the charity being those colors than any kind of organized collaboration with the attendees as I stood at the far end of the room overseeing my staff. I blended right in with my all-black, three-piece tuxedo.

Everything seemed to be running smoothly so far. The managers were running a tight ship and handling every instance of stock shortages or payment troubles, and my presence was almost unnecessary.

I would have gone home if I wasn't positive that Ava would be in attendance tonight.

She hadn't dared to reach out following the meeting with whomever she'd sent in her place. I'd considered calling the number her father had given me, but I knew that she couldn't avoid me forever—even if she had her assistant sending all of her correspondence to me. And she absolutely couldn't avoid me *here*.

"Almost done, folks. The next item for auction is a three-night stay at The Peninsula in London," the man across the room announced. He stood in the middle of the stage behind a podium and in front of the massive, curtained window, the music at the back of the room almost drowning him out. He was older, maybe nearing seventy, with almost shoulder-length hair and small glasses on his nose as he read out from the sheet below him. The crowd in front of him raised paddles in response to numbers I didn't pay attention to—my thoughts were far too focused on Ava.

I could have let a sleeping dog lie if it hadn't been for the stunt she'd pulled last week. I could have gone through with the meeting, played my part, and maybe mentioned in passing that we would never speak of what happened. But she had made a mountain out of a fucking molehill, and I was prepared to challenge her on it.

I just had to find her first.

After grabbing a glass of wine from the bar, I crossed the patterned marble floor toward the other end of the hall through the sea of people. I kept my eyes alert for a head of auburn hair, but each time I spotted her hair color, the person was either too old, too tall, or too wide to be her. But David had confirmed with me that she'd be in attendance, and I was fucking counting on it.

"Sold for two-thousand, eight-hundred, and fifty dollars."

The projected display to one side of the man presenting, showed a tally of how much money the auction had raised for charity so far, but the gauge had already met its peak. The goal had been met and exceeded by nearly two hundred thousand. I doubted there was much more that would sell for exorbitant prices, but my curiosity got the better of me.

Until a flash of perfectly waved, deep red hair snagged my attention from the side of the stage on the right.

There she is.

He was standing beside her father in a deep emerald, satin dress that clung to her upper body like a second skin before cascading down from her hips. There was a slit up to the middle of her thigh, and her hair fell pristinely around her shoulders with little sections pinned back from the front. She made me lose my fucking breath.

She'd looked beautiful when I'd seen her at the museum. But this...this was another level.

The crowd applauded for something I hadn't been paying the slightest bit of attention to, and I moved, pushing through the crowd again with my glass of wine, my eyes locked on her. But David stepped forward, one hand positioned on the top of her back, and ushered her up the steps to the stage. I stopped in my tracks.

The man behind the podium lifted one hand as a goodbye as stepped back. David left his daughter alone with the handful of men and women standing at the edge of the stage, David took up his original position where he'd been when I'd arrived.

At the microphone.

"Thank you so much for coming this evening and raising so much for researching..." He glanced down, likely checking his notes. *Don't say kids without lungs.* "...childhood interstitial lung disease."

Thank fuck he hadn't butchered that.

"I do have one more thing for auction if you lovely people have another minute to spare," he grinned.

My eyes wandered for the briefest of seconds toward

Ava, and to my utter shock and surprise, her wildly green eyes were already trained on me, wide as fucking saucers. *Ava*, I mouthed.

Her cheeks flushed pink through her makeup.

"Just to pull in a few extra dollars and maybe open the floor up to a bit of networking," David laughed, glancing across at Ava. But her eyes were still trained on me, "I'd like to offer up a dance with my daughter, Avalynn Riley."

What...the fuck?

Ava's head whipped toward her father. With nothing but anger on her face, she said something to him, but the music and the murmurs from the crowd drowned it out. All David did was laugh in return.

"Three hundred dollars!"

I turned, and roughly thirty people away to my left, the green side of a paddle shot into the air. *Fuck.*

"Five hundred!"

"Six hundred!"

Shit, shit, shit. She looked fucking mortified up there on the stage. All I could think to do in the heat of the moment was bid so she wouldn't have to dance with a stranger, but all I had was a glass of wine, not an unused paddle in sight.

I lifted my glass instead.

"Fifteen hundred," I challenged.

David rolled his eyes at me before being distracted by another paddle. "Two thousand!"

For fucks sake. "Three," I said, lifting my glass again.

Stop, Ava mouthed. I shook my head.

"Five thousand!"

"Ten," I shouted. I raised my glass.

The crowd quieted for a moment, and just as David opened his mouth to speak into the microphone, a paddle raised again. "Twenty!"

Jesus. Twenty fucking thousand dollars for two minutes with the woman who looked like she'd rather be anywhere else. How desperate were these people?

This wouldn't stop until it hit ridiculous numbers, and the horrified look on Ava's face as I raised my glass again only confirmed that I was either saving her or damning her to hell. I wasn't sure which one.

"Fifty thousand," I said.

"Seriously, Adrian?" David asked, but I was hardly paying attention to him. I didn't bother responding, and instead, I held Ava's gaze, the whites of her eyes fully visible. Her chest and neck were bright pink as she stared down at me. David didn't need an answer—I'd spent far more money on far more trivial things than this, and he knew that damn well. "All right, fifty thousand dollars, going once."

I broke my gaze away from Ava as I pushed through the crowd toward the side of the stage she'd climbed up on.

"Going twice."

I cleared the crowd and made it to the bottom of the steps. "Come on," I said to her.

"Fifty-five thousand."

"You've got to be fucking kidding me," I snapped.

The man holding up the paddle stood in the front row. He must have been pushing eighty, at least an entire foot shorter than me, and as far as I could tell, didn't have many teeth left. But his suit screamed wealth, as did the neatly pressed pocket square. *Old money.*

Literally.

"Sixty-five," I shot back. I climbed the steps, my patience waning.

"Please don't spend that much money on me," Ava said as I stepped up beside her. "You can talk to me after, just don't—"

"Any more offers?" David asked, his voice practically booming through the speakers as he leaned a little too close to the microphone. The man in the front who'd held up his paddle shook his head, turned, and pushed back into the crowd. "Sold, then, for sixty-five-thousand dollars to Adrian Stone."

———

"You didn't need to spend that much money to fucking talk to me," Ava said quietly. I had one hand wrapped around her fingers and the other on her waist as we moved in time to the music.

Thankfully we weren't the only ones on the dance floor, and I felt like I could breathe for a second without every single eye on us. There were still a few stares, though, of course. It would be hard for anyone not to notice her, not when she looked as beautiful as she did, not when she seemed to be the talk of the evening due to how much money I'd dropped on her.

I didn't quite understand it—others had spent hundreds of thousands on auctioned stocks.

"Are you saying you would have answered the phone if I tried to call your real number?" I challenged, raising one brow at her.

Her cheeks, which had finally returned to a somewhat normal color, began to turn pink again. "Probably not."

"Then I'd say sixty-five thousand dollars to speak to you was a decent enough purchase price when you're clearly avoiding me," I said.

Her lips thinned as she glanced up at me. "I...look, it must have been jarring for you when you realized, and I'm sorry about that. But we don't need to speak about it."

We shifted, and for a second, David Riley's form came into view. He was deep in conversation across the room, his back to us, and I took my opportunity to ruffle her feathers a little without worrying about his reaction.

I leaned down closer to her, bringing my lips to the shell of her ear.

"Did you think I didn't know who you were that night?" I asked, my voice barely more than a whisper. "Did you genuinely believe that you were fooling me by pretending you didn't know me?"

Her hand squeezed mine like a fucking vice as we spun again, but my position held firm with the occasional glance at the back of David's head. "You knew?"

A laugh bubbled up from my throat. "Of course, I fucking knew, Ava. You look different but not like an entirely different person."

"You should have said—"

I lifted my head, stretching my neck as I took her in. "You knew the moment you saw me. There's not a chance you didn't. And *you* didn't say a word."

Her mouth parted before shutting again, her jaw steeling. Even annoyed, she looked like a fucking dream. "I should have."

"Maybe we both should have," I shrugged. "It wouldn't have made a difference."

She took an unexpected step back, her eyes widening and twinkling due to the chandeliers above us. "It absolutely would have made a difference, Adrian. None of it would have happened if we had been honest with one another."

I slipped my arm around her waist instead of just holding it gently with my hand, pulling her body closer until it was flush with mine. "Liar," I hissed. "It would have ended exactly the same. Don't pretend like you wouldn't have let me touch you just because I knew who you were."

She swallowed, her throat bobbing as her eyes flicked up to meet mine. Her nose and her cheeks were turning a bright fucking red, and if I wasn't surrounded by a sea of eyes, I probably would have done something far more drastic than just watching her.

"Do you want to lie again and tell me you haven't thought about it?" I challenged, my lips tugging upward as I slowly released her hand. I let the fingers of my free hand brush against the front of her neck as I swept a lock of hair off of it, and the way her breath caught sent my blood rushing to my cock. "God, you have."

She didn't say a fucking word, but her eyes narrowed at me, turning almost to slits as she stared me down.

"I'll tell you a secret, love," I said, lowering my head again until I was speaking directly into her ear, minimizing the risk of anyone overhearing as the music began to dwindle. "I've barely *stopped* thinking about it."

We slowed to a stop as the song came to a close, and although it took nearly everything in me to unlock my muscles, I released her.

She took a step back, giving me just enough room to drink every inch of her in, but before I could do so much as *memorize* how she looked, she bolted.

Chapter 9

Ava

I needed air, desperately.

Pushing through the crowd, I made my way to the opposite side of the room from where my father was schmoozing someone into buying stocks. I scanned the wall, looking for any sign of an exit, but I only saw the glowing neon exit sign that definitely wasn't meant to be used by attendees.

Fuck it.

I pushed the door open and slipped through into a service hallway.

I felt like I couldn't breathe, felt like I was going to overheat and pass out. The way he'd spoken to me, the way he'd *held* me, it was intoxicating and maddening. My body had responded in ways I wasn't even sure it could in front of that many people, and if I was being truly honest with myself about it, I almost hoped he was following me.

But that would be insane. Almost as insane as the amount of money he'd spent on three minutes with me, almost as insane as my father's impromptu decision to fucking auction me off, almost as insane as how much I wanted to admit right there on the dance floor how many times I'd touched myself to the idea of him and then how many times I'd done it to the memory.

And to know that he knew who I was that night...

I might actually lose my mind.

The sound of the exit opening behind me as I pushed my way through another door sent my pulse skyrocketing, and I had to tell myself that it was just an employee, just someone pushing a cart or a keg being brought in.

Another door, another exit from me, and the cold autumn air hit me like a fucking brick to the face. *Finally.*

The balcony was fairly large with a little makeshift garden on it and a golden fence locking it in, looking out over a somewhat quiet back road. The sounds of the city invaded me, but I was growing used to that, and for a moment, I could block them out.

What the fuck was I doing?

Reality sank in like a stone in water. I'd slept with a man nearly twice my age, one whom I'd been dreaming of since I was an inappropriate age. I'd pretended to be someone I wasn't. I'd begged him to stay. I'd let him touch me in ways I'd never even considered asking to be touched.

I'd known what that would do to me, and I'd let it happen anyway.

I pressed the bottoms of my palms into my eyes, the pressure calming me just slightly, and tried to breathe through it. Emily was right—I shouldn't have avoided this for as long as I had. I should have gone to that fucking restaurant and done the interview instead of chickening out. I shouldn't have let it build like this.

The sound of the door slamming open made me jump,

and even though I knew I'd find the combination of my worst nightmares and best dreams staring at me, I couldn't resist the pull.

"Stop fucking avoiding me, Ava."

He didn't even pause, didn't give me a moment to compose myself. He walked across the balcony toward me in his stupidly attractive black tux, pushing the salt and pepper hair that had fallen in his face out of the way. I didn't know what to do. Didn't know what I *wanted* to do, other than fling myself off the fucking edge of the building.

The distance closed before I could come up with a better idea.

His mouth crashed into mine, demanding my attention, and I didn't want to do anything other than let him. Hands grasped either side of my face, and God, I felt dizzy, felt like I was back in a stupid teenage dream where I could control what he said to me and shape the scene like a painter in action.

But this wasn't a dream, and it wasn't a work of art. It was real life, and neither of us was in full control of the other.

"Fuck," he rasped, lifting his lips just an inch from mine. "Your father is going to kill me."

"Please don't tell him," I whispered.

The laugh that came from him was filled with disbelief and a hint of irritation. "If I wanted to die, Ava, there are plenty of better ways to do it than offering myself to David Riley on a silver platter."

His lips met mine again, and this time I sunk into it, my body reacting before my brain. I fisted the front of his suit jacket in my palm, keeping him tethered to me as his mouth explored mine, the taste of red wine lingering on his tongue.

But my hands weren't the only ones that roamed.

He held me behind the neck again, but his other wandered freely over the front of the corseted satin I'd put on hours before. It dipped down to the slit in my dress, hooking behind my upper thigh and lifting it up, up, up onto his hip.

I was losing it *again*.

His lips wandered, kissing the side of my jaw, my neck, the soft spot beneath my ear where he'd pressed in with his fingers before. He nipped at the skin before soothing it with his tongue, and every thought ceased. There was only me, him, and an ache beginning to grow between my thighs.

"Please," I breathed, pulling on the front of his jacket. "Please."

"What are you begging for, Ava?"

Fuck, the way he said my name when his voice sounded like *that* was exactly how I'd imagined it. No more *Lily.* "Touch me."

The air that loosed from his chest almost seemed pained as he let his fingers slide up my thigh and over the curve of my rear, gripping the little strap of the seamless underwear I'd picked out for this dress. He pulled, and they shifted down. The second he lowered my leg enough to have them drop, I kicked them off my heeled feet. "I'm not going to touch you," he rasped.

What? No, please—

"I'm going to fucking taste you."

His hands left me in an instant, and before I could process his words, he was lowering to his knees on the dirty cement floor in front of me.

My fucking heart stopped.

Fingers pushed the sides of my dress apart and up to my

hips, and I couldn't bring myself to care about the potential onlookers from the next building over, couldn't bring myself to care about the chill in the air. All I knew was that he was looking up at me from the goddamn ground, one arm hooking around the inside of my thigh and lifting it onto his shoulder.

His mouth took me immediately.

A soft hum vibrated against my most sensitive spot, and I could barely breathe. His tongue lashed against me, dragging, berating, *attacking* where I was desperate for him to, but the ache didn't calm this time. It only built, angrier and angrier, needing more, *demanding* more.

But he knew how to work my body too well.

Two fingers slipped inside of me as he sucked my clit between stilled teeth, his tongue drawing far too much from me. I covered my mouth to keep in what I could only imagine were too-loud moans, using my other to hold onto his hair for dear life.

Bright blue eyes flicked up to mine, and oh my God, he was going to make me lose my mind.

Another finger entered as his mouth continued, another little hum making me see more stars than were visible in the light-polluted sky above. As if by some kind of magic, he was already pulling me too quickly toward a release, one that I couldn't hold back from, and all I could do was let him take me there, let him destroy me *again*.

"Fuck, I...I..."

"Come," he said, and that last little bit of vibration from the word was enough to make me break, was enough to make my knees buckle, and my fingers tighten in his hair, was enough to have me putting my weight on him in the hopes that I wouldn't go all the way down to the ground.

But he wasn't done with me.

He raised from the ground as his fingers slipped out, one hand holding my waist to keep me upright as the other worked frantically at his belt. The clanking of it rang through the air, and his damp mouth met mine, the taste of red wine and *me* coating my tongue.

"Put your arms around my neck," he ordered, breaking just enough from my lips to get the words out. I followed what he said, and a second later, he was lifting me, directing my legs up around his waist with his hand. He pressed forward into the wall, letting it take some of my weight.

But then there was warmth at my opening again, but it wasn't nearly as small as a finger.

"One more time," he rasped, pulling back just an inch to meet my gaze. "You're you, and I'm me. Do you understand?"

One more time. My head was too foggy to process the reality of that, but I nodded anyway.

Not nearly as slowly as the last time, but just as gently, he pressed into me, splitting me practically in two. Little bursts of pain blinked into existence before dying out just as quickly.

"Fuck," I hissed, gripping onto the back of his head and keeping him close to me.

A hand slipped between us, and he found my overly sensitive clit, just softly brushing his fingers against it enough to take the edge off. I relaxed around him, and a second later, he was fully inside of me, filling me in a way I'd ached to know for the last week and a half. "That's it, love."

"Ah—" The sound cut off from my gasp as he readjusted, hitting a spot inside of me that made my bones turn to mush. "Please don't leave. *Fuck*, please."

"*Don't leave?*" he parroted.

I shook my head, words fully lost on my tongue as I tried to figure out a way to articulate the phrase *I don't ever want to be empty again* without sounding like a mad woman. "Just fuck me, Adrian," I breathed instead.

His answering, breathy chuckle was all the confirmation that I needed.

Slowly, achingly, he slid himself so far out that I thought he *might* actually leave—but then he was slamming in, punishingly, demandingly, leaving me gasping for air that didn't feel like it was quite enough inside of my lungs. Over and over and over.

"God, *yes*," he groaned, his nails digging into the flesh of my thigh so hard that I could feel the little half-moon indents forming. He gave me a little more pressure on my clit to compensate, and the pain morphed into pleasure, setting fire to my veins. "You're too fucking perfect."

His mouth met my neck, teeth sinking into the soft, sensitive flesh there, and I couldn't bite back the sounds I made, couldn't cover them with my hand. They'd be drowned out by the honking of cars, and the boom of the bass from music pouring out of a club nearby anyway, but something about it felt exposing in a way I wasn't quite used to.

But Goddammit, it was *exhilarating*.

Every shift in his hips came with an echoing grunt from the crook of my neck, and every gentle caress of his fingers between my thighs pulled mirroring sounds from me. I wanted more from him, wanted my dress off and his chest bare, but every time I tried to push his suit jacket further than his elbows, he resisted. I couldn't quite tell if it was a reluctance to take this further than it already was out in the city air, or if he just truly didn't want to remove his hands from me long enough to shrug it off.

But he let me pull at his tie, let me undo a handful of buttons on his crisp white shirt, let me open his vest. It was enough to slip my hand in through a gap in the fabric, and I could feel the rigidity of his muscles, could feel them flex with every movement he made.

We'd done this already, but somehow, it still felt like a fantasy, still felt like I was out cold in bed dreaming of him like I'd done almost every night for the past week and a half and intermittently for years before that. He'd wormed his way inside of my mind, and although I'd gotten him out before, it seemed almost like he'd lodged himself deeper, somewhere I didn't know how to get to.

Somewhere real.

As the post-orgasmic sensitivity faded and I craved more of his touch, I gripped what little skin of his chest that I could and pulled at the hair on the back of his head. "More," I said, my voice barely more than a choked whisper. "More, Adrian."

His chuckle as he gave me more pressure on the place I needed it most, sending a shiver up my spine. "I shouldn't like it when you say my name like that," he said. He lifted his head, his chin tipping up and meeting mine almost in defiance. "And yet...*say it again*."

I swallowed down the little hint of anxiety that flared in my throat, and just as I opened my mouth to say his name, he moved his fingers faster, pressed down harder—and the name came out contorted, half-moaned, and half-sobbed.

The rising pleasure in my gut built rapidly at his answering smirk.

"You're the worst," I laughed, and his hips shifted as he readjusted me, lifting me just an inch higher. There wasn't a single part of me that understood what the fuck was happening inside, but he was driving himself into a spot that made my breath catch, and my fingers twitch. My head tipped back onto the cold concrete wall, my vision unfocused, and oh *God*, yes, that was perfect—

"Am I?" he challenged, but his words were strained, spat out through clenched teeth and stiffening muscles. The way he gripped me, the way he moved, it told me he was close, and I was right beside him, seconds from falling off the cliff. "I could be far meaner, Ava. I could..."

His fingers abandoned my clit entirely.

"...*do that.*"

I couldn't breathe, couldn't think straight, not when he'd left me teetering on the fucking edge like that. "No, no, no, *please*," I begged, my shaking hand slipping from his shirt and searching for his. *Where the fuck was it?* "Adrian, I swear to God—"

The fabric of my dress shifted, and just above where my legs met my hips, a warm pressure bloomed. A strained cry left my throat as the pressure made me feel even fuller, as it intensified the already gluttonous sensation of him hitting that spot inside of me. I'd never felt anything like that.

My orgasm tore through me, unannounced and unexpected, from somewhere far deeper than I'd normally feel it.

I gripped onto him for dear life as he fucked me, my body seizing and relaxing over and over, that pressure remaining in place as he shook. Just when I'd thought he'd lost all control and fully broken, a brush of sensation against my clit ignited me again, just enough to have me digging my fingers into bare skin and cloth as he buried his final moan against the underside of my jaw.

And despite how long he held me like that with our combined warmth dripping down between his polished shoes, despite how much our breaths synced as we tried desperately to regain our oxygen levels, despite how still we were as the breeze off the Hudson whipped through the buildings and blew against our bodies, I couldn't cool off. I couldn't come down from the high.

He'd lit me on fire with that last little touch, and I couldn't seem to put it out.

With shaking hands, he lowered me back to the floor and refastened his slacks, fixed the little flyaways that were sticking up from my hair, cleaned up the smeared lipstick below my lip. He wiped his mouth with the back of his hand, removing any hint of evidence there, before raking his fingers through the black and speckled gray of his hair.

My feet struggled to find their balance in my heels, and I leaned against the wall for support, my chest heaving with every breath.

I had never, not once in my life, had an orgasm like that. I couldn't wrap my head around it. I wasn't lucky enough to be blessed with the ability to have a release without external stimulation, but *that*... that was the only way I could classify it.

I didn't want to admit that he might know my own body better than I did. I didn't want to admit that I'd never had someone do that to me and likely never would again. I wasn't even entirely sure *how* he did it.

But God, I wanted him to do it again. And that couldn't happen.

Using the wall as my only help, I took a step away and toward the door, swallowing down all of the words that I *wanted* to say to him. I had to go with my gut here if we stood any chance of this fizzling out—something it was clear we both wanted and needed to accomplish.

"I thought you were done avoiding me," he said, his face almost unreadable in the low light of the shadow. His fingers stilled halfway through pushing a button into its hole.

I shook my head. "No," I said. Words and whole sentences flowed through my mind, too many of them being too real, too honest, but I kept those locked behind my teeth and went with the easiest thing to say. "This is exactly why I *need* to avoid you."

Chapter 10

Adrian

The slight resistance of the wooden keys beneath my fingertips did little to take my mind off the way Ava's skin had felt beneath them, but I played on nonetheless.

The morning sun trickled in through the wall of windows to my right. Cascading beams of slightly dusty yellow bounced off the top of my closed Steinway. I wasn't normally one to play this early, but I'd hardly gotten any sleep and needed something for my hands to do besides touching myself. I'd done enough of that tossing and turning well into the morning hours, and my body's internal clock hadn't let me regain that lost time.

I'd waited the hour it had taken for Lucas to get up for school before letting myself focus on the grand piano, though.

Every note that I played filled all three floors of my penthouse. It drowned out the sound of sizzling eggs in the kitchen, drowned out the cartoons from the living room, drowned out Lucas's insistence that he didn't want to wear his vest today but would agree to wear his sweater, drowned out the clacking of his brand-new shoes against the tile as he ran across the house.

But it did nothing to drown out the sound of Ava's voice as she said my name. The memory was repeating over and over and over again in my mind. The little gasp, the strained moan of it, the way she'd laughed when she'd called me *the worst*.

Maybe I *was* the worst.

I'd be a liar if I tried to tell myself that she wasn't plaguing my thoughts or tempting me to do things I promised myself I'd never do again. Even knowing that neither of us wanted more from the situation after the charity ball, I couldn't help but feel an inkling of *what if*. But that was thinking with the wrong one of my two heads. I'd promised myself I wouldn't date seriously again—for the sake of my sanity and the fragility of Lucas after losing his mother, I couldn't do that. And even considering it with Ava came with its own challenge: David fucking Riley. Her father. My friend.

Just as I turned the page of sheet music and my fingers stilled for a moment, clacking bounded closer, climbing up the stairway outside of the music room. Lucas popped his head in just as Grace caught up with him.

"Sorry, Mr. Stone," she wheezed, out of breath. "Lucas was wondering if you'd mind taking him to school this morning. I tried to tell him that you were busy—"

"Not at all," I said. I pulled the fallboard back over the keys and pushed up from my seat. "Have you got twenty minutes to spare for me to get dressed?"

Lucas nodded over-enthusiastically before tipping his head forward and holding an imaginary hat with his fingertips. "*Aye*, captain."

I knew bingeing three *Pirates of the Caribbean* movies last night had been a poor decision.

I chuckled as I stepped around the piano, ruffling the top of his black mop of hair when I passed him. I still had an hour until I needed to be in the office—I could swing it. "*Arr*, I'll be back in a jiffy, *matey.*"

———

Lucas' question seconds before we'd walked in through the front doors of his school had left me in a sour mood.

Dad, do you think you could maybe work a little less?

I knew he didn't mean for it to feel like a knife to the chest, but it did regardless. In truth, I was working an average amount at the moment, minus a small handful of nights a week where I had an event to oversee or a meeting to stay late for, but I understood. He was getting older, and he was starting to notice my absence more and more.

A nanny didn't make up for the emptiness of our penthouse or the emptiness that Jan had left behind. But it was all I could offer him for now, save for trying to take a few more nights off.

But it left me bitter and annoyed that I couldn't do that for him now, and coupled with the nonstop onslaught of thoughts of Ava, I wasn't in the greatest of headspaces for a fucking board meeting.

"So, Les Brown has confirmed. We still haven't had confirmation from Tony Robbins yet, but his team has pretty much given us the green light," Andrew said as he aimed his laser pointer at the projected image of a man's face. He was one of the board members with the most shares in Stone & Co Global besides me.

"We can't assume that," I said, looking up from the empty document that I'd opened almost an hour ago to take notes. *So much for that.* "If he's not outright confirmed, we can't plan or price tickets accordingly. Have you gotten on his team's case?"

Andrew pushed his glasses up his nose, his glare leveled at me as if I'd just sprouted a second head. "Of course I have."

For the briefest of seconds, an image of Ava with her makeup smeared and her hair a mess flitted through my mind. I clicked the top of my pen against the table to give my hand something to do. "And what have they said in response?"

A muscle in Andrew's ginger-beard-covered jaw twitched. "Had you been listening, Adrian, you would have heard that I've already said they are dealing with a scheduling conflict and working around it."

If I could properly grind my teeth without the horrible scraping noise, I would have. Andrew and I didn't see eye to eye often, and especially not on days like today when I found it hard to sink myself into my work.

I shot him a warning glare as I clicked my pen again. "Continue, Andrew."

———

The sun had slipped behind the building opposite ours by the time I made it back to my office. For once, I was glad for it—the building headache between my temples really didn't want to deal with the harsh rays of light or having to go to each of the five massive windows to manually shut the sliding blinds.

Making a mental note to install automatic ones, I dropped my laptop onto my desk and collapsed into the leather chair, scrubbing my face with the palms of my hands.

I had to get her out of my fucking head.

I couldn't stop replaying her saying my name on a loop, couldn't get the image of her in that goddamn dress out of my head. The way she'd looked on that stage, lit up like a mirror ball, or the way she'd looked with her legs just slightly spread and her hand in my hair, my mouth devouring her.

God, I could practically taste her.

I pulled at the seam where the legs of my slacks met, giving myself just a little extra room to deal with the minor, uncontrollable swelling of my cock. There was zero chance of me getting anything noteworthy done today.

I nearly jumped at the crackle of the speaker on my desk. "Hey, it's Michael. Can you buzz me in?"

Groaning out an ounce of my frustration in the one bit of privacy I had left, I reluctantly pressed the button on the side of the speaker that unlocked my personal portion of the forty-fourth floor. It wasn't that I didn't *want* to see Michael. I just didn't have the energy to keep my mind from wandering any more than it already was, and I didn't necessarily want to inevitably dump my bad mood on one of my closest friends.

But I also knew myself. I could hold things together in front of most people, including my son—but not Michael. He knew me too well.

"Heard what happened with Andrew," Michael said as he slipped through the door. It shut behind him automatically, and a second after I pressed the little button beneath the top of my desk, it locked. "Either someone's royally pissed you off today, or something's going on with Lucas."

"Would you believe it's neither?"

Sharp, brown eyes met mine across the room. "Unless you're the person who pissed yourself off, then no."

He looked far too casually dressed for the office, but as he walked across the floor and slumped down into the wingback, black leather chair across from my desk, I bit my tongue. It wasn't *bad*, but Michael had a habit of dressing in a way that teetered between *casual* and *business casual*. At least he was wearing slacks today, even if it was with a flannel shirt.

"So that's what it is," he chuckled.

"Just because I didn't reply to that doesn't mean it's automatically true," I scoffed. The creak from my chair as I leaned back filled the annoyed silence he shot in my direction, and I made a mental note to have someone grease the hardware on it.

Michael's eyes narrowed, his dark brows knitting together.

"Don't look at me like that."

"Goddamn, you really are in a mood." His fingers twisted around the end of his sleeve and popped the button. He began to roll it up, and I could have sworn a vein in my forehead nearly burst. "Would it make you feel better to know that we just got confirmation from Tony Robbins?"

"In all honesty, I don't give a fuck about Tony Robins," I snapped. "My issue with Andrew wasn't because I was worried he wouldn't confirm. It was because Andrew, I thought, was assuming confirmation without having it."

"But that wasn't the issue, was it?" Michael chuckled. "Not really, at least. If it was, you would have been fine when you heard otherwise."

"Do we have to do this? We could just go out for a late lunch and talk about literally anything other than work," I offered.

He pushed a hand through his mop of curly black hair. He'd started graying at his temples, but that seemed to be the only lighter bit of hair that had sprung up—a stark contrast to the lighter ones that peppered my head. "I have a sinking feeling you'd be just as snippy anywhere else. So why don't you just *talk* about it, get it off your chest, and get on with it?"

"You're not my therapist."

"Oh, you finally got one?" he laughed. "I've been saying for *years*—"

"Don't." I steeled my jaw as I met his gaze across the desk.

He was my closest friend. My confidant. I could tell him anything, could trust him to the moon and back, but he got on my fucking nerves sometimes—mostly on days like today when I couldn't see past the cloud that plagued me. But I could talk to him. I knew that and so did he, and on top of that, I knew damn well he wouldn't leave my office until I actually spoke to him instead of jabbing at him. I could give him half of the truth.

"Lucas asked me this morning if I could try to work less," I sighed. Michael's mouth formed the shape of a silent *oh*. "He's at that age where things are starting to make more and more sense to him, and with one parent permanently out of the picture, my absence is...obvious. And although I can cut down my hours, there will still be nights I won't be home, there will still be trips I need to take, or meetings I need to attend. I can't do it alone."

"Right," Michael sighed. "That's fair. I mean, he has the nanny, right?"

I gripped the leather arm of my chair. Michael didn't have kids—he wouldn't fully understand how that wasn't a helpful sentence. "Yes, but ideally, he needs another parent."

"Oh. Well, you've been dating recently, right? Is that why?"

I shook my head. "No, that's more for...fun," I explained. I told Michael most things, but I didn't need to explain exactly what I got up to on those dates, and he definitely didn't need to know about my alias. "But I'm considering doing it more seriously. David's daughter, Ava, is setting up some kind of matchmaking service, and David's convinced that she can find someone to solve my problems for me. But the idea of letting another person into my life, whether they're there only for my son or something slightly more, feels like an invasion that I'm uncomfortable with."

Michael nodded along to my words, steepling his fingers in his lap. "Shall I order in a chaise lounge for your office and finally get my psych degree?"

I glared at him.

"Kidding, kidding," he laughed. "I get it. I do. After Jan, that can't be fucking easy. But really, a matchmaking service? Aren't the cool kids using Hinge nowadays?"

I shrugged. "I spoke with Ava's assistant about it, and she said that their goal is to cater to people like me. Confidentiality, expert vetting, and finding me someone who is okay with what I want would be at the top of their priorities list."

He interlocked his fingers and slid his joined hands

between the puffed leather and the back of his head. "And what is it that you want?"

"A marriage of convenience," I shrugged. "I'm not diving in head-first again. I don't want to love whoever she is. I want to like her and be comfortable with her helping raise my son. That's it. I'll hire her, find someone, and my problem will be solved."

"Right. And this has nothing to do with you chasing after Ava at the charity ball?"

My gaze snapped to his.

He shrugged. "You spent...what was it? Sixty grand, on a dance with her. Did you think I wasn't paying attention to that?"

What the fuck? "Honestly, Michael, I had no idea you were even *there* that night."

"Only for about thirty minutes to solve a supply issue," he chuckled. "I came in right as David announced that you'd snatched it up. Saw you two dancing a few minutes later. Watched, uh, *that* whole thing. Do you realize that you're an incredibly intense person? Anyway—you booked it after her, and I stored it in my noggin, and now here you are mentioning her again. I had to ask."

Shit. You need to think of an excuse. "The other people bidding on her were slimy, and she looked uncomfortable. I know her fairly well, so I bid on the dance, knowing she'd be comfortable with me."

He snorted. "She looked *very* comfortable with you. Until she went running off."

I let my head fall back against my seat. I didn't feel comfortable lying to him while looking him dead in the eye, and I needed time to think, time to steer the conversation away from her. But every time I tried to think of anything *but* Ava, she barged her way into my head like some kind of barbarian, taking over the space that wasn't meant for her.

"Look, you don't have to explain yourself to me. I was just saying—"

"You saw nothing."

He went silent for a moment, and it hung in the air like the smell of rot. "Okay."

"Have you spoken to anyone about that?"

"No."

"Good," I sighed, tipping my head forward to look at him again. "Keep it that way."

"I can do that," he said, nodding.

"If David found out—"

"I get it."

"Do you?" I challenged. I leaned forward on the desk, taking up all the space I could without getting up. The images of her on my fucking bed were still in my mind, and I really didn't need to hammer this point home by standing and making the swelling bulge in my trousers noticeable. "As much as I love him, David is not the sanest person around. He could do me *damage* if he wanted to."

"I don't think he'd have that much of an issue with you having a slightly charged dance with his daughter, but yes, I understand."

I held his gaze. There wasn't a single part of me that was sure that he grasped the extent of what this was, and I couldn't decide if that was a positive or a negative.

Michael blinked, and a second later he was groaning in frustration, rubbing his face with his palm. "For fucks sake, Adrian, it wasn't just a dance, was it?"

Chapter 11

Ava

The crescendo of a song I'd never heard before played so loudly from my speakers that I could almost feel it vibrating the walls of my apartment. My playlist had ended nearly an hour ago, and I hadn't cared enough to pull myself away from the canvas and change it.

This, the paints, the feel of a brush against the stretched linen—it was the only thing keeping my mind off Adrian. The longer I could put off the intrusive thoughts, the more I could convince myself that what we'd done hadn't absolutely ruined me or sent me back years into my silly teenage crush.

The face that had taken shape in front of me wasn't one I completely recognized. She had elements of myself—the freckles mostly and the green of her eyes. But the shape of her jaw, the sharpness of her brow line, the darkness, and the little specks of white I'd added to highlight the blacker areas of her hair, looked far too close to Adrian for comfort.

It bothered me more than I cared to admit.

She wasn't done, but the longer I stared at it, the more I

realized that I needed her to be finished. I dipped my purposely dedicated brush into the jar of paint thinner and gently pressed a fingertip against her cheek before checking it. *Perfect. Still semi-wet.*

I didn't even take the time I normally would to get the perfect stroke.

Dragging the thinner, soaked brush across the center of the canvas, I streaked the paint, pulling it at odd angles and distorting her. I pulled the brush right through the center of her face, paint smeared as if I'd taken a hand across a freshly lipsticked mouth, and she was something new and something old all the same.

But there was still too much of both of us in it.

I dipped the brush again.

Beep. Beep.

The sound of an incoming text through my speakers nearly made me knock the entire jar of thinner onto the old hardwood floor, and for a second, I could have sworn my life flashed before my eyes at the idea of how my father would react to me ruining the original flooring in the townhouse he'd bought for me.

I shuddered at the thought.

Beep. Beep.

Fucks sake.

Grunting and sore from holding my position for the last three hours, I pushed myself off my chair and hobbled over to the kitchen counter to check my phone.

I was almost grateful I hadn't had it next to the paint thinner. The text that awaited me absolutely would have sent the thinner flying.

Unknown Number: Hey. Hope you don't mind me reaching out on your real number this time.

Unknown Number: I answered all of your assistant's

questions. You haven't gotten back to me about whether you're taking me as a client.

I stared at the phone for far too long before wiping my paint-covered hands on my apron and picking it up. There was no one else that could possibly be—no one else I'd given a fake number to that had my real one now. Dad must have given it to him.

Me: That's because I'm not.

Unknown Number: Come on, Ava.

Just as I was two letters into a reply, another message came through.

Unknown Number: Can we schedule a meeting to go over potential matches?

I gulped.

Me: Find someone else.

The message sat there for a moment undisturbed before the little bubble with three dots danced across the bottom of the screen.

Unknown Number: I'd rather not.

Unknown Number: Look, client to freelancer, I need to find a mother for my kid. And I trust you to do that.

A mother for his *kid*? What the fuck did that mean?

Me: What?

Unknown Number: It will be easy as fucking pie for you, okay? Guaranteed success for your business. Just find me someone happy to have their life paid for by me while helping me raise my son. I don't need an emotional connection to her.

I stared down at the phone, trying to process what he was saying. He...didn't want an emotional connection. That was the whole fucking point of my business.

Me: I don't think I can do that for you.

Unknown Number: It will raise suspicions with your

father if neither of us follows through with this. You scratch my back, I'll scratch yours. I get what I'm looking for and you get a success story to show your father and any potential clients.

My stomach turned over, twisting, pulling at my guts. I couldn't tell his angle through text, couldn't figure out if he genuinely wanted this to go well for us both, or if he was just trying to toy with me.

Me: Adrian, please.

Unknown Number: God.

Unknown Number: Even through text, that sounds fucking sinful.

Just as quickly as those two messages arrived, they disappeared. They made the whooshing sound of my heart beating too loudly in my ears increase, made my breath catch, but then they were gone as if they'd never appeared. He must have deleted them within milliseconds.

Unknown Number: Monday morning. 10 A.M. sharp. 44th floor of the Darkwater building. The receptionist will tell you where to go.

———

Why I'd let myself be persuaded to turn up at ten in the morning on the forty-fourth floor of the Darkwater building in the financial district, I would never know. And I'd probably never live it down.

"Ms. Riley is here to see you." The young man who had walked me from the front desk of his offices to the frosted door at the back of the main room spoke calmly into the little intercom system.

The door buzzed, and he pushed it open, holding it for me. I stepped through.

"Go down this hall and hang a right," he explained. "Mr. Stone's office is clearly marked there."

I nodded and thanked him, and a second later, the door shut behind me. The space was eerily quiet—three hallways branching off in a T-formation that, from what I could tell, led to a private meeting room and a storage space.

I swallowed down the last of my pride and walked down the main hall. My heels clacked against the floor, echoing off the walls and through the quiet walkway. I wished I hadn't worn them, wished I'd dressed more casually, but this was a business meeting and nothing else. I didn't want him to get the wrong idea.

But a part of me did feel suffocated in my black pantsuit and patterned blouse. He hadn't seen me dressed like this, and it didn't feel right. It felt more like a costume with every passing step toward his office.

I took a right at the end of the hall and went down a short, narrow hallway that ended in a door that was ajar. The plaque read, *Owner and CEO, Adrian Stone*. It filled me with an intense, unending sense of dread.

I didn't let it hold me back, though.

I pushed through the open door. The office that waited for me was almost as large and beautiful as my father's. It was a wide, open space that must have taken up at least a quarter of the southwest side of the building, with floor-to-ceiling windows separated by the structural beams of Darkwater. The floor was made of large, black and gray marble tiles, and at the far end of the room overlooking the Hudson was a wide desk with a wooden bookshelf behind it. To my left, a small seating area contained three white, leather chairs, and there, in the middle, on the long matching sofa, sat Adrian.

The door shut behind me without me so much as touching it, and I nearly jumped out of my skin.

"Sorry," he said, waving something small and black in his palm. "Should have warned you."

"You think?" I breathed. My bag slipped from my shoulder as I turned back to him.

Fuck.

I had no idea how I was going to get through this stupid meeting.

He sat there in his black suit, his tie slightly too loose, his white shirt fully on display under his unbuttoned jacket. He lounged against the back of the sofa, his arms out on either side, his legs crossed at the knee. Salt and pepper hair was styled back and out of his face, save for a single clump that didn't seem to want to do what it was told.

But it was how he looked at me that absolutely demolished me.

It felt like being under a microscope, but in a way that made my skin heat and my cheeks flush. Like he could discover anything and everything he'd want to if he just *looked* long enough.

I should have insisted we did this in public.

"Have a seat," he offered, his lip lifting up at one side.

"This is strictly business," I insisted, hardening my voice. But my feet didn't want to fucking move.

"I was under no impression that it wasn't," he laughed. One hand shot out toward the chair across from him as an offer, and I swallowed, nodding my acceptance.

I shouldn't have needed that offer to move, but for some reason, my body decided it worked on his command alone. I stepped across the marble and onto the plush carpet that covered the floor beneath the seating area, sinking into the soft chair he'd pointed out.

If I was going to get through this, I needed to shut everything down. All of it, every bit of whatever wanted to come out. I needed to be cold. I needed to put on my professional mask, get this done, and then get the hell out.

I slipped my binder out of my bag and opened it to the questionnaire Emily had filled in. "How accurate is what you told Emily?"

His mouth popped open as he chuckled. "Is that her name?" he asked, shifting until he was leaning forward with his elbows on his knees. "It's accurate. I didn't hold back."

I sighed and looked down at the first page of notes. I hadn't even looked at it once—I'd managed to keep myself from giving in to my curiosity for weeks, but here and now, I had to *read* it.

Some of it was obvious—things like being interested in women, his job, his position, his primary location. The fact that he lived in *this* building was a little bit of a surprise, coupled with the exact figure of his income that made me realize that spending sixty-five grand on a dance with me was a drop in the ocean for him. It made my eye twitch regardless.

But then there were other things, things that I wouldn't have known, things that made me stop and fully read his answers.

Favorite thing to do outside of work? *Spend time with my son, Lucas.*

Favorite season? *Winter. The lights, the Christmas markets, the chill, the snow. All of it. Even the worst parts, when Christmas is over, and it's the dead part of the season.*

95

Favorite music genre? *Classical, indie, and pop. No, I won't explain.*

What is the first thing you look for in a partner? *A pulse. (I'm sorry, Ava, he wouldn't give me another answer. -Em)*

What is your favorite thing in your life? Lucas.

Ideal date? *A night at an art museum, finished with a glass of wine on my sailboat.*

"Something wrong?"

I swallowed and lifted my gaze from the sheet. "No," I lied. I just hadn't been expecting that last one. "There are a few things that Emily didn't get to when she interviewed you."

"You mean when she pretended to be you?" His smirk nearly made me break my pen in half.

"I don't know how relevant these will be considering you don't actually care that much who you end up with, but I'd rather know and try to accommodate you," I continued. I wasn't going to give his question the time of day. "Do you have a preference on a—"

"I *do* care who I end up with," he interjected. "Just because I don't want some fantastical love story out of this doesn't mean I don't want to find someone I'll be happy spending at least the next ten years with, if not more."

My lip twitched into a scowl. I'd never been good at hiding what I was feeling, but I tried regardless, covering my mouth with the back of my hand.

"Hit a nerve?"

"I just don't understand why you're talking about it like that," I snapped. "'*Some fantastical love story*'. You make it sound like that's something to turn your nose up at, like you're better than other people for not wanting that." I jotted down the phrase "fantastical love story" and put a giant X over it.

"I don't think I'm better than other people for not wanting to fuck around with the silly idea of *true love*."

I let him see the scowl that time. "See, you did it again. Silly idea. True love. Do you not hear that? Are you that dense? I'm not saying *true* love is a real thing, but *love* surely is, and you're acting as though I'm stupid for thinking that."

His jaw hardened as he looked at me, a sea of piercing blue staring me down. "Ask me about my preferences, Ava."

An uncomfortable silence hung over us for far too long as I worked up the nerve to continue. Every part of me just wanted to get out of here for reasons completely different from the ones that had flared when I came in, but what he'd said in his text was true. Dad expected me to try. And I wanted this business to fucking work. "Age preference?"

"Thirty to fifty," he said.

But I'm twenty-five. "Do you want her to be any particular height?"

"Under six foot."

"Size?"

He shrugged. "No real preference."

"Working or non-working?"

He went quiet for a moment as he looked at his watch, his brows knitting together. "Working, but not as many hours as me. Ideally, she'd be independent and would have her own things going on, but with more time for Lucas than I have."

"How many hours do you work? Just so I can ballpark this."

"Forty-five to seventy a week. It varies." He shrugged, and as I jotted down his answer, a loud crack came from him. I glanced up, and he was pushing at his neck at an odd angle before turning and doing it in the other direction. *Jesus.* "Maybe someone that can work from home if she's full-time would fit nicely?"

"Okay." I clicked the top of my pen against my lip as I tried to think of anything else that could be useful for me to know. I didn't want to have to contact him again after this unless it was to set up a date. "Is there anything else specifically that you want me to know?"

He sucked his teeth as his gaze traveled somewhere behind me, lost either in thought or in the plain gray paint job of the wall. "I have to take frequent trips for the company. So I guess someone who doesn't mind being left alone with Lucas would be good," he said. "Other than that, I guess it would just be...someone who loves children, and someone who is okay with their partner being closed off."

"You want me to ask the women I'll be speaking to if they'll be happy being unloved?" I scoffed. "That'll go over well."

"I'm sure there's someone out there who is more than happy to have their life paid for in exchange for helping me raise my son without the guarantee of more."

I shook my head. "You do realize that this service is for people who don't *need* to have their life paid for, correct? My clientele will be mostly people of *your* status."

His gaze met mine again. "You'll find someone."

I snorted. "Either you've got a warped sense of perspective, or my father significantly oversold my abilities."

"Open up the pool a little more if you need to," he said. His hands dug into his slacks on either side of his knees, and with a quick grunt, he pushed himself up until he was standing. It screamed of a power move, with him towering far above me and looking down at my discomfort. But from the way his lips tightened, from the way he looked away from me as I clocked it, it felt more like an assertion of his reluctance to keep going. "There's nothing else I need you to know."

"Wait," I insisted, flipping the page to the last little chunk of questions I'd forgotten about. He paused, and I skimmed them, picking out which would actually help me with this, since he wanted to end the meeting. "Are there any specific traits you'd like me to consider?"

He sighed. "Someone good with kids, but I figured that was clear."

"Any specific professions you prefer?"

His Adam's apple bobbed as he swallowed. "No Broadway cast members."

"What? Why?"

"Next question."

"You can't just *not* explain that," I said, jotting it down regardless and underlining it for emphasis.

"I absolutely can, and I will." He crossed the floor, stepping from carpet to marble tile, as he walked back toward his desk. "Just skip the theater industry."

The sun nearly blinded me as I turned my head to watch him collapse into his desk chair. I followed his lead and stood, putting myself back in the shade once again. "If you could just explain, I can figure out what the root of that issue is and apply it to other candidates for you."

"Ava. Stop."

I held his gaze across the room. Every part of me wanted to dive into that deeper, sink my fingernails in, and rip it out of him. It was such a random request, but I didn't know how far that went—were musicians in general off the table? What about playwrights, technicians, film actors, set designers? "I can't do this if you don't work with me."

"You can." The intensity of his voice as he said those

two stupid words across the empty space hit me in a way I wasn't expecting. It almost felt as though I were a child being scolded for something I hadn't done, like I was being spoken down to, like he wanted me to be aware that he could make or break my career with this. It felt *sour*.

He scrubbed at his face and sighed, relaxing into the leather of his chair a little bit more. When he opened his mouth again, the words came out softer, gentler, and I couldn't help but wonder if he'd realized how cutting the last couple things he had said had been.

"If we need to refine it after the first few matches, then we will. But for now, that's as far as I'm going."

"Fine." I shut my binder and shoved it back into my bag, not fully accepting his silent apology in the shift of his tone. "I'll contact you once I've figured out how to pitch this to potential matches."

Chapter 12

Adrian

The woman across the table from me smelled so heavily of sickly-sweet cotton candy that I couldn't help but wonder if she'd rolled around in a bathtub full of it before lathering herself in a similarly scented perfume.

"It's a shame they don't allow kids in here," she complained, stabbing the ice in her vodka soda with the end of her straw. For the life of me, I couldn't even remember her name. "You would *love* Veronica."

I nearly shook my head in confusion as I tried to wrap my mind around what she had said. *She had a kid? That isn't something I requested.* "Uh, who?"

The bright blue of her obviously colored contacts met my gaze as a grin spread across her brown-painted lips. I wasn't typically one to judge, but she wasn't someone I would usually gravitate toward—the overdone makeup, the bleached blonde hair, the filler, the intense cleavage of her worked-on breasts...it was someone's type, but it wasn't mine. "Veronica. Hold on, I'll show you."

She plucked her phone from her overly large handbag

that she'd insisted needed to sit on top of the table. The clack of her nails against the screen was either so loud I could hear it over the music, or the sound just simply grated on me. A couple of seconds later as the waiter rounded the corner with our desserts, she spun the phone around toward me.

"Isn't she just adorable?"

A blur of white against a black background had me backing up an inch to see the screen better without my reading glasses, and oh, *no*, who the fuck had Ava set me up with? "Is that a...pomeranian?"

"Yes! Good eye," she giggled. "Purebred, too. I'm sure she'll get along with yours just fine."

What the hell was happening? "Mine...?"

"Oh. Ava said you had a kid, too." Her brows met in the middle as she dropped her phone back into her purse.

"Uh...yeah, I do have a kid," I said. The waiter deposited a slice of chocolate cake and a small bowl of strawberries in the center of the table, and it took almost everything in me not to ask him to take it back and put it in a to-go container so I could get the hell out of here. "A child. Human child."

"Oh." Her head cocked to one side, and I couldn't help but suddenly realize how absurdly dog-like the movement was. "I'm confused—"

"Did you tell Ava *you* had a kid?"

She nodded as she stabbed the cake with her fork, shoveling a bite of it between her brown lips. *Why are they brown?* "Mhm."

"But you don't have a kid."

"I do. I have Veronica."

I thanked my lucky stars that I hadn't grabbed for my

fork yet. It would have bent in half with how much I was clenching my fists. "That...is not the same thing."

She waved at me with her fork. "My friends and I call our dogs our kids. It's not weird."

"It's weird to not clarify when you're talking to a *match-making* service," I insisted. "Do you even like kids? Human ones?"

She shrugged. "I mean, I guess. They're fine."

It took everything in me not to slam my head onto the table.

———

Me: Was that on purpose?

I pulled my jacket closer around me as I stepped out of the lobby of the building, my jaw aching from how tight I was clenching it. Either Ava wasn't nearly as good at her job as her father made her out to be, or she was fucking with me. *Ding. Ding.*

Ava: What? What do you mean?

Ava: Is this about Vanessa?

Ah, that was her name.

Me: Yes.

Ava: She seemed really nice, and she was open to your idea of a relationship. She even has a kid. I don't understand.

I stared at the phone in disbelief. Had she not fully checked anything?

Ava: Adrian?

I clicked her name at the top of the text messages and hit the call button, bringing the already freezing metal and

103

glass of the phone up to my ear. Two rings later, her voice filled my ear, and as much as it fueled me with a new sense of anger, more than anything it calmed me down.

"What happened?" she asked. In the background, a whooshing sound like wind or rain filled the gaps between her words.

"She..." I glanced over my shoulder as I crossed an intersection, double-checking that she wasn't heading in the same direction as me. "She doesn't have a kid, Ava. She has a *pomeranian*."

Silence met my words, and I lifted the phone to check that the call hadn't dropped. But then there was a squeak of something wet against the tile and the whooshing stopped. *Is she in the shower?*

I didn't want to admit to myself how relieved I was that my jacket covered my crotch. The idea of her standing there, naked, dripping wet, on the other end of the phone made it hard to think.

"But...she said she had a kid. Four years old, I think she said, named Veronica. I thought it was cute she was sticking with the V names."

"She has a *pomeranian* named Veronica," I said, side-stepping a man on a skateboard who absolutely should have been on the road and not the sidewalk. Ava's breathy, surprised laugh crept down the phone line, and for a moment, I didn't care that it was cold and wet out. Scaffolding lined the walkway, and I stepped into the gap, leaning against the wall between two shops under the street lamps. I wasn't going to give her a chance to reply. "Putting that to one side for a moment, can you explain to me why you bothered answering the phone when you're clearly in the shower?"

Another second of silence met me, and this time, it felt charged. "Because you called," she said.

Because you called. Jesus.

A man passed me as I started to speak, and I dropped my voice. "You must be cold," I teased. "Haven't heard you get out yet."

"*Adrian*," she groaned, and although I knew damn well it was a complaint and nothing more, I couldn't help but wish it was something else. Our last interaction hadn't gone well, and even though this was stupid, and there was a part of me that was still annoyed about her choice for my date this evening, it was almost...refreshing to speak to her. Like it was righting the wrong from last week when we'd argued in my office.

"I'm sorry," I laughed. "I'll drop it. Just please put a fucking towel on so I can stop imagining you standing there naked."

Whatever she said was so garbled that I couldn't quite make it out, but a second later, there was a squeak of a shower door, and the light breaths she took made me assume she was doing what I'd asked. "Happy now?"

"Do you want me to be honest?"

"No."

"Then I'm thrilled that you're in a towel," I chuckled. "*Anyway*, I'm sorry to derail us. But for the record, moving forward, Ava, I'd prefer someone who doesn't refer to their dog as a child to *that* extent. And maybe someone who doesn't smell that strongly of cotton candy."

"God, she did smell really sweet. Noted."

Chapter 13

Ava

The temptation to murder my own father had never been more present in my mind.

I stood in the doorway of the kitchen in my tank top, cardigan, and oversized joggers, my hair tied up in a messily made bun. Dad had offered for me to spend the weekend in his penthouse, and when he'd invited me downstairs for *family dinner*, I didn't think that meant anything more than he and I and whatever he'd decided to cook.

I hadn't expected to find Adrian leaning against the kitchen island with a glass of wine in his hand, midway through a fit of laughter, in a white button-up shirt and a pair of nice jeans.

His eyes met mine, and I nearly fucking bolted.

"Dad—"

"Ava! Good God, I've been calling your name for twenty-odd minutes. Dinner's done," Dad said, lifting his apron up and over his head before hanging it on the side of the fridge.

"Why...why didn't you tell me Adrian was coming?" I

asked, trying to keep my voice as level as I could. "I should change."

I glanced over at Adrian just in time to catch him mouthing, *I'm sorry*.

"Don't be ridiculous, pop tart," Dad scoffed. "Adrian's seen ya in pajamas before. I doubt he has a problem with it."

He's seen me in a lot less than pajamas.

"Honestly, Dave, I don't mind if she wants to change. We can wait a few more minutes to eat," Adrian offered. He glanced over at me, and for a split second, his eyes wandered below my chin, snagging briefly on the swell of my breasts. *I should have worn a fucking bra.* I pulled the sides of my cardigan closed at the front.

Dad groaned as he spun on the spot with a giant pot of Alaskan king crabs. "Fine. Go change clothes, kiddo. Be quick."

―――

I didn't feel *that* much more comfortable in one of Dad's hoodies and my jeans, but it was better than being braless in front of the one person I was actively trying not to be attracted to.

"So," Dad said, hooking the cracker tool around the widest part of a claw and clamping down, filling the dining room with a loud *crack*. "How's the matchmakin' going?"

"Great," Adrian lied.

"A disaster," I clarified. I shoved my tiny two-prong fork into one of the long sections of a leg and fished out the meat. "Don't listen to Adrian, he's just trying to be nice to me."

107

Adrian's gaze lingered on me for half of a second too long, and I found myself tearing my gaze away, focusing instead on dipping the strip of meat into the little bowl of melted seasoned butter.

"It hasn't been *that* bad," he said. "I just haven't found anyone I'd like to see again yet."

I shot him a glare. He was sugarcoating this—*hard*.

"Really? Ava's usually a mastermind when it comes to this kind of shit," Dad said, cracking another bit of shell with his tool. "You sure you're not being a particularly diffi-cult client?"

I snorted as I shoved a strip of meat between my teeth.

"I think we've both just been severely unlucky," Adrian chuckled. "Some of the women I've met with have been... questionable at best, but I don't think that's Ava's fault. I mean hell, one of them came right out and told me that she'd lied about being okay with kids purely to have the chance to go on a date with me. That's not Ava's fault."

"That's true, I had no idea. Lucy was very convincing," I said, popping another bit of crab into my mouth.

"Maybe you should be pulling from people who are a little less desperate to go on dates with wealthy men, kiddo," Dad offered.

I shrugged. "It's hard to keep up with all the require-ments Adrian has," I said, and it wasn't technically a lie. I didn't know how much Adrian had told my father in terms of what he was searching for, but I wasn't about to out him on it if he wanted privacy in that regard. "Widening the pool seemed like a good idea when we started a few weeks ago. I probably need to go back to the drawing board."

"After Melissa? Absolutely you do," Adrian laughed.

"Melissa?" Dad asked.

Adrian chuckled as he cracked into a claw. "The

woman I met last night. She turned up stoned to high hell and wearing a fairy costume."

A staggered coughing sound came from Dad, and for a split second, I wasn't sure if he was cackling or choking on crab meat.

"*Jesus.* Right, you two seriously need to work this out." Dad wiped his mouth with his cloth napkin as he set down his cracker tool.

"Maybe Adrian is just too hard for me to pin down," I shrugged, glancing across at him. "He'd probably do better on his own at this point."

"Ava—"

"Don't be ridiculous," Dad snapped, cutting Adrian off. "Listen, you two have barely scratched the surface. And I get that—I do, kiddo. You knew him when you were a teenager and probably barely paid attention to him."

I swallowed. *I paid far too much attention to him, Dad.*

"And Adrian, it can't be easy speakin' about all this shit with my daughter, y'know? There are boundaries there that ya don't want to cross, and I respect that."

Adrian's knee knocked against mine under the table, and for the briefest of seconds, the memory of him taking me from behind with his hand on my throat invaded my senses. The buttery bit of crab didn't taste like it should anymore—it tasted like his mouth.

"You've still got that place over in the Hamptons, yeah?"

"Yeah," Adrian said, cracking a leg in half and breaking the meat along with it. He cursed at himself before holding his hand out in my direction as a silent request for the little fork I'd been hogging. I gave it to him carefully, making sure we didn't even touch. I didn't need another flashback. "Why?"

Dad plucked another couple of whole crabs out of the pot at the end of the table and whacked them down on the serving dish in front of us. "Why don't you take Lucas and Ava out there next weekend so you two can...I don't know, iron out all the kinks?"

I nearly choked on my fucking crab.

"That's not—"

"Adrian, respectfully, hear me out, would ya?" Dad snapped, and oh no, here we went—the *I know better than you and will not be told otherwise* side of my father was kicking in. He was incapable of being reasoned with when he was like this, and I could already feel myself shrinking into my fucking seat. "If she had the chance to be around Lucas, see how you are with him, and get to know you a bit better outside of business mode, I think it could really help her get a better idea of who you need in terms of a partner. You forget she hasn't been around ya at all for the last ten years—"

"Dad," I interjected. "If Adrian isn't comfortable with it, then don't force me on him."

"No, look at him. He loves the idea."

I glanced at Adrian. All I could get from his face was mortification. "No, you've freaked him out, Dad."

"He's not...you haven't freaked me out, Dave," Adrian clarified, swallowing his food. "I just don't know how Lucas would feel about that."

Yes. Good. Perfect excuse.

"Lucas loves going to the Hamptons," Dad said as if it was the most obvious thing in the world. "He didn't have a problem when I came with you last time. Why is Ava any different?"

"I..."

"Listen," Dad insisted, leaning forward on the table

toward Adrian. My stomach twisted as the realization slowly sunk in that neither of us could fight this—not without Adrian suddenly finding someone he wanted to spend the rest of Lucas's childhood with in the next five days. "You wanna find someone soon to help with Lucas? Because this might be your best bet."

Adrian sighed, and for the briefest of seconds, he met my gaze. "All right."

Dad's joyous, *I was right* laughter filled the room, and all I wanted to do was run. This was a *horrible* idea. For both of us.

Adrian nearly jumped as Dad's hand clapped him on the shoulder, tightening fiercely and giving him a little shake. "You should feel honored that I trust ya so much with my kid," Dad chuckled. "Don't think there's a man alive who I'd trust enough to ship her off for a weekend with except you."

Chapter 14

Adrian

Taking a weekend of work off at short notice when we had an event on Saturday and Sunday wasn't my best move as CEO, but Lucas hadn't been able to stop shrieking about his excitement to go to the Hamptons when I'd mentioned it in passing, and I couldn't bring myself to break his heart after his plea for me to work less a few weeks ago.

But that didn't mean I couldn't bring some work with me to distract me from Ava.

In an effort to ensure that we weren't alone together, I'd invited Lucas' nanny, Grace, as well. At least if there were three adults on-site at a minimum, my chances of letting my cock think for me were slim.

I took up residence in the very back of the van I'd rented, with Ava and Lucas in the middle row of seats and Grace in the front with the driver. I did my best to focus on my laptop as I braved the two-hour car journey, but it was hard when Lucas kept asking question after question after question.

To my utter surprise, though, Ava had been quick on the draw for all of them.

"Why is it called the Hamptons?"

"Because it's made up of two areas named East Hampton and West Hampton," Ava grinned, leaning across the middle seat to show Lucas something on her phone. "I think I asked my dad that same question when he used to bring me out here."

"Oh, cool," Lucas chirped. His mop of black curls bounced as he turned rapidly in his seat, watching as a massive bird flew past the car window. "What's that?"

I opened my mouth to reply, but Ava beat me to it.

"Think it's an osprey," Ava answered. "Huge wingspan."

Her eyes met mine over the back of her seat, and for the briefest of seconds, I let myself take her in. She wasn't dressed for business today—in fact, she wore an outfit that reminded me more of how she'd looked when she'd been *Lily*. A mid-length, brown, flowing skirt and a cropped white sweater covered her slim frame, and her long auburn hair hung around her in waves. Her makeup was subtle, and as she looked at me, I wondered if it was possible to count how many freckles dotted her skin. How long would it take me, how many pieces of clothing would I need to remove—

"You okay?" Ava asked, her voice low as she leaned over the seat.

I pulled my lips taut and nodded to her. "I'm fine. Thank you for entertaining Lucas."

"Of course, it's no problem."

But it was a problem. It was a massive fucking problem.

———

. . .

The car pulled into the driveway of the estate, stopping only for the driver to input the code for the gate to open. We rounded the neatly trimmed hedges, and the expanse of the property opened up wide, with the house halfway between the ocean and the road. Greenery climbed the outside walls of the brick building, and for a moment, I wondered if I should call out the landscaper and have them removed—but the longer I looked, the more it charmed me, as if it were some kind of mansion in a fairytale buried deep in the woods and covered in vines.

The sun bore down on us harshly in the cool autumn air as we got out of the van. Lucas immediately began doing laps in the freshly cut grass, and I helped the driver unload the small suitcases we'd brought with us.

Ahead, in the open front door, Mrs. Henderson stood in her apron, one hand resting on the ridge of her brow to shield her eyes from the sun. The other hand was clutching a wooden spoon. "Is that Lucas Stone I see?" she called playfully.

Ava stopped to watch as Lucas booked it across the lawn, running straight for the door. "Who's that?" she asked, leaning toward me when I took her suitcase out. I didn't bother giving it to her—I'd take it in.

"Mrs. Henderson," I explained. "Don't bother asking her for her first name, she won't let you use it. She's the cook."

"Does she live here?"

I shook my head. "No, she lives on the other side of town. She comes by each day when I'm here."

I stacked Lucas' bag on top of mine and headed toward the house with Ava, all three of our bags in tow behind me.

All the other occasions I'd come here had been happy getaways—even when Lucas and I had come out here for two months after Jan's death to get away from the world. But this time...I just wasn't sure.

"Nice to see you, Mr. Stone," Mrs. Henderson said as we approached the door. Lucas' face was buried in a flour-coated portion of her apron as he clung to her. "Who's this?"

Ava stuck out a hand. "Ava Riley," she said, plastering a massive grin across her face. Mrs. Henderson shook her hand, offering her a warm smile in return. "I'm working on a project with Adrian, so he brought me along."

I snorted. *A project?*

"I'm sorry, I need to get through."

I turned, and Grace climbed up the front porch steps, her face white as a sheet in the blaring sunlight. She clutched her stomach as she trailed her bag behind her, and without thinking I took it from her grasp. "Are you okay?"

"I think I'm going to be sick," she said, slipping past the four of us and practically running into the estate.

———

An hour or so later, the smell of baking bread and searing salmon filled the living room, foyer, and kitchen. I lounged on the white sofa beneath the exposed beams of the living room, the fireplace roaring with life not ten feet from me, with my laptop on my legs and a cup of coffee in my hand.

Maybe David had a point. I *did* love it here.

Ava sat on the edge of the fireplace, her attention

focused wholly on Lucas' puzzle that they were desperately trying to figure out together. They'd managed to get two of the four edges completed already, but they seemed to be running out of steam, either from hunger or exhaustion from the two-hour drive.

"Okay, look for one with another eye on it 'cause mine only has one eye," Lucas chirped, spreading out the available options for pieces in front of him.

"Lucas," Ava laughed. "There are like, forty people in this puzzle. There are *so* many eyes."

Lucas giggled along with her and showed her his piece, and I watched over the top of my laptop. "Yeah, but this one has *black* hair, like me and Dad. So find one with one eye and black hair."

"Okay, okay," she chuckled, sorting through the pieces with him. "But let's be honest. Your dad's hair is like, half gray."

"Yeah, because he's *old*."

"Forty-five is not *old*," I interjected. "You can call me old when I hit fifty. *Maybe*."

Lucas nodded far too enthusiastically before turning back to Ava. "He's definitely old," he whispered, and Ava burst out into a full-bellied cackle.

"I can *hear* you, Luc," I said, pointing to my ear. "You'll be forty-five one day. You know that, right?"

"Will not," he pouted.

"You will. So will I," Ava grinned. She leaned in a little closer to him, her gaze snagging on mine as she whispered, "And we'll be old then."

"Oh my God," I groaned.

Footsteps padded down the hall, and what I thought would be Mrs. Henderson popping her head around the corner to announce that dinner was ready morphed into something much, much worse. Grace stepped just barely into the sitting room, her gray hair hanging loosely around her pale face.

"Oh, no. Are the meds not working?" I asked, setting my laptop off to the side and hoisting myself up.

"They are a bit," she sighed. "I think I might have some kind of stomach bug. I'm so sorry, but I don't think I can watch Lucas tonight."

"Please don't worry about that," I insisted, but the part of my mind that needed the presence of someone else to keep me from bending to what I wanted with Ava was *screaming*.

"I can watch him if Adrian needs to do some work," Ava called from behind me. "Do you want us to call the driver back? Maybe you should head home."

Grace shook her head. "As nice as that sounds, I don't think I can make it back to the city without coating the inside of the van in sick."

"You should go lie down, then," I offered. "Honestly, you deserve to relax anyway. I'll see if we've got anything else that can help you feel better."

As much as I was more than happy to take the responsibility of my son off her hands, I couldn't help but dread watching more of Ava's instinctual playfulness when it came to being with Lucas. They'd meshed the moment they met back at the bottom of the Darkwater building, and every passing second that they spent together seemed to only enhance their closeness.

I knew I should be grateful that he was happy to spend time with her when we'd be here for the next two days. But when I was actively desperate for someone who could do that with him and the person who ticked those boxes was directly in front of me in the form of Ava fucking Riley, it was my worst nightmare.

Keeping her out of my head when she wasn't around had only become *slightly* easier over the passing weeks, and I couldn't help but fear that seeing this unfold in real time would make everything that much harder.

In order of importance, my requirements went from taking care of Lucas and bonding with him, to someone I could freely enjoy the presence of, to someone who didn't need to be loved. And I knew Ava only ticked one of those—but it was the most important one. I couldn't freely be with her even if I wanted to, not with David around.

And she certainly needed, and wanted, to be loved.

Chapter 15

Ava

My reflection in the bathroom mirror stared back at me in fucking horror.

What the fuck are you doing here?

I spat out my toothpaste in the sink and tugged my cardigan closer around my body. It didn't matter that I was in the exact same set of pajamas I'd walked downstairs in at my dad's. We were in a completely different situation here. Sleeping in the same place as Adrian, two doors down from his son and at the other end of the hall from *him*, came with its own set of challenges.

I could get through this weekend without caving. I *had* to, for my sanity.

"Do you need anything for your room?"

The sound of his voice had me practically jumping out of my fucking skin.

"Shit, sorry," he sighed. "It's the fucking carpet up here. I always forget how quiet it is."

He stood in the doorway, his hands on either side of the frame, in a plain white T-shirt that clung to the muscles of his chest and flannel pajama pants. From the neckline of his shirt, a pair of rectangular glasses hung down—the ones he'd worn in the car and the living room downstairs while he worked, the ones he'd worn in bed on his sailboat when I'd climbed onto him completely fucking naked and begged him to stay.

God, I hated myself for that.

"Are you all right?" he asked. *Shit. I haven't said anything.*

"Yeah, I-I'm fine. Sorry. You just...you freaked me out." In truth, I'd been hoping to make it back to my room before he'd made it up the stairs so I wouldn't be tempted, but... here I fucking was.

He nodded. "If it's any consolation, I'm always on edge the first night whenever we come out here," he said, his jaw ticking as he forced himself to break eye contact. "Think it's because it's so quiet. Even up on my floor of the Blackwater building, I can still hear the faint sounds of traffic. But out here...just the ocean, if the wind is right."

I swallowed. "Yeah. That's probably it," I lied.

"I'm happy for you to blame it on that," he whispered, leaning a little bit further into the bathroom, "instead of me."

"It's not—"

"I get it. You don't need to explain." He pushed off the door frame and took a step back into the dark, carpeted hallway.

His eyes met mine again, and I couldn't help myself from just taking him in, letting myself linger and absorb him in this overtly relaxed version. He looked so different than he had at the charity ball, my father's penthouse, his office, his sailboat. He looked different than he had when he was completely bare and holding me to him, or than when he'd dropped to his knees on that balcony in his stupid fucking three-piece suit and put his mouth on me.

He looked at *home*. He looked like a normal person—not an unattainable figure that felt out of reach.

And as he held my gaze in the overwhelming silence, my heart hammering in my chest from a mixture of anxiety and adrenaline, I couldn't decide if I wanted to run back to my room and scream into a pillow or do something I knew I'd regret.

But I was leaning toward the latter.

I took a step forward, but the moment he opened his mouth, I stopped.

"I'll see you in the morning," he said.

What? No—

"Good night, Ava."

Adrian: You up yet?

Adrian: Lucas and I are going down to the beach if you want to meet us down there. Mrs. Henderson left breakfast out for you.

I stared at my phone in the low light of the room, my vision barely adjusting to the brightness of my phone. The clock said it was half past ten in the morning, but the blackout curtains made it confusing, and it took me far too long to understand that it was actually incredibly bright outside and not pitch black like I'd assumed.

Slipping from the bed, I opened the curtains just in

time to catch a glimpse of two heads of dark hair disappearing behind the sand dunes at the back of the property.

Me: Swimming or hanging out?

Adrian: It's cold outside. Do you genuinely think I'm that bad of a father that I'll willingly give my son pneumonia?

Adrian: We're looking for shark teeth. And maybe building sandcastles, we'll see.

A smaller, dark head of hair popped back up on the other side of the dunes, and just as I clocked him, Lucas waved wildly back toward the house. I chuckled.

Adrian: He's waving at you.

Adrian: Come on.

Adrian: Bring your bagel down.

Me: Okay, okay, I'm coming.

I grabbed the thickest sweater I'd packed out of my bag and slipped it over my head, not caring that I was still in my joggers from the night before.

Adrian: On second thought, eat your bagel first. Lucas might steal it.

The wind whipped as I crossed the dunes with my mug of coffee, one bagel fuller, and my hair up in a bun. Lucas clocked me almost immediately.

"Ava!" Lucas shouted, dropping his plastic mold and his pail and booking it across the soft sand. Adrian stayed put, in a black woolen jacket and his pajama bottoms from last night. "We found ten shark teeth! Come see. Dad has them."

He grabbed my hand and pulled me along with him. "I'm coming, I'm coming," I laughed, trying to keep my coffee somewhat stable so I didn't lose most of it.

"Dad thinks one of them is a great white tooth, but I don't think so," Lucas said.

"Really?"

Adrian sat up from his leaned-back position, wiping his sand-covered hand on his pajama bottoms before fishing through his pockets. "It's definitely a great white."

He pulled a tooth the size of my palm out from his pocket and held it out in my direction.

"Ava will know for sure," Lucas chirped, and God, he was so cute. Just because I knew what an osprey looked like didn't mean I had any clue about sharks or shark teeth, but he certainly thought I was some sort of expert.

I passed Adrian my mug of coffee in exchange for the tooth, sitting down beside him in the sand. I turned it over in my palm, inspecting it, *uhm*ing and *ahh*ing. Plucking Adrian's reading glasses from the neck of his shirt, I put them on, pretending as if they helped me see it better when, in reality, the just turned everything into a blur.

"I can confidently say, without a single doubt, and in my expert opinion..." I tried to keep a straight face as I said it, even as Lucas leaned in further and further with an adorable intrigue that made his face look almost identical to Adrian's. "...that I have no idea what this is, and you should trust your father."

Adrian's head tipped back as he laughed, the morning sun catching him at every good angle and casting shadows on the hollows under his cheekbones and jawline. It was almost infuriating how good he looked first thing in the morning, and I couldn't help but watch him, watch the way his chest rose and fell with every little sharp intake of breath between chuckles.

Until Lucas came up behind him and practically put Adrian in a headlock with his attempt at a wrestling hug. "Just google it, Dad," he bleated.

Adrian tipped forward as he held his son's forearms in place beneath his chin, lifting his feet off the ground behind him and taking his weight. "Nah, I think we should trust Ava's gut on this one."

———

Lucas raced ahead of us as we crossed the top of the dune, his short legs carrying him faster than I could even imagine in a beeline for the massive house. It left us alone for the second time, and as much as I felt the urge to cave to what I'd wanted last night, it was a little easier to fight it in the light of day when Lucas could turn around or watch us through the massive bay windows.

Adrian walked quietly to my left, watching as his son slid easily into the house. Even with the stress of his life, even with the current situation, he looked so...*calm*. It was as if being out here meant he could breathe easily for a little while.

"Can I ask you a question?" I asked, tucking a loose strand of hair back into my bun to keep it from blowing in my face. "You don't have to answer if you don't want to."

His head turned to me, but his eyes lingered on the door of the house until it shut. "Of course."

"It's fairly obvious that the reason you're looking for a match is because you want a second parent for Lucas," I said. In the sliding glass door of the kitchen, Lucas cupped his hands and smushed his face up against the glass, watching us for a second before taking off somewhere else. "But wouldn't it be better for you to find someone that you want to love as well? I don't want to overstep a boundary here, and believe me, I understand that it's not at all my place to tell you what's good for your son...but wouldn't it be better for him to see a functional, happy relationship?"

Adrian's mouth formed a hard line and his feet halted, putting me a few paces ahead of him before I could react and bring myself to stop.

"I'm sorry—"

"I know that would be better for him, Ava," he sighed. Behind him, a puffy, thick cloud slid along the blue of the sky, covering the sun. He took a deep breath in, letting it out slowly through his nose. "If I'm being completely honest, I would prefer that he saw a loving relationship. I'm not sure he even knows what one looks like at this point. Jan died when he was six, and we were on the rocks for a couple of years before that."

I didn't know what to say to that. He hadn't mentioned her to me up until now, and although I knew the small summary Dad had told me over dinner last month, I wasn't sure if I should make that known or keep my mouth shut. I *wanted* to offer my sympathies. But there wasn't a single part of me that knew if he would accept that with open arms.

His eyes met mine in a flash of blue as the wind battered us, sending his untamed hair flying. "I shouldn't, but can I vent to you for a moment?"

I blinked. I wasn't expecting that. "Of course."

"I don't know how much David told you or if he told you anything," he started, taking the smallest step toward me and bridging the gap. I still couldn't reach him if I wanted to, but it felt like an inkling of trust that neither of us should be giving each other. "But what happened with Jan...it wrecked me. I was blindsided by it completely. There were signs, of course, that she was cheating I mean, but I was so wrapped up in my work and Lucas that I didn't think anything of it. She had more *rehearsals* than normal, or so I was made to believe. But she was with someone else the whole time."

Rehearsals. Oh, fuck. Little tidbits of memories from when I was a teenager filtered in—going to a musical back in Boston with my parents and Adrian, getting to go on the stage after it was finished. That was why he had said no Broadway cast members. And I'd fought with him to try to get a reason out of him.

"I...I'm so sorry, I completely forgot she was an actress—"

A breathy, half-hearted chuckle left his lips. "It's okay. You were, what, fifteen? I doubt you were even paying much attention to us back then. You had your own things going on."

I swallowed. I couldn't tell him how wrong he was, not if my fucking life depended on it. I'd take that stupid teenage obsession to my grave.

"My point is, I didn't expect any of it. So, when my phone rang at two in the morning on a Thursday night, I didn't even check the screen. I was expecting the sound of her voice on the other end, letting me know that the final show of that run had gone well and that their wrap-up party was over, that she'd be home soon. I wasn't expecting a fucking police officer to tell me she'd been in an accident."

His gaze drifted behind me briefly before snapping back to mine. A muscle ticked in his jaw, his mouth opening and closing as he tried to find the right words. It took everything in me to not just hug him, but if Lucas was somewhere at the windows behind me, I didn't want to add anything to the confusion that would already come from this trip.

"The man that was with her in the car was in the cast for the show, too, so I didn't think anything of it then. I was a fucking wreck, yes, but I didn't doubt her for a second," he explained. The warble in his voice cracked a fucking hole in my chest. "I was grieving. I was explaining to a six-year-old over and over that his mother wasn't coming home. It wasn't until days later, when the police finally handed over her phone and the rest of her belongings, that I put the pieces together. So, I had to grieve *again*—not just for the loss of my wife, but for the woman I thought she was, for the breakdown of a relationship that I didn't get an ounce of closure from."

He pushed his hair back with one hand, his gaze breaking from mine.

"It's not that I think Lucas wouldn't benefit from seeing me happy and in love," he rasped. "I don't think I'm *able* to anymore. And I need to be honest with myself about that, and honest with whoever I'm with about it. Lucas already knows. He understands, as much as an eight-year-old can. I genuinely hope that he can learn to navigate those waters on his own when he's older, but I just...I don't think I can give him that, as much as it kills me."

His words felt like cement in the pit of my stomach. I shouldn't have pressed him on this, shouldn't have judged him for it when he'd made it clear he was comfortable before. I felt like a fucking monster for pushing him to give me answers up on the forty-fourth floor of the Darkwater building. "I'm sorry," I offered again, glancing over my shoulder to check the windows for any sign of Lucas.

"You don't need to—"

Closing the distance in two steps, I wrapped my arms around his neck and pulled him down into a hug. He froze. "I do," I insisted. "I shouldn't have pushed you on this. We'll find you someone, under your terms. No questions asked."

His reluctance to accept my hug shook me a little until his arms snaked around my back, pulling me in just a little too close, a little too intimately. His cold fingertips brushed against the sliver of exposed skin on my lower back, and I nearly lost my breath.

Calm the fuck down, Ava.

"Thank you."

"I will still need to ask you questions about other things," I clarified, loosening my arms as a signal that he could let me go. He didn't. "So maybe not, *no questions asked.* Some questions asked?"

He laughed against the shell of my ear, his arms squeezing me just a tad. "I can live with *some questions asked.*"

———

The early afternoon sun had heated the day enough that we could relax on the lawn without worrying about keeping warm. Grace was still unwell, and Adrian had given her the rest of the day off. Lucas drove around on the grass in his electric go-kart, leaving tire marks in a circle over and over as he did donuts. Adrian sat in the lounger beside me, one leg on either side of the long footrest and his laptop positioned between his thighs.

I tried to focus on the words in Jane Austen's *Persuasion*, tried to get the letters to make the right shapes in my mind so I could absorb it. But I found my mind drifting over and over again, off into daydreams or memories or the words Adrian had said to me earlier, and I had to keep rereading paragraphs or entire pages after realizing that I'd skimmed over the words without understanding them. I'd read one singular line over and over and over again, devouring it, savoring it. *You pierce my soul. I am half agony, half hope.* But it eluded me now, and it wasn't hitting like it used to.

The crunch of feet on the grass behind me easily pulled me back out of the book easily, and I looked over my shoulder in search of the sound. Mrs. Henderson approached with a platter of food in one hand, a bottle of wine and two glasses in her other, and a blanket tucked up under her arm.

She left us to it, and after a quick back and forth with Lucas to get him to abandon the go-kart for lunch, we settled quietly into an impromptu picnic.

"We could head over to the lighthouse in Montauk tomorrow," Adrian suggested, passing Lucas his plate of sliced meat and cheese and the cup of juice Mrs. Henderson had so easily balanced on the tray of food. There was even a backup ham and cheese sandwich for him.

"Yes! I can race Ava up the stairs," Lucas beamed.

Adrian poured out a glass of wine for me and handed it over, his face deadly serious. I didn't bother checking the label—I didn't want to know how much it cost this time. "He will absolutely beat you. It's not worth it."

I didn't doubt that for a second.

"Dad, don't *tell* her that," Lucas groaned, taking a bite of the backup sandwich before tucking into a slice of what looked like chorizo. "That ruins the fun."

"A lie is still a lie if it's by omission," Adrian said, barely containing his chuckle as he took a sip of wine. "Would you be up for heading over there and losing in a stair-climbing race, Ava?"

"You know what? I think I'd quite enjoy losing a race to him," I laughed, leaning over toward Lucas and ruffling his hair.

He leaned into it, his body swaying back and forth like a dog, in a fit of infectious giggles—

And his juice spilled all over my top and lap.

"Shit—Wait, sorry, I shouldn't say that in front of you," I stammered, lifting myself up onto my knees and pressing a handful of napkins that Lucas handed me into my shirt. The red splotch spread across the white fabric, deepening, *staining*.

"Dad says *shit* all the time."

"Lucas," Adrian groaned. "You know better than to say that."

"There was an opportunity!"

Adrian rolled his eyes as he pushed himself to his feet, holding a hand out. "Come on. Let's see if Mrs. Henderson can get that stain out before it sets."

I took his hand, and he hoisted me up to my feet.

"Don't touch the wine, Lucas. And stay there."

———

"It *should* come out," Mrs. Henderson said, lifting and dunking the fabric into the deep basin in the laundry room.

"It's honestly fine if it won't," I insisted. With my arms wrapped around my mostly bare torso, I felt a little out of place in front of a woman I didn't know very well. But it was just the two of us in here, and I could live with her seeing me in my bra. "I thought you were a cook?"

She shrugged. "I do a bit of everything, too. But cooking is what I prefer to do." She lifted the shirt again, and the stain had paled significantly. "The only shirt I've got in here is Lucas' from last night. You might need to make a break for it back to your room."

For *fucks* sake.

I turned the handle on the door and slipped out into the little hallway that separated the laundry area from the kitchen. The house was so quiet I could have heard a pin drop, and I assumed my modesty was safe—until I turned the corner and nearly ran into the back of Adrian as he leaned against the kitchen counter, his gaze fixed on the window that looked out at Lucas.

"Shit," I breathed, slipping my body back behind the corner to cover myself.

Adrian turned, his eyes meeting mine. I covered the bit of me that he could potentially see from my position, my skin flaring with heat almost instantly. "Why are you—"

"There weren't any other shirts in there," I hissed. "Can you go..."

My sentence trailed off as I realized what a horrible, catastrophically terrible idea it would be for him to get me a shirt out of my bag. *Why the fuck did I bring my vibrator?*

"...actually, scratch that, can you just get me a pillow or something from the couch?"

His eyes rolled dramatically. "A *pillow*?"

131

"Please."

"Christ, Ava, just have mine." Before I could even protest, he was hauling the fabric up and over his head with one hand, baring his goddamn *chest* to me as if it was nothing. Every curve, every ripple of muscle that pulled at his skin drew my attention like a blazingly bright, neon exit sign.

He held the shirt out to me.

It took *everything* in me to grab it and look away.

———

The sound of the sliding glass door opening behind me cut through the crickets and the toads, and I didn't need to look to guess who it was.

"He was out the moment his head hit the pillow," Adrian said, appearing beside my rocking chair on the back porch with a glass of wine held out. I looked up at him, taking in the softness of his face now that his one worry was sleeping upstairs. "Have a drink with me, Ava."

Hesitantly, I took the glass from him and pulled my knees up to my chest. "Okay."

His jacket snugly around him, he sank into the rocking chair beside mine with a huff, his breath forming a little cloud of steam in the significantly colder air. He lifted his glass to his mouth, the deep red of the wine slipping past his lips, and *God*, all I could think of was how they'd tasted after he'd kissed me on the boat.

That hint of wine, but also the rest of him.

"Think it's your turn to open up," he said, breathing out a chuckle as he swirled the wine in its glass.

God fucking dammit. I should have expected this. "What do you mean?"

"Can I ask you some questions for once?" he asked, his gaze meeting mine as his lips tipped up in a smirk.

Reluctantly, I nodded and took a sip of my wine. It tasted suspiciously like the wine he'd given me on his boat, but I wasn't a connoisseur. It could have been anything.

"Why the alias and alter ego?"

I snorted. "Easy. Because I didn't want my dad to find out that I was going on dates with all types of different people. He wants me to end up with someone who can provide for me, but I think he forgets I'm the only person in his will."

His lips tightened. "Thought that might be why," he said. "Can't be easy growing up with a father like yours. I love the guy, don't get me wrong, but he's made some...*questionable* choices. And he's impossible to say no to."

"Yeah. I dated this guy in my junior year of high school, Henry—it was right after you and Jan moved to New York, and right before my dad followed you and moved his business," I explained, cringing at myself for even letting it slip that I remembered exactly when he'd left. "He was the first guy I ever slept with, and Dad found out. I thought he'd be mad at me, but instead, he hired a private fucking investigator to find out everything about the family. Income, address, degrees, the whole nine yards. He was proud when he realized that Henry was well off. I didn't even know it."

Adrian sucked in air through his teeth. "Why am I not surprised?"

I hugged my knees a little tighter, the relief of just *talking* about the stress my father added to my life helping me relax into whatever this conversation was. "I did get my masters in contemporary art, for the record. That wasn't a lie. But my dad fucking hated it. My BA in business wasn't enough, apparently."

"I'm sorry—"

"And he won't stop badgering me to *find* someone," I continued, not even caring that I was steamrolling whatever he was saying. Adrian had opened a faucet in me that I didn't realize needed to be opened. "I'm twenty-fucking-five, for God's sake. And I know damn well that unless it's someone he deems appropriate, he'll tear the whole thing down. No one under a certain income bracket. No one *unsuccessful*, whatever that means. Preferably someone in finance, if he has a say in it."

"Damn, out of the running, then," Adrian joked. The stone in my gut that he was so aptly named after only sunk further.

"Honestly, Adrian, if you were anyone other than my father's friend, he'd probably celebrate that I found a *decent* guy to fuck me." My cheeks heated instantly as I realized what had slipped out of my mouth, but I couldn't take it back. I downed the rest of my glass of wine and avoided meeting his gaze at all costs. "He'd hound you to put a ring on my finger and knock me up. Probably force me into some gigantic puffy white dress and throw us an extravagant wedding, invite everyone he knows, and fill it with photographers to sell my image to the press, who couldn't give two shits about who I am."

"Aves—"

"What?" I laughed, forcing myself to stare out at the darkness of the dunes. "Doesn't sound good to you? I'm not surprised. I don't think there's a person on earth who could handle being with me when my father is the way he is."

The answering silence that hung around me was far too thick to breathe through. I set my glass down on the little table between our chairs, using both of my hands to pull my knees just that tiny bit closer to my chest.

"And without someone in my life that can handle him and satisfy what he wants out of a partner for me, my only other option to please him is this fucking business," I continued. My chest felt too tight, like I was breathing too little air, and for a horrible second, I wondered if I was going to pass out—at least I was already sitting down. "But if I can't even get this right for you, someone I know well, how the fuck am I supposed to do it for strangers? How am I supposed to do *anything* right when he's breathing down my neck?"

"I'm so sorry," Adrian said. His hand moved, and I watched from the corner of my eye as he carefully swapped my empty glass for his half-full one. "Maybe I can talk to him. Get him to calm down about it."

The backs of my eyes burned as I reached for the glass. I needed it. "I don't think he'd listen."

"Could be worth a shot, Aves."

I took a sip of the wine, holding it on my tongue and letting it linger for a little longer than I had before. That *had* to be the same wine. "I'll think about it," I sniffled, wiping my nose on the sleeve of my sweater.

I looked across at him finally, meeting his eyes around the curve of my wine glass. The way he watched me, the intensity of his stare, for once felt more like a thousand helium balloons tied to my body and lifting me up instead of cement blocks. The silence felt less heavy, the weight of the world falling off of my shoulders, the crinkles in the paper ironing out—if only a little.

But it was charged, too.

We hadn't outwardly spoken about what we'd done outside of that night at the charity ball, and even mentioning it out loud felt like a sin. But I felt lighter, too. Like whatever sense of calm he gained from being out here was infectious, oozing into me and claiming all of my problems for itself. The walls were down. The barriers were gone.

For both of us, it seemed, from the way his gaze dropped to my lips.

"Adrian," I breathed. "Don't."

He swallowed, his Adam's apple bobbing, and it looked as though it took everything in him to turn away from me. "I won't."

Chapter 16

Adrian

The downpour of rain I'd woken to at five in the morning did absolutely nothing to ease the sting of a cold, half-empty bed.

I'd made it almost two full days now without caving to my instincts with regard to her. The temptation was maddening, driving me to depravity every time I stepped into the shower, and this morning had been no different.

But as I relaxed on the sofa and watched her play a board game with my son, I couldn't help but feel bad for imagining her the way that I had after she'd nearly cried last night. A part of me, as basic and absurd as it was, had risen to that—I'd wanted to fix it. Whether that was making her forget about it for as long as I could, or talking to David to get him to get off her case a little, it didn't matter. I just wanted to make it better.

But more than anything, I just wanted to fucking *cave*.

Especially now. She was in her pajamas, her hair up, her attention focused wholly on Lucas. She was far better with him than I could have ever imagined, and my mind kept pointing out that she was exactly what I was looking for. She ticked the most important box.

"I'm sorry we can't go to the lighthouse today," Ava said quietly as she rolled the dice on the board. She moved her little figurine six paces forward. "Maybe another time?"

Another time.

"It's okay," Lucas shrugged. "This is fun, too. I like hanging out with you."

It was such a flippant sentence, but it felt like a fucking dagger to my chest.

————

With the cookies in the oven and Lucas practically coated in flour and sugar, the calm settled in again. I could get through today. We all could.

Even with the rain battering the house, Lucas found a way to have fun with it—he drew little stick figures in the pile of flour on the counter, coating his hands further, much to Mrs. Henderson's dismay as she tried to clean around him.

"Lucas," I said, trying not to crack a grin as he drew another little figure right in the spot she'd just wiped down. I made a mental note to make her tip this weekend heftier than usual. "Why don't you go take a shower, bud?"

"Okay!" He jumped down off the step stool, sending a cloud of flour dancing through the air.

"Oh my God, he's covered," Ava laughed.

I pushed off the counter I'd been leaning on and walked up to him. "Arms up, Luc."

He lifted his arms above his head. I tried to keep most of the flour contained in his shirt as I pulled it off of him, but it rained down through the neck hole and onto the top of his head.

"You're so lucky you're cute," Mrs. Henderson deadpanned.

"Just use the downstairs shower. Walk *very* carefully, and do not shake your head," I instructed.

He fucking *nodded* before taking off in the direction of the bathroom.

Ava and I helped with the cleanup—I couldn't bear to leave it entirely up to Mrs. Henderson. But the moment she'd left the kitchen to put Lucas's shirt in the wash, I couldn't help but bring myself closer to Ava, couldn't help but see her in that light again.

She'd done so much unnecessary work this weekend, so much that hadn't been expected of her. I'd hoped that this would at least give her a bit of a vacation, but with Grace unwell and the amount of work I had to do, parenting had somehow fallen on her.

"Hey," I said, slotting in beside her against the kitchen island.

"Hi," she replied. She lifted a brow at me.

I rolled my eyes at her questioning stare. "I'm sorry if this weekend hasn't gone how you were hoping."

The brow dropped, and instead, her eyes narrowed. "What do you mean?"

"I *mean* that I wasn't expecting you to have to help me so much with Lucas, and I appreciate what you've done," I explained.

She let loose a breath. *She... fuck, she thought I meant something else.*

Does she want that? Still?

"Oh, don't worry about that. He's a good kid." The little smile she gave me didn't quite reach her eyes. "And the stain came out of my shirt, so he's done literally nothing wrong, apart from driving Mrs. Henderson insane."

I snorted. "Yeah, I'll tip her well for that. Don't worry."

Her gaze met mine and held.

"You're great with him," I said, and I didn't care how she took it. I wanted it known. "I know I insinuated that maybe Lucas wouldn't be okay with this back at David's, and I should have clarified sooner, but it's been eating me up all day. If it wasn't clear, I said that to try to get out of it. Not because of any preconceived notion I had that you two wouldn't get along for whatever reason."

Her chuckle and the genuine little smile that accompanied it made my chest ache, made my hands twitch in her direction. "I figured, but thank you for saying that."

The green of her eyes was dulled in the artificial light of the kitchen, but they captivated me nonetheless. Rain pelted like bullets against the glass sliding doors, and in that brief flicker of the time we had alone, all I wanted to do was take her outside with me. I wanted to feel the rain on my skin, wanted to live in the moment for a minute and think about nothing but her and the way it coated me like the never-ending downpour. I wanted to let it try to wash it all away and be okay with the realization that no amount of scrubbing would get her out of my skin.

I wanted to fucking kiss her.

"You're doing it again," she breathed.

"Doing what?"

"Looking at me like that." She swallowed, the sound almost audible. "One of them will be back any minute, Adrian."

The longer I watched, the more obvious it was that she was disappointed. I should have done it.

I shouldn't have backed down.

———

The rain didn't let up for a second for the rest of the day, and as Ava and I sat beside each other on the floor by the fireplace, the heat of it felt like a heaviness that I couldn't quite shake. She looked up at me, her hair a mess, covered in a thin, satin pajama set that I was *positive* didn't include a bra. My will was fucking breaking—I had no one to hide from with everyone in bed, nothing to hold me back except the glass of wine in my hand.

"The ideal first date you told Emily about," she said, breaking the beat of silence as she looked back down at her open binder. She sipped at her third glass of wine. It was the same wine I'd served her last night, and the same one I'd served her on the boat. "Do you want me to book your dates for that kind of thing? Art museum first, and then you can decide where it goes from there?"

"Fuck, no," I scoffed. It wasn't a lie—I didn't want that with someone else, and I'd been unable to avoid that realization all day. "Dinners are fine."

"But that's what you—"

"I know what I answered before, Ava."

She looked at me, her gaze bouncing between my lips and my eyes, and temptation flared again.

"I don't want to do that with someone else," I said.

Okay, she mouthed. She wrote something beside my

141

original answer, but her hand obscured it from sight. "If you could do anything else for work, what would you choose?"

"Travel photographer," I answered.

She hesitated again, but marked it down. "I know you said you don't care what profession she has," she said slowly, tapping her pen against the paper. "But in an ideal world, if you could choose...?"

I swallowed another hefty sip of wine. My inhibitions were on the fucking floor, and I wasn't going to try to hide that from her right now. I didn't *want* to. "I don't know, Ava. Aspiring art teacher. Matchmaker."

I set my glass down on the coffee table in front of us as she watched me, her mouth parted just a hair, her gaze locked on me. "You can't just say things like that to me."

"I can," I insisted. "I did."

The red on her cheeks spread, little blotches of pink sprouting across her neck, her jaw. "Please—"

She stopped herself the moment my hand pressed into her cheek, the intense warmth of it heating my palm. I tucked a hanging lock of auburn hair behind her ear and her breathing quickened, her body frozen despite the heat of the fire that I could feel behind her.

Her eyes flicked back and forth between mine rapidly.

"Ask me who I'm looking for," I rasped, dragging my thumb across her bottom lip. So fucking soft. "Ask me what I want. The answer is the same."

She swallowed, and I could feel her throat move against my pink finger. God, I wanted to wrap my hand around it. "Who—"

"You."

I leaned in closer, bridging the gap, giving myself the one thing I'd so desperately craved for days, for *weeks*.

But the heavy padding sound of footsteps stopped me just before I could reach her lips.

"Mr. Stone?"

If looks could kill, I was certainly trying as I turned to look to the entrance of the living room. Grace stood there in a nightgown that covered her from neck to toe, the color back in her face tenfold with a hefty painting of blush across her cheeks.

"I-I'm sorry, I didn't mean to interrupt."

It physically *pained* me to retreat from Ava. She hadn't looked away from me with her eyes as wide as saucers, but her mouth fell a little bit more open as I pulled back. My hand left her cheek. "It's fine," I said to Grace. "How are you feeling?"

She nodded. "Much better. I wanted to let you know that I should be good to go tomorrow morning if we're still planning on heading back to the city."

I swallowed. "Glad to hear it."

Chapter 17

Ava

Dad had my office finished up over the weekend, so there was at least one happy ending there.

"We've got six more male clients," Emily said, her fingers counting off each of the updates she had for me. "The website's up and running, too, so we can start to vet people before they fill in their questionnaires. I've run a few ads on Instagram, and we've had a *ton* of female sign-ups. I've marked a few of them down for you in the binder that I think could be a good fit for Adrian."

I wanted to throw up.

"You don't look happy."

"I'm not," I said. I rested my head in the palms of my hands, resisting the urge to slam my head against something hard.

"Bad weekend with him?"

I shook my head.

"Oh no. You slept with him again."

"No. I didn't," I mumbled.

"Oh," she lilted, dragging out the sound. "You *didn't* sleep with him, and you regret it."

144

The backs of my eyes burned as I lifted my head in the overwhelming glow of the fluorescent lights. It shouldn't have bothered me as much as it did, but I'd never felt so frustrated in my goddamn life than I did when he'd stopped and walked Grace back to her bedroom. It felt like I'd stepped into a fever dream when he'd come back and suggested we go to bed before we did something we'd regret.

Because I *did* regret this. I regretted doing *nothing* when I had the chance.

"I feel like he's fucking edging me, but it's my emotions," I explained, taking a deep breath to calm the rising tide in my chest. I'd barely been able to calm down since it happened.

"Edging can be fun," Emily said.

"Yeah, during *sex*. Which we didn't have," I snapped. "This was so much easier last month when I hadn't been building him up in my head, when I could pretend like we barely knew each other, when sex wasn't this thing hanging over my head like a banshee screaming at me."

"Oh, Aves," Emily cooed, her hand wrapping around my forearm and squeezing gently. "I'm sorry. That can't be easy."

"It's not," I said. "And now I have to find him a fucking match, because it couldn't just be easy, could it? I couldn't have just had a fun little fling with him and moved on. No, my father had to get me involved in his life. With his *son*. And I'm going to have to pick out women for him that I think he'll like when I'd rather shove my fingers into my fucking eyes, and I'll have to be *okay* with it."

. . .

The sun had long since set in the quiet retreat of my office, and Emily had already gone home by the time I'd picked three somewhat satisfactory choices.

The first was an art major. She had a parrot, but he could probably deal with that. She liked children.

The second was a history major, but she was a curator at the MOMA. She liked children, too.

And the third was a film buff with an interest in photography, traveling, and teaching. More importantly: she liked children.

I didn't want to give him any of them. And if I was honest, maybe I'd overlooked some of the red flags in the others without realizing I had done it on purpose. But this felt different, and despite each one of them confirming a day and a time this upcoming weekend, I didn't want to tell him. I didn't want to have to do any of this.

I couldn't even bring myself to text him. His potential response churned my stomach, and I couldn't handle the idea of seeing it right away. E-mail would have to do.

I wrote out something short and sweet, a quick message to let him know that he should find someone to take Lucas for the weekend so he wouldn't need to worry about coming and going from his apartment. I wrote out the times, the schedules, their names, and the locations. I wanted to change every single one to my name, to my address. But I didn't.

I stared at it for far too long before hitting send.

Chapter 18

Adrian

I checked my watch as I shoved my laptop into my bag. I had about two hours until I was expected at my date, and I couldn't have dreaded it more.

Grace had already picked up Lucas from school and brought her back to her home in Queens. Her daughter had a son who was roughly his age and although they hadn't seen each other in a few months, he was more than happy to spend a weekend having sleepovers with him. But I still needed to get up to my floor and change, still needed to pull myself together.

I could handle it.

An unexpected, angry knock at my door had me spinning on the spot. I hadn't pressed the buzzer. Whoever it was must have come from my wing, and considering a meeting had just let out...

For fucks sake.

"What do you want, Andrew?" I asked, pulling open the door and taking a step back to let him in.

"Do you realize the shit you've got us in?" he snapped.

147

His glasses were too low on his nose, and he stared at me over them as they bounced with every word from his mouth. "You disappeared during one of the most important weekends of the year. You didn't get anyone to cover for you. You barely gave notice. We had to fucking *scramble*." The door slammed shut behind him.

I truly fucking hated Andrew.

"Something came up with my son last minute." I shrugged. "You may be a board member, Andy, but you don't have control over me. I saw the reports from the weekend. Everything went fine."

"Because of *me*," he hissed. Spittle collected on the sides of his ginger mustache. "Because I took time away from my family to be at that event all shitting weekend."

"You think I don't do that every single time we have an important event? My son is *eight*, Andrew, yours is twenty-four." I threw my laptop bag over my shoulder and huffed out an exhausted sigh. I could have walked around him if I wanted, could have walked away from the situation, but I just couldn't be bothered. "If you have a problem with how I'm running things, take it to the board."

"If it happens again, I will. You're clearly far too focused on other things to lead this company properly."

I blinked at him. "You realize you sound insane, right? I took a weekend off to be with my son. This is *my* company. I felt comfortable leaving it to Michael and you to handle, and it went fine. It's not like I took some out-of-the-blue two-week vacation playing golf like half of the CEOs in this city."

Andrew shook his head, his glasses bouncing again. "And you realize that I have the majority of shares in this company, right? Besides you. My vote will sway the board."

"Fucking try, then," I laughed. "*Try*."

. . .

———

I was back to square one with Ava, and all I'd done was touch her cheek.

Every second that I spent getting ready, riding the elevator, getting in the back of the car, sitting in traffic, she swarmed my thoughts, claimed her territory in my head, and took up residence. The grave I'd dug for her was fully unearthed and packed back in, and she sat atop it in her dark blue satin pajama set, boring a hole through my fucking skull.

I couldn't *stop* thinking of her. I thought of her playing with Lucas, thought of her at five in the morning in my lap on the boat, thought of her staring at that fucking shark's tooth, thought of her almost crying on the porch, thought of her not telling me to stop that final night. I thought of the way she laughed when Lucas hounded her with questions, thought of the way her breath hitched when I touched her throat.

I thought of her, and her, and her.

The closer we got, the more I wished that I wasn't meeting this Heather. I wanted it to be Ava, and I didn't want to have to worry about doing this anymore—I wanted my weekend to be her, and only her.

But I would do it. I'd do it despite feeling like it was wrong. I'd meet Heather at least, and go from there, see how I felt when she introduced herself. This, *none* of this, was ultimately for me, and I had to take that into consideration.

I stepped out of the car one block from the photography

gallery. Sitting in a barely moving car for another ten minutes when I could walk it in two seemed absurd, and if I could just get the worst part of this out of the way, I'd be fine.

I'd be *fine*.

Chapter 19

Ava

"You're psychotic. You know that, right?"

The bitter wind whipped at my back as I crossed at Essex and Delancey with the phone to my ear. I quickened my step and narrowly avoided getting clipped by a taxi, but I could see her from here, could see her looking around anxiously as she waited. "I'm not," I snapped. "I just want to see how this goes."

"You're...what, at least thirty minutes from home? If you don't want him to do this, just call him," Emily groaned, the tinniness of her voice through the line hitting something angry in my skull.

"She's here," I said. "And I don't want to make that decision for him, Em."

Heather's chestnut hair blew in the breeze, and she pulled a few strands away from her lips. I glanced down Delancey Street, double-checking for any sign of him, before tucking into the southern side of Essex in case he got out of a passing car.

"You're just going to upset yourself. What's your plan,

Aves? Stay out there all night? Buy a balaclava and follow them inside?"

I crossed over Essex and positioned myself at a right angle to Heather—just around a corner. I leaned against the edge of the wall and kept my sights set on her. "I don't know. Probably not."

"*Probably* not?" Em laughed. "A normal answer would be 'no, definitely not'."

"Where *is* he?"

"Are you even listening to me? Should I just let you go so you can stake out your crush in peace?"

"Yes, I'm listening," I sighed. "What time is it?"

"Seven thirty-one."

"He's late."

"Ava. There's probably traffic. You know damn well no one gets anywhere on time here." The unmistakable sound of a nail file scraping filtered down the line.

The crosswalk's light turned green across the street not ten feet up from me, and as the crowd moved and shifted, a head of gray and black hair came into view. "Shit, shit, shit, he's here."

I tucked myself further back around the corner, giving myself just enough space to be able to see him if I leaned out from the wall. Adrian seemed to suck the air from everything around him, and the closer he got, the less I felt like I could breathe. He looked nice in his black slacks and sweater. He wore the same jacket he'd taken to the beach.

"Ooh, what's he doing?"

"Walking toward the exhibit, obviously," I hissed.

I watched as he stepped up onto the sidewalk, my chest fucking cracking as he spotted her.

"He found her."

He crossed the steady flow of foot traffic, and I moved

further up the wall so I could poke my head fully around the corner.

"Great! You can go home now," Em said.

His brows furrowed, but he grinned at her, his lips moving around words I couldn't quite make out except for one: *Heather*.

"Shh," I said.

He held out a hand to her. From where I stood, I couldn't make out her face anymore, and as she shook his hand and her body pitched forward with a laugh, I focused in on Adrian instead. He was speaking again, his brows curving up at the center, and two words were easily readable: *thank you*.

She took a step back and turned, and a second later, she moved around him and started walking down Delaney away from either of us.

"What the fuck?" I breathed.

Adrian waited where he stood, watching her for a fraction of a second, before taking a step back toward the crosswalk.

This didn't make fucking sense.

"What? What's happening—"

I hit the button on the side of my phone that would end the call and shoved it into my pocket. Fuck hiding, fuck watching him from the corner, fuck *all* of this—I'd spent an entire day's work finding potential matches for him, spent my time and my energy on something that emotionally hurt me, and he was just going to *send her away?*

I stepped out from the corner that hugged Essex Street, putting myself fully in view of him. "Adrian!"

His head whipped in my direction, and for a second, it felt like time slowed—like the people around me were walking at half speed, like sounds of the cars were filtering in through cotton wool, like I couldn't *breathe*.

Bright blue eyes met mine, and he froze.

"Ava?"

I didn't want to imagine how jarring it must have been for him for me to pop out of nowhere. Not when I couldn't fucking wrap my head around this. But he moved toward me, and I didn't know what to do, didn't know how to *react*. I watched him, watched as he grew larger in my vision, watched as he took up parts of me I didn't want to give up. Two steps before he reached me, his eyes glanced down to my mouth, and I finally got words out. "What the fuck was that..."

Warm hands cupped either side of my face, and before I could finish what I wanted to say, his lips met mine.

He kissed me, and everything just...stopped.

Chapter 20

Adrian

his. This was what felt right.

And maybe it was a mistake—maybe I'd acted too quickly, too irrationally, the moment she'd appeared out of what seemed to be thin air on the corner of Essex and Delancey. Maybe I should have taken longer than half a second to register that she was here as if by some miraculous answer to a prayer, maybe I should have considered the harm I could cause to not only myself but her and Lucas by proxy.

Maybe I should have done a lot of things differently.

But I just couldn't bring myself to fucking care, because it just felt *right.*

I tucked her up against my chest with an arm around her waist. Her mouth tasted of strawberries and sin, and in the glow of the streetlights with the occasional passerby hurling abuse at us for taking up too much space on the sidewalk, I didn't care that her lipstick was staining my teeth or that she was grabbing for the buttons on my shirt.

Scratch that. I cared a little bit once I realized she'd managed to get half of them undone.

"Car," I rasped, coming up for a breath of freezing cold air just an inch from her mouth. "Now."

Eyes half-lidded and mouth parted, she nodded, her nose brushing against my chin. "Okay."

My heart hammered in my chest as I forced myself to pull back enough to look at the sea of traffic. It had been maybe ten minutes total since I'd left the car, and considering traffic was moving at a snail's pace, my driver couldn't be that far.

I pulled my phone from my pocket with shaking fingertips. Adrenaline was dumping into my system—none of this felt real, not really. Why the fuck was she *here*? To tempt me? To get me to finally break and give in to what I'd wanted from her for weeks?

If that's what her motivation was, she'd won. I didn't have it in me to fight it.

My driver's voice filtered down the line after a single ring. "Mr. Stone?"

"Where are you? Change of plans." I kept Ava pressed against me, the warmth of her body enough to dull the sting of cold air against the slit of visible bare skin between the two sides of my shirt. Part of me worried she'd run the moment things became too real, and I wasn't about to let her go anywhere.

A laugh came through the phone. "I've barely moved. I can see you," Oliver said.

Roughly six cars back from the traffic light, a black car flashed its headlights.

"You see me?"

"Yes." The crosswalk light turned green, and in a moment of haste, I pulled her with me toward it, braving the bitter wind. I didn't care what I looked like as we crossed the street together, didn't care that I likely had lipstick on my face or that my shirt was half undone. "Get the privacy screen up."

"Good God, Adrian," Oliver huffed. "I'll put in my headphones while I'm at it."

"Pretty sure that's illegal."

"And what you're about to do isn't?"

"Completely fair." I hung up the phone and shoved it into my pocket.

In the time it took to get her to the car, I could use half of my brain to take her in—all five and a half feet of her. Whatever her plan was seemed to be last minute from her choice of attire. The black leggings, the oversized tee shirt covered in splotches of paint, the pull-on boots, the wool coat that looked like it had seen better days...she must've been cold. It was freezing outside.

I shot Oliver a text that just said *turn the heat up* as we stepped onto the road near the car. He gave me a thumbs-up through the windshield.

"Where are we going?" Ava asked, her voice smaller than I expected.

I opened the door to the backseat for her. "Does it matter, Ava?"

She hesitated, her green eyes raking over me as if she were trying to come up with a reason to run. But she didn't find one. "No. It doesn't."

Thank God.

I ushered her in and across the leather seats before ducking down and sliding in beside her, closing the door with an audible *thud* behind me. The privacy screen was up and filled the gap between the back seat and the front, and even from here, I could hear the steady bass of whatever music filled Oliver's ears.

My twitching hands wouldn't let me stay put. It would have to do.

I climbed across the seats, twisting her in them with my hands the moment my mouth met hers again. She sighed into me, the warmth of her breath filling the space between us, and dear God, I couldn't wait another second. I needed to touch her. I needed to *have* her.

I pushed her jacket off her shoulders and grabbed the collar of it from behind, wrenching it down her back. She let it fall from her arms, and a second later it lay forgotten in the footwell.

With one hand on the door and my knee on the cushioned seats, I pulled her body closer, forced her thighs apart so I could seat my hips between them. She worked at my shirt again as her kiss turned needy, her fingers in my hair and on my buttons, and I shrugged my coat off my shoulders to give her that extra bit of help.

I pushed her old band T-shirt up her stomach, my hand roaming along her skin, and just as I crossed over her ribs...

No bra. *She's going to be the death of me.*

"God," I groaned, breaking my lips from hers long enough to get the shirt up and over her head. "You drive me fucking crazy. You know that?"

My nails dug in so hard to the door that I could feel my nailbeds screaming and the leather scratching. It took everything in me not to do the same to her soft skin as I dropped my mouth to her neck, my fingers kneading at the flesh of her breast, the scent of her shampoo and body wash filling my senses.

I kissed the slope of her throat, over her collarbones, down her sternum. The car moved forward an inch.

"Is it bad that I like that?" Ava whispered, a little chuckle shaking her chest beneath my mouth.

"Driving me insane? No." I laughed. Her hands gripped the sides of my shirt and pulled, freeing them from where I'd tucked them into my slacks. "I can't get enough of it."

She gasped a squeak as my mouth closed around her nipple, my tongue gliding across the erect little bud. Blood pooled in my already aching cock, and every movement I made, every stroke of my tongue or squeeze of my hands, was so goddamn controlled so I wouldn't devour her with everything in me at once.

Her hips ground into me in response, and I nearly lost every bit of patience I had.

I pushed her down into the seat beneath her with my free hand and bit down gently on her nipple as a warning. "Why were you there?" I asked, the words muffled through my teeth as I hooked my fingers in the back of her waistband.

She pushed the sides of my shirt off my shoulders, forcing the fabric to pool in my elbows and pull taut across my back. Her fingers felt like ice across my skin, but everywhere they touched seemed to catch on fire, burning me, consuming me.

"Ava," I growled.

I glanced up at her face, and even in the low light of the car, I could see how flushed her cheeks had gone. Splotches popped up across her jawline, her neck, almost down to her chest. "You know why," she said, her voice barely more than a breath.

"Tell me." I pulled on her waistband, bringing it down over the curve of her rear.

She swallowed, and the curve of her throat shuddered. "I wanted to know if you'd like her. And I was terrified that you would."

"Why?" Releasing her waistband, I grabbed for her feet,

pulling the little zippers down on her boots and popping them off. They clattered into the footwell.

"*Please*," she begged, her voice turning whiny as more splotches of pink appeared across the top of her chest. I bit down harder on her nipple. "Fuck, okay, *ah*—I picked well and that scared the shit out of me, okay? I don't want to avoid you. I want you, and that's pretty goddamn obvious right now. I want you. *I want you.*"

God, that felt like fucking opium in my veins.

I pulled my mouth from her chest, taking a brief moment to take her in like this—her top half bare, her leggings askew at the hips, her hair a mess and her lips swollen, laid out like a goddess along the backseat of the car. She was mine, for now, and that felt more charged than when I'd let myself play along on my boat or when I'd followed her at the charity ball.

"Please tell me you want me, too, so I don't feel like such a loser for saying that."

"I want you," I said, dipping down to her again and hovering just above her lips. I pulled at her leggings again, getting them down to her knees, and brought her legs together between us to tug them off all the way. "Why do you think I walked away?"

Unfocused eyes searched mine, and the moment her legs fell back apart astride me, she kissed me.

Fully bare in the back of the car, she morphed into a goddamn animal. Her nails clawed at my chest as she searched frantically for my belt, my zipper, the button on my slacks. She undid each one with scary precision, her kisses so aggressive that it felt as if she were devouring me. When she'd accomplished her mission and there was nothing between us, she only barely calmed—her hips pushed up into me, her warm, soaked entrance pressed firmly against the tip of my cock.

"Please," she begged. "*Please.*"

"Oliver is *right there*," I laughed against her mouth, tipping my nose in the direction of the back of the driver's seat. The bass from his music still played steadily, but the car was moving now, and when I glanced out of the windows, the busy scenery of Delancey and Essex had disappeared and was replaced with the shimmering lights of Union Square. We were at least half of the way home.

That didn't mean that I didn't want to bury myself in her right then and there, though. The temptation of heat escaping her was almost enough to make me break.

"I don't care," she mewled. Her hips pushed against me again, her clit dragging against my swollen, aching head, her chest heaving with little gasps. I could have sworn I saw stars when she lifted her hips higher, forcing my cock to slip inside just an inch. "Adrian, *please.*"

God, the way she said my name was sinful. *Guess I'll be torturing myself, then.*

There was no chance I'd have enough time to take her fully before we got back to Darkwater, but I could give her what she needed in the interim.

"For fuck's sake, love," I grunted as I wedged my free hand—the one not gripping the door for stability—between her waist and the leather seat. I pulled her up and she flushed against me, twisting us in one quick movement until my rear was on the edge of the seat and her legs were on either side of me. With her on top and the tinted windows keeping the view from onlookers, I could focus entirely on what she needed.

I could mess with her, too.

Grabbing her hips, I pushed her down onto me, impaling her on every inch of my length at once. She cried out as her warmth enveloped me, swallowing me, bending and breaking for me—and it was music, it was heaven, it was every painting she loved and every photograph that enraptured me. It felt too good to be true, and every second she sat there unmoving and adjusting made my head swim.

"Ride me, Ava," I rasped. I didn't even think about it—I grabbed her around her throat, my fingertips squeezing gently on either side just enough to send her pulse racing but not for one second affect her breathing, and slipped my free hand into the space between our bodies. I grazed over her clit and her walls shuddered around me, those wild green eyes trained on mine. "Come for me before we get home or so help me God, I'll use you in every way I want to instead."

She swallowed, her neck bobbing against the palm of my hand.

She started to move, and I could have fucking died right there, could have spent eternity in hell for what I was doing if I had to. Why couldn't she be *anyone* else?

The sounds from her filled the hot air of the car, little whimpers and moans that set me on fire. I quickened my pace against her clit, gave her just a little more pressure on it —and dug my fingers deeper into the sides of her neck.

She yelped.

"Fuck, *yes*," she said, and I used my hand to pull her closer to me, bringing her chest to my mouth.

I bit down on the flesh of her breast, soothed the ache with my tongue, groaned my own pleasure against her skin. I didn't want to leave the fucking car, not with her on me like this, not when I could spill everything inside of her right here, not when I could pretend the world didn't exist and it was just me and her—

The car slowed, and a quiet, "Parking now, Mr. Stone," from the front seat made Ava jump.

Pink splotches sprouted back to life across her skin, and I lifted my mouth from her breast, grinning up at her. "Don't stop," I ordered, slipping my fingers down to where we joined and forcing her walls to make space for more than just my cock.

Her nails dug into my chest so hard I wondered if she'd made me bleed.

I hooked my digits on her pubic bone, pulling her body forward from the inside. She got the message, even if her brain wasn't entirely with it.

"You've got about one minute until we're parked," I warned, "and then that privacy screen comes down."

Panicked eyes met mine as she moved quicker, my fingers still seated inside, my thumb rubbing against her most sensitive spot. "*Adrian.*"

"Or I could open the windows," I said, my breathing unsteady as she fucked herself on my cock. The sensation was driving me insane, sinking me deeper into a pit that I knew I couldn't crawl out of, that same one I'd dug for her in my mind and tried to keep a solid foundation on top of. It would seal us both inside. "Let all of Manhattan hear you."

Her walls clamped down on me as the rest of her body began to lock up. I pulled her along to keep her moving. She was close, so close.

"Let them *see* you looking so goddamn helpless for me," I rasped. "Let them see how depraved Ava fucking Riley really is."

The moment she hit that peak, I released her throat,

flooding her with the blood I'd been slowing the movement of—and ever so gently pressed the button for the window, cracking it just enough that she could hear the sound.

Just enough to get a rise out of her.

She pitched forward in an instant onto my chest as the car stopped, all of her going slack, a guttural cry leaving her body as she broke and shook. The sound hit my ears like music, ebbing and flowing, charging like a bull. Completely naked and out of breath, she clung to me.

"You're an ass," she laughed breathily, and I couldn't help but join her. Maybe I was.

Her hips moved forward, pushing me further inside. I grabbed for the soft flesh of her rear, holding her in place, keeping her from antagonizing me further.

"But you—"

"I'd rather have my way with you upstairs."

———

Her cheeks and neck stayed red as a strawberry as she picked at the skin on her lips, her leggings and band tee tucked under her arm, her jacket buttoned up around her bare body. I'd barely been able to contain myself as she walked through the lobby of the Darkwater building like that, her hand clutching mine.

The second the elevator doors shut and I scanned my keycard for a direct ride up to my penthouse, her hands were on me again.

The moment the floor counter on the screen went from showing numbers to showing two dashes and we traveled express past the offices and lower residential floors, her fingers found the button of my slacks. I hadn't bothered buttoning my shirt back up or redoing my belt when I knew it could be hidden beneath my jacket, and she pushed it all back open, exposing my upper half in the small, enclosed space.

Despite her orgasm, she was still just as desperate as I was.

The warmth of her hand wrapping around my length was nearly enough to set me on fire, and as the elevator dinged and opened up into my private foyer, we stumbled backward into it together, letting the elevator door close behind us.

I couldn't even get my keys out of my pocket before she was kneeling down on the tile, her jacket halfway off and pooling around her elbows.

I couldn't breathe.

"Christ," I choked, pushing the hair from her face while she worked at pulling my slacks down enough to free what raged beneath. "You look so fucking pretty on your knees."

She beamed up at me.

I dipped my hand into my boxers and helped her, sighing in relief the second her warm breath hit my cock. I was stupidly hard, so much that it was making me light-headed and I *ached* under my palm, and *dear God*, her lips were parting, a string of saliva connecting them—

My fingers knotted in her hair as her mouth closed around the tip.

Damp, soft heat moved across the underside of the head, and I had to lean against the wall for support, my breath catching and my heart racing. "*Fuck*, Ava."

She hummed her reply, and the vibration of it against the most sensitive part of me sent me into overdrive.

Clutching her hair in my hand, I steadied her head, forcing her blown pupils to look up at me. Her jacket slid from her arms and landed limply on the floor around her, every inch of her on show for me, and all I wanted was to claim it, own it, keep it forever—keep *her* forever. What the fuck was wrong with me?

I pressed myself further between her lips, dragging my cock along her tongue, tapping gently against the back of her throat before retreating and starting again. She let me control her, let me guide her head onto me, let me pull her away.

Every dream, every thought, every imagined scenario of *this* that I'd come up with, touched myself to, driven myself mad with—none of it compared. *Nothing* compared. I wasn't sure if it was the way she felt or if it was truly just *her*, but it made me feel as if I'd been starved of touch for decades, as if I'd been burning up for as long as I could remember and had finally found water, as if I was experiencing everything anew.

It was psychotic. It was insanity, it was utterly absurd, and I knew better than the choices I was making. But I couldn't bring myself to care if this hurt me, and out of all of it, that was what horrified me the most.

With the back of her throat against my head, she held herself there, unmoving despite me attempting to pull her head back. Her lashes fluttered up at me, and just before I could ask her what on earth she was doing, her throat...*opened*.

She took me further. And further. And *further*.

Those same lashes turned damp as her lips touched base, her throat twitching around me. I couldn't think straight. I couldn't feel anything but her.

"You're going to ruin me," I whispered. My fingers loosened in her hair, and I smoothed it down, stroking my nails across her scalp. "And *fuck*, I want you to."

She pulled back, popping her mouth completely off of me and replacing it with her hand. Little strings of sticky saliva connected us as she grinned up at me. "Then I guess we're even."

Chapter 21

Ava

I didn't have the bandwidth to process how nice his penthouse was as he carried me through the front door, my bare body wrapped around his front and his mouth on mine.

I didn't have the bandwidth to *care* about what this meant or what I was admitting to myself as he took me up the curving stairs and through a set of double doors.

I didn't have the bandwidth to question how he felt or why he'd walked away from Heather, because his hands and fingers were on me, in me, teasing me, filling me in the low light of his master bedroom, dark gray walls on one side and a floor-to-ceiling window on the other. My dad's penthouse didn't compare to whatever this place was, and for a moment, I wondered if I'd been hit by a fucking car back on Delancey and was vividly dreaming in the hospital.

None of it felt *real*.

But then he was slipping into me again, with his hand in my hair and his lips in the crook of my neck. His body pressed into the backs of my thighs, my knees hooked around his torso, my fingernails digging into his back. He

168

moaned my name, and it sounded like heaven, like sin, like the only thing I ever wanted to hear for the rest of my life— and I didn't have the bandwidth to care about the consequences of this.

At that moment, I would gladly be Icarus if he were the sun.

And I was insane for it.

———

I woke the moment Adrian's arms unknitted themselves from me stitch by stitch. The room was cloaked in darkness as I blinked my eyes open, the sky out of the window only slightly brighter than it had been when we'd fallen asleep. *Was he up early again?*

I rolled to face him, catching him off guard as I slotted into the empty space of his bare chest. Half asleep and groggy, my mind was screaming at me that he was trying to leave, and I wasn't going to let that happen again.

He chuckled softly and pressed his nose into the top of my head. "I didn't mean to wake you."

"Stay," I mumbled, the sound muffled.

"I'm not going anywhere." Gently, he played with my hair, smoothing it down and pushing strands behind my ear. "This is just what time my body wakes me up."

"Your body is stupid," I insisted. "The sun isn't awake yet. You shouldn't be either."

He laughed as he pulled me in just a little closer. "Go back to sleep, love."

"I don't want you to leave."

He went silent. There was no sound except our breathing and the steady hum of the heat, and even his fingers paused in my hair, the steady drum of his heart against my forehead slowing. I could feel myself slipping back toward sleep, and I wanted to fight it, wanted to make sure he wasn't going to run away like he had on the boat or like I had after the charity ball. This was his home, but that meant nothing when he had other places he could go.

"Okay," he whispered, pressing a kiss to the top of my head. "I won't."

———

By the time I'd woken back up, the light of the room had increased dramatically, and the steady inhale and exhale of Adrian's breathing was still all around me. He was still holding me exactly the same way as earlier that morning.

I pulled my head up from his chest and looked up at him, fully expecting a bored, awake Adrian to be looking down at me. But his eyes were shut, his lips just barely parted...

He'd fallen back asleep with me.

Bleary-eyed and exhausted, I reached up, dragging my fingers across his cheek. The fine lines in his face seemed to smooth as I touched them, and I did it again, touching his forehead, the little lines beside his eyes, the one that ran from his nostril to the edge of his lips. He was relaxed out in the Hamptons, but seeing him like this was another level that I didn't think was possible for him to achieve.

He blinked awake and blue eyes found mine in an instant. "Hi," I said.

He studied me for a moment before glancing at the window behind me, a flicker of confusion washing over him. "Was I asleep?"

I nodded.

"Hmm." He cupped my cheek, his thumb moving back and forth across it. "I can't remember the last time I slept later than the sunrise."

We were slow-moving as we made our way from the bed. He offered me a shirt that didn't have paint stains on it and I took it from him, opting not to wear bottoms for both comfort, and in case things became heated again. The shirt hung low enough over my rear that I didn't feel a need to, anyway.

As we made our way from the bedroom and passed the handful of closed, mysterious doors and one that said *Lucas*, I wondered where exactly he'd sent his child for the weekend.

"He's with Grace," Adrian said, intensely nonchalant as if he hadn't just read my mind. "She's got a grandson about his age."

The walkway on the second floor opened up, over-looking a massive, bright living room with windows lining the entirety of the far wall. Two sets of stairs lined each side, and at the far end of the walkway, an open doorway led to a room I could barely make out the contents of, but I could see what I thought was the corner of a grand piano.

gray walls carried through to the living room as he took me down the stairs. His place was sleek and modern with a hint of an almost academic feel, with white couches and wooden furniture filling the space. A handful of oversized Legos sat in the corner in the shape of a castle, and beside them, an abandoned train beside a set of disconnected tracks.

"Are you a savory or sweet breakfast kind of person?"

I turned my attention back to him as he pulled me into the kitchen, depositing me by the island with high-top chairs along one side. "Oh. Uh, sweet."

"Pancakes?"

I grinned. "Do you have chocolate chips?"

"I have an eight-year-old," he laughed, pulling out a box of flour. "Of course I have chocolate chips, Ava."

———

"It's *freezing*."

"The water's hot, love."

Adrian slid the glass door open onto the hidden balcony. I couldn't for the life of me understand why this was tucked away on the other side of the penthouse, the only access point hidden in the room I'd spotted earlier that housed nothing but a grand piano, massive mirrors, and a bench to sit on.

Frigid air whipped my hair as he pulled me out into the cold, my bare feet expecting frozen ground but finding warm paneling. I stared down in confusion, wondering why the hell my toes hadn't gone numb.

"Heated floors," he said casually. He pressed a button on the wall and the cover on the pool began to shift, retracting toward the left side and revealing roiling, steaming water. By the time I'd finally pulled my gaze from the floor and the pool, Adrian was already half undressed, standing in nothing but his flannel pajama bottoms. "Come on."

The wind picked up again, his unstyled hair lifting and blowing lightly. He pushed his pants down to his ankles and kicked them off, baring himself entirely, and I couldn't tell if it was the cold of the wind or just *him* that stole the air from my lungs.

He held out a hand for me, and I took it.

Shivering in the cold, my body naturally gravitated toward him as he pulled me backward in the direction of the pool. His hands snaked beneath the oversized shirt he'd given me, lifting the fabric up my body as his fingers glided across my bare skin.

In one quick move, he pulled the shirt up and over my head and hooked his fingers beneath the curve of my rear. He lifted me up, hooking my legs around his waist.

"Hi," I breathed, my teeth chattering.

Step by step, he descended slowly into the pool. "Hi," he grinned.

The moment the water touched my toes, I trusted him. Warmth enveloped me as it rose up my calves, my hips and thighs, my waist. It was almost as warm as a hot tub but was large enough to be considered a small pool, stretching maybe twenty feet wide. It backed right up against the side of the building, and the lack of railing on the edge made my heart rate spike.

"Is that...safe?" I asked, clutching onto the back of his neck. Heights weren't my worst fear, but they were up there, and the possibility of being thrown over the edge or accidentally lifting myself when we were almost high enough to touch the clouds made my hair stand on end.

Little by little, he edged us closer to the edge. "The drop is just to the lower balcony," he said. Damp hands pushed the hair from my face. "A fall would hurt, but you're not dropping sixty floors."

I clung to him like a fucking koala anyway. "Do you let Lucas out here?"

He snorted. "Not a fucking chance. He can swim out here when he's ten. Until then, he can use the building's community pool."

I watched him, studying him in the confusing mixture of freezing air and warm water. If he didn't swim with Lucas out here, then this was either solely for him, and he swam alone, or he saved it for occasions like these. I wasn't sure why that made my stomach twist. It shouldn't bother me that he'd been with other people—he had a son, for God's sake. But the idea that whatever this was would just be another name on his list made me feel as small as a fucking grape.

He propped me up on a seat that jutted out from the inside of the pool, just beside the edge. I could see the balcony he was talking about down below, and the wooziness washed over me, a mixture of adrenaline and fear from the height and a sickening feeling that maybe, this meant nothing to him. Sure, the sex was incredible, the tension between us was finally breaking. We'd shared one of the best nights of my goddamn life, and we'd spent far too long together today to be considered healthy, but that didn't necessarily point toward anything real from him.

He'd said he wanted me last night. That on its own had shot me into the goddamn stratosphere, and the longer I stayed here, the more I worried I wouldn't be capable of coming down—and that was fucking terrifying if he was down on earth and not beside me.

"We shouldn't stay out here for too long," I said, and the squeak my voice made as it cracked on the word *long* made me wish I'd shut my mouth instead. "You, uh, you have a date at seven."

His lips pressed into a thin line as he stared at me, his brows dropping. "Ava." He pushed my thighs apart and pressed me into the corner of the pool, invading my space again as he slotted his hips between my legs. A hint of firmness pressed against my inner thigh, and heat swept over me even in the cold. "Do you honestly think I have any interest in that?"

"I—"

"I walked away because I wanted you," he said, his chin dipping as he dragged his nose along my cheek. "Is that not what I said last night? I already canceled the two tonight and the one for tomorrow morning, Ava. This is the only date I want."

I swallowed to dampen my dry throat, my breath catching the moment his hand dragged up my thigh. *You can want this.*

You can properly want this now.

"On a fucking Saturday? Are you kidding me?"

Weak-kneed and wrapped in a towel with the light-headed aftermath of another two orgasms flooding my senses, I stood beside the grand piano as Adrian shut the sliding glass door a little too hard, a little too angrily, his phone pressed against his ear.

"Fine. I'll be down in twenty."

He hung up, and those lines of stress popped back out

on his face. Gone was the absolute calm I'd gotten used to. "What's wrong?"

"Crisis at the office," he sighed. The clock on the wall showed four thirty— surely they should be finishing up. "I'm sorry, I need to sort this out. I'm not sure how long I'll be down there but I can try..."

"It's okay," I insisted, a sinking feeling in my gut. Insecurity had always lingered a little too close to me, and I couldn't help but worry about the worst possible scenario here. But he'd insisted that he wanted me, and I needed to *try* to believe that. "I need to pick up a few things from my dad's anyway."

He closed the distance, damp feet padding across the wooden floors, and pressed a kiss to my forehead. "I'll call you when I'm done. We can meet up later tonight if you want."

Of course I fucking want that. I looked up at him, trying to get a read on whether that was a sincere offer, but he spoke before I could even question it.

"Lucas is with Grace until tomorrow afternoon. I don't want to waste that time on anything else."

Chapter 22

Adrian

Michael's call had ripped me from the stressless bliss I'd been floating in for almost an entire day. Part of me wanted to be angry with him about it, but the other part, the part that had been significantly calm yet ignited in ways I hadn't been in years, could find a single morsel of understanding.

Until I pushed through the door to the private wing of offices and came face to face with Andrew.

Michael stood about ten feet behind him, his fingers rubbing at his temples as he leaned against the far wall of the meeting room. But Andrew, his ginger beard freshly trimmed and the lines in his forehead about half an inch deeper than yesterday, looked seconds from blowing his lid.

"What on earth is so important that you two have pulled me from my home on a fucking Saturday?" I asked, pulling at the slightly too snug collar of my shirt. *Goddammit, I must have grabbed the one that was too small for me.* That's what I got for rushing and spending five minutes with my tongue down Ava's throat. "I had to leave my goddamn date for this."

"Adrian," Michael started, but Andrew beat him to it.

"You're aware of the conference all day today and tomorrow upstate, correct?" Andrew asked. He stared me down with a level of irritation I'd never seen in him—and I'd seen him *furious*. He was practically shaking, each part of his body vibrating in his deep maroon suit. "Or were you not paying attention?"

"The Tomorrow's Vision one? Yes. Of course." There was a part of me that wanted to throw the name of it in his face, *show* him that despite his insistence, I was fully invested and present here. "What about it?"

"It's a disaster," Michael mumbled.

A rock dropped in my stomach.

"We did what we could without getting you involved. But it's gotten to the point where we need to shut it down, *now*, and you have executive power," he added.

"What the fuck does that mean?" I asked.

Andrew shifted one foot to his left, stepping between me and Michael and blocking my view. "It means that shit wasn't checked out," he said. "It means that somehow, we double booked every ticket, resulting in twice the amount of people and far exceeding safety numbers. It means that security wasn't vetted, and only a quarter of the necessary detail that we needed arrived. It means that we had to shut down ticket scanning because almost every single one was coming back invalid, so it's a free-for-all all, and it's filling up with random passersby."

Dear fucking God.

"How the hell did this happen? Why didn't you contact me sooner?"

"*That* one," Andrew started, jutting a thumb back at Michael, "refused to bother you. But we've run out of food, we've run out of drinks, and the hotel is insisting we shut it down before both they and we get a hefty fine, or worse, insurance claims."

I opened my mouth to speak, but Andrew cut me off.

"This ship is not fucking tight enough," he continued, spittle flying in the fluorescent lighting. "Do you understand what this will do, Adrian? We have to shut it down. We have to refund everyone. We have to eat the cost of this, both in revenue and *reputation*. Cedarwood will be furious. We could lose them as a client over this. We could lose *multiple* clients over this."

My fingers twitched inwards, my hands curling into fists. The temptation to hit him square across the jaw crept up on me, starting low and small and increasing to a high-pitched ringing in my ears by the time he'd finished speaking. "You think I don't know that?" I seethed. "Respectfully, Andrew, I am not the one in charge of final checks."

Michael pushed off the wall behind Andrew, his jaw steeled and his gaze averted. "I should have..."

I shook my head. "You know damn well that isn't your responsibility either."

"You should have been there to oversee it," Andrew snapped, his gaze locked on me. "This is your company. Take the fucking responsibility. Handle this."

Silence, or as much of that as one can get on the forty-fourth floor in downtown Manhattan, settled in around us. It nearly crackled with charge.

None of us wanted to be the one to make that call. None of us wanted to be the reason the conference shut down. None of us wanted to be on the receiving end of the damages, the consequences, the wrath that this would bring.

It would be corporate suicide.

Andrew would never. He was too proud, too pompous, too up-on-his-high-horse to ever come down. And Michael...

Michael was my best friend. The second he opened his mouth again, I knew what he was doing. And I couldn't let it happen.

"Shut it down," I said. "Shut it all down. *Now.*"

———

There wasn't a chance in hell that David Riley wouldn't find out about this in the next hour, and considering his company was one of the few showcasing at the conference I'd just had to obliterate. I figured it would be better coming from me.

Nervously, I fidgeted with the cuff of my sweater as I sat in the back of my car. I didn't love turning up at David's uninvited, even if he was one of my closest friends. But the anxiety of what I'd just done was eating away at me, and it was mixing in a horribly nauseating cocktail with the knowledge that Ava would be there, and I'd have to keep my hands and thoughts to myself.

And I'd have to look David in the fucking eye after everything I'd done to his daughter. Somehow that seemed harder than doing the same thing weeks ago when I'd only slept with her once and everything else was simply a cacophony of debaucherous, debased thoughts that filled my head—now I had to speak to him with her a foot away, close enough to reach out and grab and beg for her to drop to her goddamn knees again. I could do it. It just wouldn't be easy.

But none of this was easy, not now.

Chapter 23

Ava

hy the fuck didn't he text me?

Dad's phone had gone off thirty seconds before Adrian's tall, overwhelming form had stepped through the doors of my father's penthouse. I sat on the sofa opposite Dad's recliner, the lighting low and the curtains drawn, in my leggings and paint-stained band shirt from last night. I wasn't dumb enough to turn up in one of Adrian's shirts, even if there was a chance Dad had never seen it before.

But I knew what the heat that filled my skin meant, and it had crept across my cheeks and neck the moment Adrian's eyes had locked with mine.

Before they turned to my father.

I just had to hope that the unexpected arrival was enough to keep Dad's attention off me while I got myself under control.

"David," Adrian said, his eyes wide and chest heaving as if he'd run up the sixty flights of stairs instead of taking the elevator. "I'm sorry. I need to talk to you, *now*."

What?

"Yeah, I figured as much."

What does he need...

Bile crept up my esophagus as the immediate, horrifying worry hit me: *Is he going to tell him?*

Adrian's name crossed my lips, slightly cracked, slightly hoarse, and sharp blue eyes cut across to me. He shook his head, just a quick, little action that was nearly imperceivable, and he turned back to my Dad as he pushed himself up from his recliner.

"Office, then."

Dad padded across the floor in his full suit without socks or shoes, the fabric clinging unnaturally to his small beer gut. He beckoned Adrian to follow, and both of them slipped away, leaving me alone on the couch with a glass of wine that I could only imagine Adrian would gush about. But I felt too nauseous to drink it now.

What the *fuck* was going on? Why was he here, now, when he knew I'd be here? How did he expect me to act calmly when he and my father were alone in the same room?

Seconds after they disappeared, my phone screen lit up.

Adrian: Not about us.

Adrian: Try not to worry.

Trying not to worry about that was like trying not to breathe.

I knew I needed to be okay with things. Whatever the hell we were doing wasn't going to magically vanish from memory, and Adrian was close friends with my dad. They would *have* to be alone together sometimes. But with whatever the hell was going on that had brought him here with almost no announcement, two hours after he'd last had his hands on me before basically rushing us both out of his apartment, I couldn't help but feel nauseous and panicked and fucking *worried*.

Sinking my fingers into the warm, plush fabric of the throw blanket, I pulled it from its neatly folded spot on the back of the couch and draped it over myself. I wanted to hide beneath it like a child, but I was old enough to recognize how insane that would look to my father if he stepped out of his office with his friend to his twenty-five-year-old daughter lying on the couch with a dark blue blanket over her head.

I had to wait this out. I *could* wait this out.

————

"Stay for a bit. Have a drink with us."

Two sets of footsteps padded down the hall along with my father's voice, and it took everything in me to not whip around to look at both of them. Whatever they were discussing wasn't meant to concern me, and if I tried to insert myself...

"David..."

"Don't try an' get outta it. You need it."

For fucks sake.

I waited until they'd both entered my line of sight to lift my head from my phone. "Everything okay?" I asked, the warble in my voice almost entirely gone.

Adrian stood at the far end of the sofa, his gaze flicking back and forth between me and my dad. "It's fine," he said. A muscle in his jaw twitched, and *God*, the lines on his forehead looked so much deeper. "Nothing you need to worry about, Ava. Just having some issues with Stone & Co. It shouldn't affect David too much."

Dad's hand pressed down on my shoulder as he passed me, and it should have been a comforting touch—it was something he'd done hundreds, if not thousands of times before. But with everything hanging over me, it felt heavy.

"I'll get you a glass, Adrian," Dad called over his shoulder.

He disappeared around the corner a second later.

"I'm so sorry," Adrian whispered. "I should have warned you I was coming."

"What the fuck is happening?" I asked, keeping my voice low enough that Dad wouldn't hear two rooms over. The muffled sounds of clinking glass didn't help with my anxiety.

"I'll explain later. Please, Ava, don't worry about it."

"I'm *already* worried about it."

His gaze flicked to the entrance of the hallway and back to me. "I know. I'll get out of here as quickly as I can."

"That's not..."

Dad's footsteps echoed heavily as he walked back toward the room, and all I could do was shut my mouth. I pulled up my texts with Adrian instead.

Me: I'm not worried because you're around my dad.

"Grabbed another bottle," Dad announced, setting down a glass in front of the space beside me on the sofa and filling it with freshly opened wine. Adrian hesitated before sinking into the couch a healthy distance from me.

Me: Okay, that's a lie. I am a little worried because of that. But mostly because you look like you just got hit by the metro.

"Thanks, Dave," Adrian sighed. He picked up the glass

of wine and leaned back into the cushions. With one hand, he shot me back a reply.

Adrian: I had to shut down an event while it was happening.

Adrian: Your dad's business was one of the sponsors. I had to speak to him.

Adrian: I'm sorry for worrying you.

"Aves and I were chattin' about her matchmaking schtick before you turned up," Dad said, filling the dead silence as Adrian and I stared at our phones. "How's that goin' for 'ya, Adrian? Heard you were on a date earlier."

I nearly choked on my sip of wine.

Adrian looked across at him, his thumb hovering over his screen. "How did you...?"

"When I got the call earlier about the conference, I asked to speak with 'ya but Andrew said you were out galavantin' with some girl," Dad laughed. "Figured I'd let 'em sort it out and speak to you if it got worse."

Me: Adrian.

Me: Adrian what the fuck do we say to that??

"Oh. Andrew was who called you?"

Me: ADRIAN.

"Yeah, seemed real worried 'bout the whole thing. I told him to do whatever was necessary and I'd worry about the ramifications later," Dad explained.

"Right. Got you," Adrian said.

Adrian: I'm working on it.

"Yeah, it was a second date, actually," he continued, shutting off his screen and shoving his phone into his pocket. My hands went clammy, and all I could do was pretend they weren't and that it wasn't getting increasingly hard to hold a glass of wine in my hand. "All of Ava's choices after we went to the Hamptons have been spot on. That was a great suggestion. But I'm really liking this one."

"Oh, that's fucking great news!" Dad boomed, pitching forward in his chair in excitement as if he'd won the goddamn lottery again. "What'ser name?"

"Heather," I interjected. "Her name's Heather."

Dad's grin only grew. "See? Told 'ya she'd do 'ya right."

Do not read into that, Ava, oh my God.

"And I told 'ya that trip would help," he chuckled. "I could see it all from a mile away. You're goddamn lucky I trust ya, Ade, 'cause that never woulda happened with anyone else."

My throat closed in.

"Even after today?" Adrian asked, a breathy, barely-there laugh tainting the words.

"Of course."

————

"Are you going?"

The words flew out of my mouth as Dad and Adrian rounded the corner from the kitchen. They'd migrated there ages ago to talk business, leaving me alone and anxious in my boredom for two fucking hours. The clock was ticking toward ten in the evening, and I just wanted to go back with Adrian, wanted to spend the time I had left with him before Lucas came back tomorrow.

"Yeah, I'm heading out," Adrian said, plucking his coat from the closet by the door. "It's getting late. Do you want a ride home?"

The way his eyes glinted as he met my gaze told me everything I needed to know.

"That would be great," I grinned.

"You can just stay the night, Aves," Dad said. "It's cold out there, anyhow."

Shit. I needed to get him off of that idea before he could settle on it and enforce it. "I would, but I've actually got a ton of work to do before I see Em tomorrow."

"I can set ya up upstairs..."

"I haven't backed up all my client files yet to the cloud," I lied. "Sorry, Dad. Maybe tomorrow night?"

Dad sighed and knocked back the rest of his wine. "*Fine.* Movie night?"

I pulled myself up from the sofa and grinned at him. "You got it."

Dad pulled my coat from the closet and I slipped it on before shoving my feet into my boots. He and Adrian idly talked business while I gathered the handful of things I'd come in with, and with a quick hug and a promise to come back tomorrow night for a screening of *The Goonies*, Adrian and I slipped quietly out the door and into the private landing that connected us to the elevator.

We didn't dare say a word. We didn't even touch, but the air between us felt thick enough to slice, and as we stared at each other in absolute, horrified silence while we waited for the elevator, I searched for words I wanted to say when we finally could.

But the moment the elevator doors shut behind us, he was on me instead.

He kissed me hard enough to send me back into the mirrored steel wall, his hands cupping my cheeks, his knee between my thighs. And so easily, again, he made me dizzy.

Chapter 24

Adrian

As much as I wanted to get her back home, I didn't want to touch the Darkwater building with a ten-foot pole at that moment.

"Are you warm enough?" I asked, clutching her hand in mine as we walked along Fulton Street. I'd asked Oliver to wait at the corner of Church Street in case David tried to insist that we ride separately, but I just didn't want to go back there. I wanted to be out and about with her, I wanted the fresh air, wanted to feel what it was like to be around her in public without hiding away in my apartment. And as the lights dazzled off One World Trade Center at the end of the road, it only solidified how much I wanted to stay out here. "We could grab food. I know it's late, but..."

She huffed a chuckle, her breath fogging in front of her lips. "I'm warm enough. We can do whatever as long as it's out of eyeshot of Dad's floor."

"Dear God, yeah, as far away from your father as possible," I laughed. I pulled her closer to me, her shoulder brushing against my upper arm. "Feels like we're sneaking around like teenagers."

The stress from Stone & Co hung over me like a fucking storm cloud, but with her this close and this *touchable*, it felt more like I had an umbrella, like I wasn't drowning under the weight of whatever would come of this. Andrew wanted to take it to the board—he'd outright said it to me before I left, said that he would follow through on his threat. And in complete honesty, for the first time, I was genuinely worried.

There was a chance he could sway them after this. I was the one who had pulled the plug, and he was betting on using that to prove I couldn't do my job, I was sure. But there was no other choice to be made there. If the board wanted to pull me out of my position, I would have to let it happen.

But I felt like I could handle that with her by my side. And that, more than anything, was the most unnerving thing of all.

We wandered through the streets of downtown Manhattan together, the harsh wind dying down as they cut through the buildings. The cold wasn't anywhere near as punishing as it was higher up, but the chill still soaked into us, enough to have her teeth chattering and her fingers freezing against mine. I shoved our joined hands into my pocket.

"We can go back to my place," I offered, slowing as we made our way through Tribeca. Up ahead, a bagel cart with its lights still on sat on the edge of the sidewalk, and a little sign next to it read, *Best Hot Chocolate In The World!* I didn't believe it for a second, but it would do the trick. "Or..."

"Don't tell me you genuinely believe that's the best hot chocolate in the world," Ava laughed.

I popped my mouth open in an O as I pulled her toward

189

it, stepping in front of her and walking backward. "You don't think they're lying, do you?"

She tried to hold back the adorable, stupid little grin sprouting across her cheeks. "Adrian."

"*Ava.*"

The pink that had cropped up on her nose from the cold spread outward, darkening her cheeks dramatically and making her freckles stand out even more.

"What? Do you like it when I say your name?"

She breathed out a laugh. "I do. But I like it even more when you say it like that."

"Like what?" I teased.

She gave me a knowing glare, unable to keep her smile tucked away any longer. "Breathy," she said, her voice lowering. "Sounds like you're moaning it."

"Oh, like this?" I grinned, pulling her closer as I stopped just short of the bagel stand. I leaned down, bringing my lips against the shell of her ear. "*Ava.*"

I cupped the side of her face, feeling the little shiver she did in response. "You can't just..."

"*Ava,*" I said again, forcing my breath to catch at the very end of it, putting just a little more emphasis on her name.

She cackled with awareness of me. Her head tipped back, her auburn hair shining in the light from the street, and my fucking God, she was beautiful. Paint-stained and makeup-less and not a fucking care in the world, she looked like something straight from the goddamn heavens, distracting enough to make Orpheus turn to look and magnetic enough to tempt Icarus.

Everything about her was just...*everything.*

"That one was bad," she laughed. "You can't convincingly moan on command."

It didn't matter that it was a thinly veiled, joking insult, just as it didn't matter that she was twenty years my junior or David's daughter or a light in the dark that I'd desperately wanted to ignore, just as it didn't matter what had happened today or what could happen tomorrow. "I don't care," I said.

I kissed her, and she sunk into me, her hands resting gently on the sides of my neck. I hadn't felt like this with anyone in years, and even then, there was always a stiffness to it, a hesitance that I couldn't quite break through. Even with Jan.

It was terrifying, and yet, it was okay.

"Can I be honest for a moment?" I breathed, keeping her lips not an inch from mine as we huddled in the vague warmth that emanated from the bagel cart. I dragged my thumb across her cheek, feeling the little shift she did as she nodded. "I want this. For real."

Her breath caught, and unfocused eyes searched mine as she pulled back enough to look up at me. It hit me, then, what I'd said, what it meant, what I'd admitted—and for once, it didn't make me panic. I was just...*calm*. "You don't mean a bagel, right?" she whispered.

I snorted. "No, I don't mean a fucking bagel, Ava. I mean *you*, and the thing I've been trying so desperately to avoid."

"I thought you didn't want that," she said. Her throat moved on a swallow, and that little shiver was back, her lower lip bouncing ever so slightly. "You *said* you didn't want that."

"I didn't think I did," I admitted. "But then there was you."

"But Lucas..."

"I'm willing to figure that out." The wind kicked up, her

191

hair blowing forward into both of our faces. I fought to push it back behind her ears. "Are you?"

Her mouth popped open, closed, open, closed, open. I couldn't help but hyper-focus on how little the risk of her presence in my life scared me—my only worry was that she would say no, that she wouldn't feel ready to explore something real with me, consequences be damned. I would find a way to be okay with it if that were the case. I'd buried heartbreak before, and I could do it again.

It might just take me another two years.

"I am. I want that," she said, her voice so soft it was nearly lost in the noise of the city. "I just don't know what to do about my dad."

Relief washed over me, but if I was honest, it felt like a wash of *her*, like the air in my lungs was her, like she'd personally lifted the weight from my shoulders, like she alone held the earth in her hands and kept it afloat. It was absurd, it was psychotic, even, that she'd forced a one-eighty from me by being nothing but a breath of fresh air. And I didn't want to lose that feeling.

"We'll have to tell him," I said. I pressed a kiss against her cheek, letting myself linger. "If he can handle what happened today, then he can handle this. Hopefully."

"He'll lose his mind."

"I know."

"If we do that, we have to do it right," she said, but her teeth were chattering harder, and the chill was sinking in despite the little bubble of heat we'd found and the warmth I was trying to give her.

I tucked her into my shoulder with one hand around the back of her neck. "We'll figure out the best way to do it. And I'll shoulder the consequences of it."

The sliver of warmth I found in my pocket as I grabbed

my phone out wasn't enough to shake the bitter cold that was overwhelming both of us. I shot a quick text to Oliver with a link to our location, and in the spare few minutes I had left before the car would whisk us away to privacy, I ordered Ava the best hot chocolate in the world.

————

The thought process was simple: with Ava staying the night again, I'd inevitably wake up at my usual time, and if she wanted me to stay in bed with her, I could at least get started on damage control from the canceled event while she slept. But that meant I needed files and my spare hard drive from my office on the forty-fourth floor.

Get in, get out, take her home, and bury the last of my stresses by being with her, touching her. Andrew and Michael had long since taken their work home with them, and with no one left in there, it wouldn't raise any eyebrows to waltz through the office blocks and the private wing with David Riley's daughter.

And it didn't.

We made it all the way to my private office before she'd tempted me enough that I broke.

Half-dressed and with bare breasts pressed against the floor-to-ceiling window, she shuddered and sputtered a moan as I sank fully inside of her from behind, her knees resting on a single filing cabinet I'd kicked the contents off of. With one hand between her thighs and the other around the front of her throat, I pulled her upper body back toward me.

Heavy-lidded eyes looked up at me upside down, her mouth parted. She was the most beautiful thing I'd ever seen.

Just like a fucking painting.

Half of me wanted to get into Shibari just so I could tie her up beautifully and hang her in a goddamn museum. But the other half, the half that had control and thought mostly logically, wanted to keep her entirely for myself.

I lost my mind with her, *in* her, and she took all of it, warped it, made it her own. The way she grinned up at me as if she were the devil herself with my hand gripping the sides of her throat, the way she gasped my name as I harshly squeezed her nipples between my fingers, the way her body responded to absolute filth that I couldn't keep myself from saying —all of it was too much, too tempting, too grounding, too perfect, wrapped up nice and neat in a pretty little package that fit me so well in so many ways.

"You've ruined me for anyone else," I rasped, my teeth playing with the soft flesh of her earlobe. Pleasure knotted in my gut as she tightened around me, her little, raspy moan the only reply.

I'd known what I was doing when I had told her that I wanted this. I'd known what I'd been admitting to—that I saw a pathway to falling harder than I'd wanted to with anyone, that I'd end up somewhere I'd told her over and over I couldn't handle. The words weren't all there to explain how I felt but I showed her in the ways I could muster at this point, in the ways I touched her.

And for now, that would have to do.

Chapter 25

Ava

"Ava. Please. Think about this for two seconds."

I set down the steaming cup of peppermint tea in front of Emily as she lounged on my cracked, vintage leather couch. She was fully dressed for the office despite me deciding we would work from my apartment today, and although she looked absolutely incredible in a full, dark pink pantsuit, it clashed with my pajamas and made it feel a bit like I was being talked down to by a therapist.

"He's twenty years older than you."

"I'm well aware of that," I said, trying to keep the snark in my voice to a minimum as I sunk into the matching chair opposite her. "It doesn't bother me."

"Just because it doesn't bother you doesn't mean it won't bother other people," she explained. Her braid fell over her shoulder as she leaned forward, wrapping her fingers around the hot mug. "Others will question it. *Constantly.*"

"Like you're doing now?" I snapped, and her mouth shut. "It's no one else's business. It doesn't matter if they have a problem with it."

"I get that. I do. And please understand that I'm talking to you about this as your friend, as your *confidant*, and I don't want to upset you. I'm genuinely thrilled for you, but I'm worried, too. You guys have such different lives and I don't want that to come between you, but you should be aware that there are risks here for that kind of thing."

I narrowed my eyes at her. "What do you mean?"

"Well, for one, he was a fully grown adult when 9/11 happened and you were still in diapers," she deadpanned. "He has a different perspective on the world. Hell, he probably has a different perspective on this *city*. One that probably clashes with yours, at least a little."

"I can handle clashes in perspective. I'm not five years old on the playground fighting over toys any more." The longer I stared at the swirling steam of my cup of black filter coffee, the more her words sunk in. She wasn't *wrong*, necessarily. There was an inherent oddity in the idea that he was a legal adult before I was even born.

"I know."

I sighed and lifted my cup to my lips, wincing as the contents burned my tongue. *Fucking ouch.* "Look," I said. "If Adrian was anyone else, if he was the same person he is now, but in the body of a man my age, it wouldn't change anything. I'd still want him. I'd still be drawn to him. And maybe that's naive of me to assume that, because he probably wasn't as well-rounded twenty years ago as he is now, but I honestly don't think it would change a thing. He would still be him. And he's who I want."

Her lips pressed into a thin line.

"I can't change the fact that he's the person I stumbled into blindly. I can't change my stupid, incessant teenage crush that I had on him, and I can't change how that's playing into things now. But in all honesty, if I had a time

196

machine and could pluck anyone out of a crowd to do all of this again with and feel the same way about, I wouldn't. I'd choose him. Over and over again."

Her shoulders sagged as she leaned back, resting her cup of tea on her knee. "I love that. Genuinely. It makes me insanely happy, even though I don't look it," she said, huffing out a weak chuckle. "But you know I have to ask about the other part of this."

I averted my gaze. "Lucas?"

"Yeah. You're twenty-five. Are you ready to be a mom to an eight-year-old?"

I'd spent a lot of time thinking about that since I'd left Adrian's yesterday. He'd kept me with him up until the moment he'd gotten a call from Grace to let him know that they were on their way, and even then, he hadn't *wanted* me to leave. But we'd agreed it was the right thing to do so we wouldn't confuse Lucas.

But it was still a heavy topic, one that I didn't take lightly even though Adrian had insisted we'd figure it out. I had enough of my own issues from growing up in a family that wasn't happy, and I didn't want to inflict any unintentional trauma on the kid by taking on responsibilities I wasn't certain about.

"Honestly, I don't know," I sighed. "And I know that's a make or break for him. I love Lucas, he's great, but the fear of ruining his childhood by just being in proximity and doing the wrong thing at the wrong time is...terrifying. It's not like I don't want to be a mom at all, but I never expected to have to make that choice just because of someone I wanted to be with."

"Do you feel like you're ready to have a kid at all?"

I shrugged. "Maybe. When is anyone really *ready*, you know? My mom had me when she was seventeen, she wasn't *ready*, but she and my dad figured it out until they stopped working well together. And I'm..."

"Insane?" Em laughed.

"A little," I chuckled. "But I mean I'm not terrified of being a mother. I'm terrified of filling someone else's shoes."

"Do you think he'd be okay with you not filling that role immediately?" She sipped at her tea, and her lack of a wince from the heat of it made me irrationally jealous. "Like, do you think you guys could take it slow for a while, and once you feel certain, he could bring you in?"

I shook my head. "That's not what he's looking for. You know that. He wants someone who can help him raise Lucas."

"Yeah, but he also wants someone he doesn't have to love."

Fuck. I knew it would come up —she'd helped me with his file, had done the initial interview. She knew this. "I think...I think he's changed his mind about that."

"For you?"

"Yeah. For me."

———

Why I'd agreed to Adrian's somewhat last-minute invitation to come over for dinner with him and Lucas was beyond me. He'd be insane to try to broach the topic with his son about me this early, and I'd made entirely sure that wasn't his plan before I'd said yes. But even over text message three hours before he wanted me to arrive, he seemed overly care-free about the situation.

I could handle tiptoeing around Lucas. We'd basically done that already back in the Hamptons, but we also hadn't acted on our instincts fully then—the temptation had been overwhelming, sure, but it wasn't as easy to slip up as it could be with this. I just had to make it long enough for Lucas to go to bed.

The moment I typed the code that gave me access to his floor into the elevator, my phone chimed in my bag.

Adrian: I'm so sorry. I need to stay a little later at work. Damage control.

Adrian: I'll be out as soon as I can, but I understand if you want to cancel.

I stared down at my phone as the elevator rose rapidly. Ten seconds in, my ears popped, and I wondered if I was passing his office at lightspeed on the way up to his penthouse.

Me: I'm in the elevator. Do you want me to go?

His reply was almost immediate.

Adrian: Fuck no, I don't want you to go. Stay. I want to see you. I was just trying to be polite.

Adrian: Lucas and Grace are up there. If you're okay to wait around with them, I'll try to be as quick as I can.

The elevator slowed, stopped, and dinged on the sixtieth floor. The doors opened up to the private foyer, the same one I'd knelt on days ago, and it took everything in me to shove those memories down as I stepped out of the metal cube.

Me: I want to see you too. I'll wait. :)

Heavy footsteps grew louder and louder on the other side of the door.

"DADDY?"

Shit. I have to be the one to tell him?

. . .

199

Taking a deep breath and hesitantly opening the door, I came face to face with a boy half my height, with curly black hair and his father's blue eyes, a little set of glasses resting on his nose. His smile didn't falter, but his brows furrowed as he took me in.

"Hi, Ava," he said, but the way he said my name sounded more like a question than a greeting.

"Hi, Lucas." I grinned at him as I shut the door behind me, desperately trying not to show how uneasy this made me. "Your dad is still in his office. He's got a little more work to do but then he'll be up."

His nose scrunched up, and his glasses wiggled. He looked adorable in them—like a miniature version of his dad. "Did he send you to tell me that?"

I shook my head. "Nope. I'm having dinner with you guys tonight if you're okay with that."

His mouth popped open in surprise, his brows raised straight up his forehead, and he did a little happy dance. "Yay! Dinner with Ava!"

He grabbed my hand immediately, and within seconds, he was hauling me through the hallway and past the couch I'd spent far too much time on with Adrian. "Those new glasses?"

Lucas shook his head, his loose curls bouncing. As we passed Grace in the kitchen, I gave a little wave, and she answered back with a small nod and a smile that told me Adrian had at least warned *her*. "Nope! I gotta wear them to read like my dad. Can you help me with my homework?"

Four hours later, I'd eaten chicken parmesan, helped Lucas finish his homework, and watched an entire Legos movie with him. It was nearing ten in the evening.

Adrian still hadn't come up.

Me: Adrian?

Me: Lucas is saying his bedtime is 1 AM. I do not believe him.

Me: Are you okay?

Grace had already packed up and gone home after I gave her the green light. I didn't know what else to do short of calling Adrian or going down there with Lucas in tow. The nausea in my stomach came more from worry than it did from irritation, and in a last-ditch effort, I snuck away from a yawning Lucas to call his father.

It took four rings for him to pick up.

"Fuck, I'm so sorry," Adrian said. In four little words, I could hear the overwhelming stress in his voice, could *feel* the realization hitting him about what time it was and what had happened.

"It's okay," I insisted. "Grace went home about an hour ago. We're just watching TV. Are you all right?"

"I'm just...I'm dealing with a lot. I'm really sorry, Aves," he sighed. "Actually—fuck this. I'm coming up now. I'll deal with it tomorrow."

"Are you sure?"

I could hear the sound of his computer shutting and his chair squeaking. "Yeah. I'll see you in a few." He hesitated for a moment, and a second later a light, barely-there laugh echoed down the phone. "And for the record, no, his bedtime is nine. But it's not on you to police that."

He said a quick goodbye before hanging up, and as I rounded the corner of the private little alcove I'd stood in, a photo that hung on the wall opposite caught my eye in the low light. I lit the space with the flashlight from my phone, and to my absolute surprise, found a version of my father from at least ten years ago, if not more.

And beside him, a younger Adrian.

They stood in the backyard of the house my mother still lived in, my dad in his barbecuing apron and a set of tongs in one hand, Adrian in stars-and-stripes shorts and a plain white shirt. It must have been the Fourth of July—I couldn't see him wearing those for any other reason.

There wasn't a single crease on his face, and every little gray hair that ran through the black that I'd come to adore was absent. It was nearly the exact same version of him that I'd obsessed over as a teenager.

My chest tightened. I'd always been fond of him. *Obviously*. But looking at him like this, seeing a version of him in the past, comparing that to who he was now and who *we* were...there wasn't a part of me that felt I could explain how it made me feel even if I wanted to. It made a lump crop up in my throat, made my eyes water, made a blockage form in my nose.

This was Adrian before Jan. Before Lucas. Before us.

And for some reason unbeknownst to me, it solidified everything. I could be what he needed, if he wanted that. I could love him, if I wanted that. I was probably way too far along the path than I should be, and I only had my teenage infatuation to blame.

Chapter 26

Adrian

Each key from the piano hummed around me, vibrating the walls, and filling the space.

For once, I wasn't doing it as a distraction. I was doing it because I *wanted* to, because I *could*, and because I had nothing else to do on a rainy Saturday afternoon since Ava was at her father's. We'd agreed to hold off on telling him until we could figure out the best way to go about it, and for now, that was okay with me.

Gentle footsteps climbed the stairs, and just as I finished up the song I was playing, Lucas' little head appeared in the doorway.

"Hey, Dad?"

"Yeah, bud."

I pushed my glasses up my nose as he slipped into the room quietly, his bare feet padding across the floor. He crossed to me, still half asleep from when he'd taken a nap unprompted in the middle of a movie earlier, and practically crawled up into my lap.

He fit in just as snugly as he used to when he was half as big as he was now.

I wrapped my arms around him and pulled him in tight, resting my head on top of his. "What's up, Luc?" I asked, shifting slightly so I could lean back against the wall to my left.

"I missed you this week," he mumbled into my chest.

It cracked me wide open.

I'd spent so much time in the office. At the bare minimum, it had worked out to roughly twelve hours a day—and most of the days were longer than that. Damage control was eating my time, devouring it and throwing it away. Even with Michael working around the clock to help me with every individual thing I needed to deal with, it hadn't been enough to make it to bedtime twice with Lucas.

"I missed you too." I squeezed him tighter. "I'm sorry. I promise I'm trying to get to a point where I don't need to work as much."

"Can you get there faster?" His little face peeked up at me, and the pout on his lips broke my fucking heart in two. "Please?"

I pressed a kiss against his forehead. "I'll try," I said. "I will."

Part of me, for a single fleeting moment, wanted Andrew to succeed in turning the board against me. At least then I could have enough time for my fucking kid.

We sat in relative silence, him just resting in my arms as I thought about every option I had in terms of freeing up time. I'd had one single evening alone with Ava this week outside of the night I'd come home late after inviting her over, and it cut far too deep that she was the only removable factor right now. I could have gone to work today, could plan for tomorrow, just to get through the damage control as quickly as possible—but that seemed like taking time away, not adding it.

I didn't have good options here. I hated all of them.

Lucas reached out, idly fiddling with the keys on the piano and playing a little sequence I'd taught him earlier this year. I watched him, studying him, but then he stopped.

"Is Ava gonna be my new mommy?"

I stilled.

"What?" I breathed.

Lucas poked his head back up, questioning eyes meeting mine. "She was here the other night."

"For dinner? I just thought it would be nice since you guys got along so well in the Hamptons." I swallowed down the acid rising from my gut. "I didn't mean to be gone so long..."

"No," he said, shaking his head and scratching his chin against my chest. "I heard her two nights ago. I went to pee and saw you guys on the couch."

Fuck.

Fuck.

Two nights ago. If we were on the couch...

There wasn't a chance he'd seen anything bad. I'd been smart enough about that to keep things confined to my locked master bedroom, but we had been drinking, and I knew damn well that I'd kissed her more than a handful of times. She'd had her legs in my lap at one point, and at another, she'd been leaning back on me, her hand in mine.

God, I was a fucking idiot.

"What did you see?" I asked, trying my absolute damnedest to not show a hint of panic. But his head was against my chest, and there wasn't a chance he didn't hear how quickly my heart was beating.

"You were having wine," he said plainly.

Oh, thank gGd.

"And when I came back from the bathroom, you were,

like, standing over her. Like, *leaning* over her. Your face was super close to hers."

I swallowed. *Shit.* "That's it?"

His eyes narrowed slightly, but he nodded.

"I was just telling her a secret."

I hated lying to him. I hated it more than I hated anything in the world, more than I hated the way Jan had made me feel when she'd died and I'd found everything out, more than I hated Andrew, more than I hated how much I had to be away from Lucas. This was our one thing, our *only* major rule, and I seemed to be breaking it far too much lately. *No lies.*

"Were you worried about that?" I asked.

He shook his head again, his chin going red from rubbing raw against my shirt. "No. I like Ava."

I leaned my head back against the wall, taking deep breaths to calm the racing in my chest. I needed to broach the topic with him—this wouldn't necessarily go away anytime soon, and even if things didn't work out with Ava, I'd have to do it at some point. He was already asking about it, and I had to be okay with that. "Does the idea of me dating someone upset you?"

He scrunched his mouth up to the side as he thought about it. "No," he said. "Are you dating Ava?"

I swallowed again, and it felt like sand. "Yes," I breathed. Fuck the lies. "Is that okay?"

Lucas nodded as a little grin spread across his cheeks. "You *like* like her."

I huffed out a half-hearted chuckle. "Yeah."

"Do you think Mommy would like her?"

Dear fucking God, I was not ready for that question.

I didn't know how to answer it, couldn't breathe life into a single word in response. It was as if every bit of air left my lungs at once, like I'd slammed into the ground after jumping off our balcony, like I'd drunk myself stupid into a blackout.

"Dad?"

How on earth was I supposed to answer that? How was I supposed to keep Jan's good name in my mouth when he asked questions like that? I promised myself I would never talk badly about her in front of him, promised myself I wouldn't ever let him know what really happened—but even the *thought* of her approving or disapproving from beyond the grave was enough to send me reeling.

What the fuck was I doing?

She'd damaged me.

She'd broken my heart and smiled at me in my dreams with the pieces stuck between her teeth.

And here I was, two years later, offering the remnants of that to someone else. And not just my own, but the mostly untouched, only slightly damaged heart of my fucking son.

I needed to take a step back.

I needed time.

I needed to get my head on right.

"Yeah," I lied, and fuck, it hurt. "I think Mommy would like her."

Chapter 27

Ava

Three days. That was all it took for me to start feeling antsy about not having seen Adrian in person.

The hold he had on me was intense, and although we'd been texting, he'd wanted to spend the weekend with Lucas after barely seeing him all of last week. Of course I understood, and I didn't dare question it or push him on it.

But the palpable relief I'd felt when Adrian had texted me to meet him at the cafe across the street from the Darkwater building for lunch today was...significant.

The chill in the air had gone from bitter to downright freezing, and as I clutched my jacket shut and held my scarf in place for dear life while walking along the front of Darkwater, I nearly ran directly into him as he stepped out of the building. It took him a moment to register it when his gaze was focused intently on the cafe opposite, but after a couple of seconds, recognition flickered across his face.

The face that looked nearly ten years older from stress.

"Hey," he said, wrapping his arms around my waist and

pulling me in tightly. He picked me up and moved us closer to the wall of the building and out of foot traffic, setting me down only once I'd loosened my grip around his neck.

"Hi," I grinned. "Lunch?"

———

The silence that hung between us felt...uncomfortable.

We ate our food with small talk in between, him giving me little updates about the sheer amount of damage canceling the conference partway through had done, and me telling him about how we'd finally gotten the walls painted in my little office block back in Dad's building. But something about it felt wrong, like there were things left unsaid, like we were walking on eggshells.

I couldn't put my finger on it directly. But it made me feel smaller than I already did, and that was fucking horrible.

"So," Adrian sighed, resting his head on his knuckles as he leaned onto the table. "Lucas knows."

Oh, shit. "You...told him?" I didn't want to ask the unspoken questions—*what does this mean for me? I've barely come to terms with potentially being a parent to him and I have to start that now?*

His jaw ticked. "No. He saw us on the couch last Thursday." He reached across the table with his free hand, lightly dragging his fingers along the tops of mine. "He asked me directly. I couldn't lie to him."

I nodded, but I was fucking reeling. I wanted to ask him

why, but I wouldn't question his judgment on this. He was the parent, not me. For now. "Okay," I said. "What the hell do we do about that?"

"I...have no idea," he huffed. "He's happy about it, for the record. The kid fucking loves you. But I think we need to take a step back and give it a little more time before confronting what that could mean for him."

A step back? What the hell did that mean?

"I think we should wait to tell your father," he said softly. "At least a little bit longer. I'll keep Lucas away from him in case he lets anything slip. I just need time to figure this out."

The relief from the idea of not confronting my dad was soured from whatever this meant. "What do you mean by *taking a step back?*"

He shook his head. "Nothing major. I'm spending a lot of time at work right now and I need to allocate some of my time off for you, but mostly for Lucas," he explained. "I barely got to see him last week and he's noticed. He's begging me for time that I can't produce out of thin air."

"So..." I blinked as I tried to arrange my scrambled thoughts. I couldn't help but feel slightly defeated, rejected, even—but I knew he had good reasons. I couldn't and wouldn't expect him to put time with me over Lucas. But after the chaos of the last few weeks, it felt like we were hitting the pause button, or even worse, erasing the whole tape. "I'm sorry, for my own peace of mind, I just need to make sure...you're not saying we're done, right?"

His hand wrapped around mine and squeezed the living daylights out of it. "No, Ava. I'm not saying we're done. I'm just saying we should take it a little bit slower until I can figure things out."

I didn't know why, but I didn't quite believe him.

He hadn't invited me over after Lucas went to sleep, but he had texted me at five-thirty in the morning telling me that he couldn't get me out of his head, so that was a positive. He hadn't been expecting my reply so early.

But I'd barely been able to sleep.

My anxiety over the situation had turned into never-ending nausea. I'd spent half the night next to the toilet, scrolling through my phone for a distraction. His texts hadn't helped abate the bile, but it was enough to keep me occupied for a little while until he had to wake Lucas up for school.

But the handful he'd unexpectedly sent a couple of hours later as I pulled myself up from the bathroom floor had made me feel miles better on the anxiety front. Not so much the nausea, though.

Adrian: I can bring some soup over to your place for lunch if you want.

Adrian: Or some anti-nausea meds.

Adrian: Or both.

I sank into the shitty swivel chair I desperately needed to replace. I wasn't going in to work today, but I could at least try to get some shit done at home.

Me: That's really sweet, but if I have a stomach bug I'd rather not give it to you.

Me: Let me see how I'm feeling in a little while. I'll let you know.

I shot a text to Emily, too, to let her know why I wasn't

in the office this morning as I flicked open my planner and booted up my laptop.

Tuesday...

Tuesday. Complete Tori's, Adam's, Cypress', Hilary's, and Daniel's profiles. Tax calcs. 3 pm appt with Heather. 4 pm appt with web maintenance. 5 pm appt with Angela...

Perfect. Completely doable.

But that red star on the previous Tuesday's date was glaring at me, and I wanted to throw up all over again.

I must have used the wrong color marker. That can't be right.

I flipped the calendar back one month, and there it was, twenty-eight days before last Tuesday.

The month before?

Twenty-eight days before.

Twenty-eight days before.

Twenty-eight days before.

Twenty-eight days before.

I was never late.

I was up and moving before I'd even decided. Jacket around my body and wearing nothing but pajamas that smelled of vomit and a pair of old Crocs, I ran out of my apartment with my keys in hand, out into the freezing, wet morning. Ice had formed on the tops of the cars, and as the little droplets of rain fell, it slowly melted away.

The bodega was quiet at this hour. And I was counting on that.

––––––

I threw up again when I turned the test over and two pink lines stared up at me.

I took four more of them.

Eight more pink lines.

With shaking hands, I shot Adrian a text. So many fucking typos.

Me: Def a bug. Don't come over. Gonna try to sleep.

I couldn't breathe. I couldn't think. I left my phone abandoned on the bathroom counter amongst the discarded pregnancy tests, barely registering Adrian's reply as panic, and panic, and *panic* set in.

Adrian: Shit, I'm sorry. I hope you feel better.

Adrian: Text me when you get up so I know you're okay.

How the fuck was I supposed to text him later when right then, in that goddamn moment, I didn't feel like I could even say a word to him without breaking down?

How did this happen?

I'd been careful. I'd taken my pills. I'd been so fucking careful about doing it at the right time every single day. If for a single second, I thought something had gone wrong—if I'd taken it an hour late, if I'd forgotten—I would have run to a goddamn pharmacy for the morning-after pill.

But here I was.

Twenty-five, sleeping with and seeing a man who was both twice my age and my father's closest friend, a failed art student with a stupid fucking career that my father had funded, and *pregnant.*

Porcelain chipped my nails as I threw up again.

I was screwed. Horribly, utterly screwed. I'd known since I was little that although I had no problem with others exercising their right to choose, I wouldn't be able to pull the plug if the time came that I needed it. That's why I was so careful, down to the fucking minute. And even now, even faced with the reality of it instead of it being a hypothetical, I knew I couldn't. I couldn't do that. I didn't have it in me.

I hadn't realized I was crying until the salt hit my tongue.

I had to tell him.

But I couldn't tell him.

How the *fuck* was I supposed to tell him when he'd literally just told me yesterday that he needed to slow this down? How the *fuck* was I going to tell him when he already had one kid to worry about?

How were we going to handle this when we couldn't even tell my father?

And to think that Adrian was already dealing with stress upon stress from work, from Lucas, from *me* — to add another thing to the mix would be insanity. Pregnancies were among the most stressful things to go through. I could have sworn I'd read that somewhere once.

One more stressor and he could drop dead from a heart attack for all I knew.

But how was I going to keep this from him? How could I lie to him, how could I hide it and push it down until the time was right? I was falling for him, completely, totally, unabashedly, and dangerously— was too far in this to not be damaged forever, and now he was a permanent part of my life without my choosing. I wanted to love him, felt like I *could* love him, and probably already did. And I wanted to crawl in a fucking hole and die.

I was spiraling there on the bathroom floor, the cold tile biting through the jacket I still had around my shoulders. I shucked it off. I took *everything* off.

I reached up and turned on the shower, setting it as hot as possible. Waiting for it to warm up felt like personalized torture from the old pipes, but as soon as steam started billowing up, I dragged myself through the glass shower door.

I sat there, naked and scalding on the floor.

And all I could fucking do was sob.

Chapter 28

Adrian

Two weeks passed, and I'd only seen Ava three times.

Our schedules started colliding. My meetings would overlap with hers, or Lucas would beg me for an evening of just the two of us, or she would be at her Dad's when I finally had time. Each time we'd managed to line up, she'd come over after Lucas had already gone to bed, and we only had a handful of hours to ourselves before we'd inevitably pass out from exhaustion.

I'd mastered the art of sneaking her out in the morning without Lucas noticing, though.

But I fucking missed her, even if I shouldn't. My guard was up, and for good reason—but it felt uncomfortable.

So when she'd turned up unexpectedly at my door at ten in the evening with her hair a mess, her clothes soaked, and her eyes puffy, all I wanted to do was erase the struggle the last two weeks had been. I wanted to hold her, wanted to keep her here for longer than she'd let me, wanted to unashamedly have her here in the morning when Lucas woke up. I wanted to have her properly.

I cupped her cheeks, held her to me as I stood in the doorway with her.

"What's wrong?" I asked.

She shook her head. "I'm just so fucking stressed," she said. Her bloodshot eyes went glassy, her lower lip wobbling. "And I missed you."

Slowly, gently, I removed her dripping jacket from her shivering form. "I missed you too," I breathed. "But you're going to get sick again going out in this weather. We need to warm you up."

Quietly, I took her upstairs to my bathroom, starting the shower for her. She sniffled in silence as I undressed her, taking each bit of damp clothing and peeling it from her flesh. She practically hyperventilated more and more with each layer I took off of her.

"I'm sorry," she said, but her voice warbled. "I know you wanted tonight with him."

"He's in bed," I insisted. "It's okay."

I helped her into the shower and followed closely behind her, stepping under the hot water with her. There wasn't a single part of this that felt sexual to me—something was clearly wrong, and I just needed to fix it. I just had to piece this back together. Just add one more puzzle to the pile.

"What happened?"

She shook her head before burying her forehead in my bare chest. "I can't stop panicking. I feel like I've been having an anxiety attack for three days straight. Em wasn't answering my calls and I just..." She took a few deep breaths, but they sounded more like gasps. "I didn't know where else to go."

I wrapped my arms around her body and leaned against the wall, holding her freezing, shivering form to me. I knew how she felt—I'd been feeling it too lately. "I'm sorry," I said. "I'm so sorry. Is there anything I can do to help?"

She didn't answer, but the little choked wheezes coming from her told me plain enough that she was crying. I couldn't remember if I'd ever seen her cry before. Certainly not as an adult.

"You're okay," I whispered, holding the back of her head as it slowly began to warm up. "You're okay."

———

It shouldn't have bothered me when I'd offered for her to stay the night and she'd said no. It shouldn't have bothered me when she'd declined to stay a little longer and have a drink with me.

But it did.

She'd calmed down enough after the shower, and after a handful more apologies and my insistence that she at least borrow some of my clothes and use my driver to get home, she'd left.

And that was it.

An hour, tops, of time with her—enough to get her stable and thinking somewhat clearly. But her refusal to stay at all left me questioning things.

I almost felt used, but I wouldn't ever assume she'd come here just to leave me feeling empty. But that was the result anyway, and although I didn't want to push her on it or make her feel any more uncomfortable than she clearly was, it felt almost as if she was pulling away.

As if she was struggling to separate herself from all of it.

As if she needed a quick hit and was weaning herself.

I'd been distant, sure, and I knew it wouldn't be easy for either of us. But I couldn't stop myself from worrying that maybe she was rethinking everything. Maybe she was considering this done and over despite my insistence that wasn't what I wanted.

But maybe it was what *she* wanted. And that was fucking horrifying to think about.

Chapter 29

Ava

I hadn't been able to bring myself to reach out to him for four days after I'd turned up at his apartment.

The stress of deciding whether or not to tell him about the life growing inside of me was eating me from the inside out, devouring everything in its wake. I was nothing but a walking panic attack, and despite him calming me down for a couple of hours and enabling me to actually get a good few hours of sleep, I felt like a zombie in my own skin.

"Ava," Emily said softly, brushing my heat-curled hair away from my face as she looked at me in the bedroom mirror. She'd done everything in her power to make me look presentable—my makeup, my hair, even spritzing me down with perfume. "I'm sorry, but the...the dress doesn't fit."

She let go of the zipper on my back. The backs of my eyes burned.

"Do you have anything else?"

I reached around to my back and unzipped what she'd managed to zip up. "I'm not going," I croaked.

"You have to go, Aves," she insisted. "That will raise so many more questions."

"Just tell my dad I'm sick."

"I think he might insist you see a doctor if you use that excuse again," she sighed.

"I don't care."

"Won't Adrian be there? He'll be worried if you don't turn up." She pushed the straps off my shoulders and helped me push the dress down over my thighs. "You've got to go."

I didn't want to, though. There wasn't a single part of me that wanted to go to the stupid fucking charity event tonight. I wanted to sit in my room and cry and try to get my life under control, but I wasn't allowed to do that.

"How far along do you think you are?" she asked, her voice low as she pulled me toward the closet.

I watched as she started furiously going through my closet. She pulled out option after option, throwing them on my bed behind her as if we were children having a fashion show. "The last test I took said I should be about eleven weeks," I mumbled.

Eleven weeks set me back to roughly the first night. The night we'd spent on his sailboat. The first fucking time.

I could see it in the mirror. The curve of my stomach, even though it was slight. I'd seen it for the last week and a half. I'd panicked when Adrian had undressed me the other night, worried sick that he'd notice it and question it. But he hadn't.

"That one," I said as Emily held up one of my least favorite dresses. Long and black and A-line, with a lace-up back. It would work. "That should fit."

. . .

"Where have you *been*?"

Adrian stood in front of me, looking down at me as I leaned against the wall of the ballroom. He looked downright magnetic in his maroon and black tux, but the worried green eyes that bore into me made me want to peel my gaze from him. "I'm sorry," I said. "I've just been dealing with a lot."

"So have I," he insisted. "But that doesn't mean I don't have space for you. You're blanking me."

"I'm not trying to." *Liar. Fucking liar.*

Music filled the empty space for far too long. "Do you not want this anymore?"

I snapped my gaze back to him. *How the fuck can he ask me that?* "What?" I croaked, my voice cracking before I'd even had the chance to steady myself. My emotions had been all over the place for weeks now, and I'd grown almost accustomed to not having a solid grasp on when they would switch or why, but right then, I felt betrayed by my own body. "I want you. I've always fucking wanted you."

"Then talk to me," he begged. "You disappeared for four fucking days, Ava. You left without much of an explanation. I've been worried sick."

Nausea swirled as I realized exactly where his mind had gone, exactly what he'd been through before. At least with Jan, he'd gotten a phone call from the police, but she had been his wife—he would have been her emergency contact.

If something happened to me, he'd have to hear it through the grapevine.

Dad's eyes met mine across the room as he stood beside

a man I vaguely recognized, two whiskeys deep in conversation. His brows furrowed.

"Can we talk somewhere private?" I asked, my voice breaking yet again and fucking betraying me.

He followed my gaze, and everything about him changed. He turned more casual, plastering a friendly smile on his face, and mumbled a quick, "Yeah."

And then he was moving.

I waited until Dad's eyes left me to slink around the corner after Adrian.

The hallway was filled with staff from his company. Men and women dressed to the nines in tuxedos wandered with trays full of food, bottles of champagne, checklists, and cases of soft drinks. I followed Adrian in dead silence as he turned another corner, and then another, leading me further and further away.

The panic only rose.

He opened a door for a stairwell and held it open for me, and we slipped inside, finally finding a bit of privacy and silence.

"Talk," he said. "This is as private as we're going to find."

My lower lip shook as I tried to find the right words, but my mind was moving at lightspeed, leaving my body in the dust. There were so many things I wanted to say. So many things I *needed* to say. But they wouldn't form coherent words, wouldn't come together to form a sentence.

I moved toward him, looking for some sort of security, some sort of support, but he took a step back.

"Please," I begged.

"Ava," he sighed, his hands coming to rest on my shoulders. "I'm not just here to comfort you when you're feeling overwhelmed. You have to fucking talk to me."

My heart raced in my chest, my skin chilling, and chilling, and chilling—until I realized that wasn't actually a chill, it was a sheen of sweat. "I'm sorry," I sobbed, and oh, God, when had the tears started? *Am I ruining my makeup? Dad's going to notice.* "I'm sorry. Please. I'm sorry."

It was all I could get out of my mouth. Nothing else formed.

"You can't just tell me you're sorry with no fucking explanation, Aves," he snapped. "What am I supposed to do with that? Accept that you disappeared for four days and have basically blanked me for a week, and not worry about why?"

"I'm sorry." The words were more of a whisper, barely breaking past my lips. Everything swayed, from the floor, to the stairs, to him. It felt like the earth was turning on its axis, like my heels broke at the same time.

"Jesus fucking Christ. *Why?* Just tell me *why* so we can figure this out!"

His voice boomed and echoed through the stairwell. I gasped for air. "*Please.*"

"I've put my heart on the goddamn line for you. I've been so fucking patient. I've been on the verge of breaking down the last few weeks while trying to keep my job, make sure that you were okay, and that my son had enough time with me. I know you're having problems but this isn't *okay*."

Darkness crept in at the edges of my vision. "Adrian."

"I can't fucking do this with you if you won't..."

It took over entirely.

———

The scent of chemicals hit me before the stinging pain in my left hand and the light jostling of whatever I was on forced me to open my eyes.

A woman in all blue stood over me, with deep brown skin and braided hair up in a ponytail. I'd never seen her before in my life.

"You're okay," she said, patting the side of my arm. "We're almost there."

"Where?" I asked, but the sound was so muffled I almost couldn't make out my own voice. Something large and pliable rested over my mouth, and as I lifted my hand to touch it, I found a full plastic oxygen mask.

"Oh my God, you're awake."

"Stay there," the woman said, her gaze locked somewhere beyond my feet. I tried to follow it, but my head pounded, and I couldn't bring myself to look down enough. "Give her a minute."

Letting my head fall back onto the pillow, I looked up above me at the ceiling of whatever place I was in. Wires and medical equipment hung against a white background, but everything was so fuzzy, so blurry, so bright...

Just as quickly as I'd come to, I was out again.

———

The bed shook, and I was back, but so was the panic.

"Hey, hey, you're okay."

A blurry, tall figure stood next to me, squeezing my hand, their body draped in maroons and blacks. I blinked, over and over and over, and the fog started to clear. Blood-shot blue eyes met mine.

Adrian.

"Is there space for her yet?" Someone behind me asked, but I couldn't hear the reply.

"I don't understand," I said.

He leaned over me, pressing his forehead to mine. "You went down," he croaked. "You scared the shit out of me."

You went down.

The memory of it slowly filtered back in—the stairwell, the way my words hadn't worked, how he'd shouted at me when I reached for him. The blackness that crept into my vision and ate it alive. The clamminess of my skin.

"I thought you were fucking dying," he rasped.

"I'm...I'm sorry." I didn't know what else to say, didn't know what else I *could* say. I'd traumatized him twice, now, and that fell entirely on my shoulders.

"I couldn't find your dad," he continued, completely ignoring my apology. "I think I left my phone back in the stairwell. I don't know his number by heart but if you do..."

"No," I insisted. "Please. I don't want him here."

"*Ava.*"

"Please," I begged. The realization was starting to set in —I was at the fucking hospital. I was eleven weeks pregnant. The truth would come out, sooner than later. And having Adrian here was bad enough, but I needed to keep my father out of this as long as possible.

"We've got a space for 'ya." A man in all blue sidled up beside my stretcher, a far too wide grin on his face. "We just need to run some checks on you and then we can get this all sorted. You seem to be all right, though. Looks like you just fainted. That normal?"

"No," Adrian and I said in unison.

226

"Right."

He stepped behind my stretcher and slowly lifted the back so I was sitting upright before wheeling me inside.

Harsh, fluorescent lighting bounced off nearly every surface as we moved in silence down the squeaky-clean hallway. I tried to wrack my brain for any other time I'd passed out from a panic attack, but I couldn't place a single time. There had to be something—something I could tell them and get sent home for without further tests.

As much as I was thankful for Adrian being here, I couldn't help but wish it was anyone other than him or my father, or even no one.

The man parked me in a small square space separated from other triage banks by hanging blue curtains. He didn't say a word before he disappeared.

"They should have your dad's number on your file, right?" Adrian asked as he slowly sank into the chair beside my stretcher. He didn't dare release my hand, but his leg bounced incessantly, his cold blue eyes fixed on me.

My eyes burned again. "I need you to not call my dad." I enunciated every word to make myself as clear as I possibly could. "You don't want him here. I can promise you that."

"I don't think he'll think it's suspicious that I rode in the fucking ambulance with you, Aves," he said, his voice a little too loud, a little too aggressive. "I'm sorry. I'm trying to stay calm."

"It's not that." I squeezed his hand half because I needed it and half to try to calm him down. *Oh —that was the sharp pain. I've got an IV port.* "I need to tell you something and I need you to not..."

"Ava Riley?"

A beaming woman with jet-black hair and white scrubs

rounded the corner of my little cubicle. Fuck. "Hi," I said. "Can you give me a minute?"

A single brow rose. "You want me to give you a minute?"

I nodded.

"You realize you just arrived by ambulance and we need to run diagnostics on you as quickly as possible, right?"

I nodded again.

She looked across to Adrian. "Did she hit her head when she passed out, or...?"

Adrian snorted. "No, but she's certainly acting like it."

The woman clamped a little clip onto my first finger and a heart rate monitor popped up on the screen behind her. It took a second, but one-hundred-and-seven flashed up and stayed steady. "Hmm," she said. "That's a bit high, but you're stressed out, so we'll see if it calms down."

"Can I please just have a minute?" I asked again, and the beeping increased. One-hundred-twenty-five. "Please."

She completely ignored me as she grabbed a clipboard from the mobile set of drawers beside her. "So you fainted?"

"Yeah, she passed out," Adrian confirmed.

"Any issues with blood pressure in the past?"

"No," I sighed.

"Have you eaten and drank enough today?"

"Yes."

"Have you taken any drugs or had any alcohol in the last twenty-four hours?"

"She had a cocktail about forty minutes ago," Adrian said.

"No," I clarified. "I had a *mocktail*."

His brows knitted together as he looked at me.

"Any history of heart problems?"

"No, none," I sighed.

"Are you pregnant or is there any chance you could be pregnant?"

I opened my mouth to speak, but the words wouldn't come. The woman looked at me expectantly, her eyes glancing at Adrian, but I could feel his gaze locked on me, could feel it tearing me apart with every second that passed that I didn't answer the question.

"Can I *please* just have a minute?"

Chapter 30

Adrian

This tux was too fucking tight. The lights were too bright. The room was too small, and the sounds were too loud.

If I was anywhere other than a hospital, I might have been concerned that I'd go into cardiac arrest and die on the fucking spot.

The woman who'd entered the little square of space Ava had been given turned on her heel. "I'll, uh, be back in a minute."

She disappeared.

"Adrian," Ava whispered.

"You're pregnant." The words felt hollow, like they didn't exist even though I'd spoken them. They felt cheap. They felt baseless, absurd —she was on birth control. I'd checked.

"I wanted...I wanted to figure out how to tell you," she said, her voice breaking. I watched her like a hawk, watched as the tears welled up in her eyes. Anxiety brewed in me, swelled, broke, crashed. I couldn't for one second tell if I was elated or disturbed. "You've been dealing with so much and I didn't want to make it worse."

"How did this happen?" I asked. It felt as if I was being piloted on a course I didn't select. I couldn't even remember deciding to ask that.

"I have no idea," she said, her knees pulling up to her chest beneath the thin blanket. "I'm never late with the pill."

"How far along?"

"Eleven weeks."

Eleven weeks. So...almost three months.

"I'm so sorry," she said again, her hand squeezing mine. But I didn't know what to say to that.

This felt like a blessing and a curse, like a violation of trust and a shot in the fucking head. "How long have you known?"

"Three weeks," she croaked. "Please don't hate me, Adrian."

I rested my forehead against our joined hands, trying to make sense of this. Three weeks—she'd had a stomach bug three weeks ago. Was that real? Or was that morning sickness? When she'd turned up at my house four days ago, she'd known. She'd refused a drink. She'd left before anything else could happen. Was she showing? I hadn't even been looking, hadn't been paying attention when she was naked in my shower with her body up against mine, hadn't thought to look while she was sobbing into me because why would I? I'd just wanted to help her. I'd just wanted to fix her problem, but knowing what that problem was now was more overwhelming than I could have imagined.

She'd kept this from me.

For three weeks.

"I don't hate you," I breathed. "I just don't understand why you've done this."

She sniffled as a tear broke free, streaking down her cheek and taking a line of makeup along with it. "I found out the day after you told me you wanted to slow things down," she said. Her voice broke as she spoke, her throat visibly tightening. "I panicked. You've been doing so much at work and trying to make time for Lucas. I didn't want to add to the stress so I've been trying to figure out the right way to do it. I'm sorry, Adrian."

She wiped at her eyes with the base of her palms.

"I'm just so fucking sorry."

The woman slipped back into the room with a cart and a clear, hanging bag, her eyes warily darting between both of us. She unhooked the clipboard from under her arm and slowly approached Ava, hesitating slightly as she reached for our joined hands. "Sorry," she said. "I'm going to get a drip going just in case."

Ava clung on.

Slowly, painstakingly, I loosened my grip and slid my fingers out from between hers.

The woman got to work connecting her to the IV drip despite Ava's sniffled objections, but Ava barely watched her, barely paid attention to her incessant questions about how far along she was, the date of her last period, and the symptoms she'd had so far. She gave the woman one-word answers where she could.

Instead, she kept her attention on me, glassy, tear-filled eyes watching every microscopic movement I made. The heaviness of it, the chaos behind it, struck me in a way I hadn't felt in two years.

Betrayal.

I swallowed down what felt like a mouthful of sand. "I

need to make some calls," I said softly, gripping the arms of the far too uncomfortable chair. Her eyes widened, her mouth opened, and the heart rate monitor beeped faster behind her. Sighing, I added, "Not to your father."

Her lips locked as she nodded. I couldn't tell if it was aimed at me or was more of a self-soothing gesture, but it made my chest ache.

"Will you be moving her any time soon...?" I asked, turning my head to the woman in scrubs.

"Ashley," she grinned. "She'll probably stay here for another thirty minutes to an hour. We need to run some blood tests. But if you give me your number, I can call you if she gets moved early."

Ava's heart rate spiked again, filling the little area with louder, quicker beeps. I tried not to think about it. "I don't have my phone on me. I was hoping I could use one of the ones here."

"Oh," Ashely said, her smile faltering for just a moment. "There's one on the wall a few cubicles down. You're welcome to use that. Just dial nine to get out."

I nodded my thanks. "I'll be back in a few, Aves."

———

The air in my lungs felt too heavy to exhale, like I was holding in the smoke from a cigarette or had stood too close to a fire. No amount of internal reflection seemed to fix that, no matter how long I stood there looking at the closed curtain that Ava sat behind.

I'd called Grace, warned her that I wouldn't be home until late and asked her to put Lucas to bed for me, asked her to stay until I could get home. I'd called Michael, warned him that I was no longer at the event and given him as brief of a rundown as I could. And I'd resisted every urge to call David and tell him his daughter was in the hospital.

Because she was right. If he came down here, he'd find out she was pregnant. That on its own would spark questions.

So as I stood in the hallway of the triage area of the emergency department, leaned up against a wall with the hardest parts of my palms pressing into my eyes to relieve some of the overwhelming pressure in my skull, all I could do was think.

Think about what this meant.

Think about what she'd done.

Think about how fucking horrible it felt.

There was a part of me, of course, that was thrilled. That part of me was bursting beneath the pressure of the rest of it, though—all of the bad was smothering it, stamping it down, burning it, digging it a grave twenty feet beneath the surface of the earth and filling it with concrete.

Because more than anything, this brought me back to the lowest point I'd ever been at.

It felt as if Jan had clawed her way out of the ground and wrapped her manicured, white-tipped nails around my ankles. Like she'd dug them in and drawn blood for the first time in a year. Like she was screaming my name as if it were her dying breath, like her mangled body was in front of me on that cold, metal table again, like I was searching the small bit of skin they'd let me see in search of her tattoo of Lucas' name. Like I was identifying her, giving her back her name, breathing life into a lifeless corpse that would only hurt me days later.

Jan hadn't been honest with me. I'd given her every

ounce of my trust, and she'd crushed it under the heel of her leather boots that still sat in the back of my closet.

And Ava—someone I'd opened myself up to, someone I'd risked shattering myself over, someone I'd thought was worth letting inside of my head and my heart and my life despite feeling unwaveringly sure in my decision to never do that again—had kept this from me.

She hadn't been honest.

She'd made me break the one rule between Lucas and me. And if she could do that for three weeks, could she genuinely fit into our family dynamic? Could I trust her to?

The twisting in my stomach made me worry that I couldn't.

But the sounds of quiet sobs behind the curtain begged me to.

Chapter 31

Ava

"What did he say when he came back?"

I stared at the easel on the other side of the living room and the canvas that sat atop it, half painted and abandoned for nearly three and a half weeks. I couldn't bring myself to look at Emily, even with her sitting less than four feet from me on the other side of the coffee table with a cup of steaming hot mint tea in her palm that she'd made for herself. "Nothing," I said, the word barely audible.

"Nothing?" she asked.

I nodded. Emily scoffed.

"I can't believe him," she snapped, setting down her tea a little too hastily. "Did you ask him to talk to you? Or did you just sit there, Aves?"

I winced. I wasn't ready for a spiteful Emily today—I'd just wanted company instead of sitting alone in my apartment and crying over the volatile, fragile state of my relationship with Adrian. "I...I asked him where he wanted to go from there. He said he didn't know."

I watched from my peripheral vision as she pushed her

hair back in frustration, her hands lingering on the sides of her head. "What the fuck?"

"I hurt him," I croaked insistently. "I don't blame him for not wanting to speak to me."

"You're carrying his child, Ava!"

I swallowed and pulled the throw blanket up over my chest. "I know."

"And he's more than old enough to not be acting like one," she added.

"He's not acting like a child. He's acting like someone who has been hurt, and I'm trying to respect that." The lump in my throat grew tenfold. It felt as though I could barely breathe around it, felt like I was hyperventilating, but I counted my breaths and forced myself to calm down enough to speak again, even if it was with a wobbling lower lip. "He stayed with me until they discharged me. His driver took me home. I have no idea how he got home or what happened, but it was about an hour later when my dad called asking me what happened."

Keeping tight-lipped about what had happened had been hard, especially when I was struggling to think coherently with the way Adrian and I had left things, when Dad had called. I couldn't tell him that my body was flooded with an excess of progesterone to the point that my blood vessels were expanding too much and directing too much blood to the baby and not quite enough to my brain. Somehow, in that hallway, my blood pressure had dropped significantly enough to cause me to pass out, and it had hovered just above that fine line between overwhelming dizziness and fainting since then.

Dad hadn't been happy with my excuse of, "I just hadn't gotten the chance to eat yet and my blood sugar dropped." And he'd be furious once he realized that Adrian hadn't contacted him the moment it happened.

Emily sighed exasperatedly, her gaze lingering on me. "I swear to God, Aves, if he just leaves you high and dry when you're pregnant with his goddamn kid, I'll storm the Dark-water building myself."

I shook my head and wiped my eyes with the back of my hand, the smallest sob breaking through and shaking my chest. "I don't want him to do that but he already has one he needs to look after," I insisted. "I have to be careful."

Her head dropped in frustration.

"I need to tell my dad," I said hoarsely. "I can't hide this forever and my stomach is getting bigger every goddamn day, it feels like."

Slowly, I turned to look at Emily as silence crept over her. Her blonde hair fell in perfectly styled ringlets around her cheeks today, her makeup nicely done, her clothes casually professional. I felt like a mess in comparison in my paint-and-tear-stained pajamas and unwashed hair as she lifted her head just enough to stare directly at me. "You know he'll question whose it is."

I gulped. "I know."

"And you want to just outright tell him it's his best friend's?"

There wasn't a single part of me that wanted to do it without Adrian beside me, but with every passing hour that he didn't reach out, my mind was spiraling toward the idea that he wouldn't want to do that. I wasn't even sure if he wanted to be near me right now, and considering he was the one who had insisted weeks ago that we take it a bit slower and put off telling my father, I couldn't see a future where he'd agree to that just because I was pregnant.

But I was only going to get bigger. And I worked on the same floor of the same building as Dad.

"No," I choked. "I want to do it with him."

She sighed. "Then you need to call him, Aves."

"He doesn't want to talk to me." The words were broken, spoken through my snot-covered lips and the lump in my throat that just wouldn't go away. "I don't think he even wants me at all anymore."

Her lips pursed together as she reached forward, sliding my phone across the coffee table toward me. "You won't know if you don't try."

I stared at it for longer than it took for her to sigh, pick herself up, and settle in next to me on the sofa. She pulled me into her, and only once I'd settled enough to calm my breathing and relax slightly into her side-on embrace, she grabbed my phone and slid it into my hands.

I wanted to throw it across the room. But I didn't.

Me: Can we please talk?

Chapter 32

Adrian

I didn't know what to say to her. It felt like hours passed as I stared at her message, watching as the little dots bounced at the bottom of the screen over and over before disappearing time and time again as I sat in my empty office.

I wanted to reply.

But every time I went to move my thumbs, it was as if my brain wasn't quite connected right to my hands, and everything just...stopped. I couldn't think of the right words to say, couldn't come up with a good enough answer that I would be happy with.

Days had passed since she'd been in the hospital, and I knew that although her anxiety the last few weeks had likely stemmed from the worry of telling me about the pregnancy, it was almost certainly still there for reasons obvious to both of us, now—I was uncomfortable with our situation. She was likely still anxious, and I wanted to fix it, but I found myself...stuck.

Until my phone started ringing, and a different Riley name popped up on my screen.

Funnily enough, my thumbs worked again. "Hey, David..."

"My office. Immediately."

Click.

I pulled the phone from my ear, checking if the call was still connected.

It was gone.

What...the fuck?

My heart rate kicked up as my hands grew sweaty, and horror hit me like a freight train. Does he know? How could he know? Did Ava tell him?

Is that why she texted me?

It felt as though an arrow had pierced me straight through the gut, bleeding me dry as I pushed myself up on unsteady legs. My chair moved behind me, slamming into the bookshelves behind my desk, knocking over a framed photo of Lucas and a strange glass bowl of clear pebbles someone had placed in here long enough ago that I'd never thought to ask about it.

I didn't bother packing away my laptop or the paperwork that was strewn across my desk. I shoved my phone into my pocket and grabbed my jacket, slipping from my private office so quickly I couldn't even remember making the decision to do it.

Michael stood in the hallway with a binder clutched to his chest. "Adrian?"

"Emergency," I said. "Hold down the fort."

His brows came together as I passed, but the subtle nod was enough to give me the tiniest glimmer of calm. "All right. Good luck with...?"

"Don't fuckin' ask, please."

. . .

Every second of the walk to the car, every second I sat in traffic, and every second spent in that goddamn elevator on the way up to David's floor felt like torture. I'd texted him three times on the way over, trying to get an answer out of him regarding what this was about.

He didn't reply.

But even as I stepped through the hallway and his assistant buzzed me in, the smallest glimmer of hope remained that I wasn't about to walk into what could be the second-worst conversation I would have to have in my life.

Three steps.

Two steps.

One.

Pushing open the door of David's office, I came face to face with the man I'd considered one of my best friends for nearly fifteen years, his face made of stone and his blood-shot eyes trained on me.

I could feel the blood drain from my face.

He didn't move as I shut the door behind me. He didn't move as I took a breath in, still as a statue, for once feeling small under his gaze—and he was a full foot shorter than me.

His mouth opened, and before the angry, spiteful, seething words came out, I knew. I knew it in my gut. "What the fuck is wrong with 'ya, Adrian?"

Spittle flew from his mouth as he took a single step toward me.

"I trusted 'ya. Wrongfully, apparently. You lied to my face, 'ya took my daughter to the goddamn fuckin' Hamptons at my request, you pranced around telling me about all

242

these women you're seein'," he scolded, one fat finger pointed in my direction. "Meanwhile, you're fuckin' her behind my back. She's twenty-fuckin'-five, Adrian. She's my kid!"

I didn't know what to say. I didn't know if there was anything to say. I'd fucked up, horribly, and I knew I would pay the price for it at some point, but at least when I envisioned this happening Ava had been beside me. She was supposed to be here for this.

But she wasn't. She was somewhere else, nearly twelve weeks pregnant.

Oh, God, did he know about that, too?

"David," I gulped. "I need you to calm down."

"Calm down?" he laughed, that pointed finger flying in my direction. "You expect me to calm the fuck down when you've been fuckin' my goddamn kid? Is it that hard for 'ya to find something to get your dick wet that it had to my own flesh and blood?"

My pulse thundered in my ears as he took another step toward me. Had anyone asked me before today, I would have confidently told them that David Riley was not the type to lay hands on someone else—but what I'd done might have changed that. "That's not it..."

"Don't fuckin' tell me what it is or isn't," he barked.

"Just let me explain." I took a hesitant step toward him, trying to remain hopeful he wouldn't swing at me. "I didn't mean..."

"I didn't mean to," he parodied, putting on the most average accent he could instead of his usual half-Boston and half-New Yorker twang. Bile rose up my throat, burning the dry flesh. "What, 'ya tripped and fell and landed cock first in my goddamn daughter? Were 'ya ever actually goin' on dates, Adrian, or was that all just a dramatic show for me?"

"I was," I insisted. I shoved my hands into the pockets of my suit jacket to conceal the shaking. "Genuinely, I was."

He scoffed as he spun on his heel, sauntering over to his desk with his freshly polished black loafers clacking on the ground. "As if I can believe 'ya after all this," he barked.

He watched me from across the room, his hands closing into shaking fists. I didn't understand how this had happened, how we'd gotten to this point, how everything had seemed to fall apart in a matter of days. This felt like psychological torture.

"Is that why 'ya didn't call me when she went to the hospital?" he said, a hollow laugh creeping up his throat. "I saw 'ya chatting to her at that event. Looked back five minutes later and both of 'ya had fucked off. Didn't want me to know you'd snuck off together, huh?"

I steeled my jaw. Fuck. At least, from that, I could make the assumption that he probably didn't know she was pregnant, but it felt like shit to be called out for doing the one thing she'd insisted I not do. Part of me wished I hadn't forgotten my phone in that stairwell and had called him while we were in the ambulance. At least then this all would have come out at the same time, with both of us in attendance.

But she'd done this without me.

She'd left me to deal with the consequences, and a single text of "Can we please talk?" would never have fixed this.

"Fuckin' disgusting," he said, leveling a glare at me. "Stay the hell away from my kid, Adrian. And stay away from me, too, while you're at it."

"You're just going to throw away fifteen years of..."

"Oh, don't fuckin' fifteen years me. Clearly, those meant fuckin' nothin' to 'ya," he spat. The veins across his bald head protruded, one of them coming all the way down to his eye and making it look as if it were bulging. "You said yourself that 'ya have enemies on your board, did you not?"

I blinked. What the fuck did that mean?

"Get within a hundred feet of my daughter again, and I'll see to it they've got everything they need to kick 'ya off."

I stilled. My nails dug so hard into the palms of my hands that I worried I was drawing blood. "David, please."

"Nah," he laughed. "Don't fuckin' please me. You're hangin' on by a thread at Stone & Co., and I will gladly take a pair of fuckin' scissors to it."

I tried to breathe in, but my throat felt so raw, so swollen, it was as if the air wouldn't go anywhere. Adrenaline rushed through my system, sending my pulse skyrocketing to the goddamn heavens. I couldn't deal with this, couldn't handle it, couldn't fathom how I'd let things get so out of control that I'd found myself here. "We wanted to tell you together," I said, my voice barely level, barely calm. "I didn't mean for this to happen."

"Together?" he laughed. "Christ, do 'ya love her or some shit? How deep does this go?"

"I..."

Fuck, did I?

Surely not. I hadn't allowed myself to think long enough about that to have come to any sort of conclusion—love had been off-limits for so long, and although I'd let myself believe that it could be possible with her, I hadn't stopped to consider if it was genuinely in the works or if I was following a path of potential and not certainty.

And if I did...

Surely, that feeling wasn't returned. Not when she'd done what she'd done.

"Get the fuck out of my office, Adrian."

Chapter 33

Ava

Adrian: *Meet me by the fountain in Washington Square.*

I stared down at his text for the fiftieth time as I stood beside the fountain, the bitter wind keeping most of the locals away. Gray skies loomed above with the promise of the first hint of snow—it wouldn't stick for another month or so according to Emily, but flurries would start soon, and despite the double layer of jackets around me, the smell of ice in the air made my teeth chatter.

But maybe that was just the stress.

I'd managed to calm down enough that the dizziness had abated for now. But I worried that no matter what I was expecting out of this, the dizziness would come back with a vengeance.

Tearing my gaze from my phone, I monitored the archway that stood at the main entrance to the park, looking for any sign of him. Tourists in I Heart NY merchandise strode past, some of them overdressed for the weather and some not wearing nearly enough, clutching tote bags full of gifts or souvenirs that would inevitably break before they'd even made it home. The man working the hot dog stand argued loudly with a customer, and across from them, a leashed dog barked and jumped at the pigeons nearby, sending a massive swarm of them flying off overhead.

"Are you happy with yourself?"

The voice behind me had me spinning on the spot, giving me just an inkling of vertigo as I came to a halt in front of Adrian.

His face was almost entirely expressionless, but the tic in his hard-set jaw was enough to tell me he wasn't happy. His thick wool coat was buttoned nearly all the way up around his neck, his nose just slightly pink in the cold.

He narrowed his eyes at me.

"What do you..."

"Your father called," he started, and just the mention of him made my stomach twist. "Asked me to come see him. I came from there."

I blinked up at him, searching for whatever he was trying to tell me in the sharp blue of his eyes, but there was nothing but steel to see.

"You're lucky I'm even here," he said, a hollow chuckle breaking from his lips. "I could have disappeared off the face of the fucking map. I could have not given you the ounce of grace I'm giving right now to allow you to explain yourself and never speak to you again. But against my better judgment, Ava, I'm here, again, giving you the smallest bit of trust that I absolutely shouldn't be."

I recoiled from the minor lashing, taking a step back as I clutched the sides of my jacket together. "What?"

"I know we're on the rocks, Ava, but we were supposed to do this together."

The nausea roiling in my gut doubled, tripled, quadrupled. "He knows?" I asked, my voice nothing more than a whisper. The backs of my eyes burned, but before a tear could even form, the cold air evaporated it.

Adrian didn't answer me.

No, no, no. No. Panic set in again for the millionth time, creeping up my spine and making me feel as if I was sinking into the concrete beneath my aching feet. "Fuck," I said, pushing the hair out of my face as if it would help me think clearer. "Fuck!"

Adrian's jaw ticked again as he watched me, not making a single move in my direction. This didn't make sense.

"Why?" I asked, my fingers catching on a knot and pulling regardless, making little blossoms of pain sprout from my scalp. "I don't understand, why?"

A flicker of something rippled across his face, but it was too quick, too small to decipher. "I was hoping you'd tell me that, Ava."

What? I opened my mouth to speak, but the words were trapped again, locked behind the building lump in my throat that I was so, so tired of.

"Thought so."

"I didn't..." I cut myself off as the words ran out, wracking my brain for more, for anything. How could he think I'd done this? "I didn't tell him, Adrian. I didn't."

He shook his head, his lips forming a tight line. "Who else would have?"

"I...I don't know. Maybe he asked for my discharge paperwork, maybe he worked it out..."

"You're an adult, Ava," he scoffed. "He can't just ask them for that. That would be a fucking HIPAA violation."

He stretched his neck from side to side, his eyes glazing over as he looked anywhere but at me.

"You told him. You conveniently left out the pregnancy, but you didn't consider the consequences for me."

A ringing started in my ears, loud enough it felt as though it blocked almost everything out—but I could hear him breathing, could hear the thunder of my own heartbeat, could hear his sigh as I struggled to find words to say. I hadn't done this.

I fished my phone from my pocket and hastily pulled up my texts with my dad. I hadn't gone into a fugue state and dropped that bombshell, I was goddamn sure of it.

I pressed my phone into his chest. "Look," I croaked. "Just look. I didn't. You can go through my whole fucking phone if you want to, Adrian."

He sighed as his hand covered mine, peeling back the screen from his jacket. He glanced down at it, his mouth scrunching up on one side for a second. "This means nothing when it could have been a phone call or a chat in person."

"You think I wouldn't have warned you?"

"I think you tried." He tapped on my screen a handful of times before turning my phone around, pointing out the last message I sent him.

Me: Can we please talk?

"That was an hour before David called me," he clarified.

I stared at the text, trying not to look at the last one above it from him that simply said, *I miss you.* "I...I wanted to talk to you about where we were at and how we were going to tell my dad..."

"So you told him yourself when I didn't reply."

"No," I snapped. The feelings from his insistence that I was lying were morphing from horror to irritation, and it was getting hard to keep myself from lashing out and screaming at him for even entertaining this idea. "Do you honestly believe that if I'd done that in person, I'd have been let out of his sight within an hour? Do you think that if I'd called him, he wouldn't have immediately come to my apartment? How would that have worked, Adrian?"

"You could have told him earlier. Yesterday. I don't fucking know, Ava, I just know that there is no one else who knew enough about what this was for him to have found it out," he said, his shoulders rising and falling in defeat.

But it was what he'd said in the middle of that last sentence that I latched onto in panic.

...who knew enough about what this was...

...what this was...

...was...

Was.

I choked on the only word I could focus on. "Was?"

He watched me for a moment, his gaze hard and unnerving, before looking away. "Was."

Everything in my mind came to a screeching, crashing halt. The sinking feeling was worse, now, and it felt as if the ground beneath me had cracked and split, eating me whole. That single word hung in the air, sharp and final. Was. He didn't want to be with me anymore. He was giving up.

"Your father told me that he would ruin me if I got within a hundred feet of you again. And I don't doubt him for a second," he said, squinting his eyes just barely as he looked toward the overcast sky, forcing his crow's feet to deepen. "I'm taking that risk right now, but I can't again. Not when everything I've worked for, everything I have, everything Lucas has, is on the line."

My chest tightened, the breath caught in my throat, and the sting of tears pressed hard behind my eyes, but I couldn't move, couldn't speak. A choked sound left me, but that was all I could get out.

"I don't know if you thought he'd come around or if

this was what you wanted, Ava, but either way, I can't fight this. I can't fight him." His throat moved as he swallowed, his gaze slowly moving back to mine. "This is over."

Instinctively, my hand moved to my stomach and the little bump that was barely visible through my double layer of jackets.

It felt like I'd been kicked.

"I'll talk to him," I croaked, the sting of cold air feeling harsher against the trails of tears that freely came now. If a passerby saw and looked at me strangely, I wouldn't have noticed—I was so focused on Adrian that it was as if everything else melted away. "Let me talk to him, please. I can fix this. All of it."

He shook his head and took a further step back, his eyes glancing down at the hand on my stomach. He winced. "It wouldn't help."

"It would. It would. Please, Adrian, don't do this." The words were broken, battered. Everything about me felt raw, from my throat to my heart to my brain. Nothing felt okay. Nothing.

"Even if I could bring myself to be with someone who has lied to me twice now," he scoffed, "you and I both know that when your father sets his mind to something, it's not changing."

I didn't want to accept the potential truth in what he'd said about my dad. "I haven't lied," I sputtered, my breath hitching with each word. "I've admitted over and over that I should have told you sooner, and I've apologized just as much. But I didn't do this. I didn't. I'm fucking pregnant, Adrian, do you think I'd want him to hate you in the midst of that?"

Another step back, and he was further than arm's reach.

He looked away again and it felt as though he were ripping my goddamn heart from my chest.

"Do you expect me to do this alone?" I sobbed. I truly, wholeheartedly couldn't give a shit if everyone could hear me, if everyone was judging me. Tourists would come and go. This was too big for that. "Do you want that?"

For the briefest, fleeting second, his lower lip trembled. "I will help you, Ava, and I will take care of the baby in the way I need to as a father once we know that David won't literally cut off my head for it. But that doesn't change anything." He took one more step back, almost hesitating. "I'm sorry."

Before I could get another word out, he was halfway across the park.

Chapter 34

Adrian

I 'd never been one to disassociate often, or even at all. My first real episode with it had come the moment I'd learned about Jan's death and I went into overdrive to handle it. I'd gone in and out of fits of shock the weeks and months after, somehow managing to get work done and be a parent despite it, even when it felt as if I were taking a backseat in my head and letting someone else control my body.

But now, as I sat on the floor against the wall of windows in my office, still wearing my coat and my hands frozen from my walk back from the park, I was gone entirely.

It was as if I wasn't even in my body anymore. Everything around me—the office, the floor, the plants, the mumbling of high-ranking staff passing by my door, my own heartbeat—felt distant, muffled, as if I were watching it all through a dusty, fogged-up window. I blinked, trying to recenter myself, but nothing I could see felt real anymore. My hands, my body, my breath felt so far away that it was like I was drifting away, somewhere safer where the weight of everything couldn't touch me.

I knew I should feel something. I knew I should force myself, somehow, back into reality. But there was only what was before me and the feeling of an empty, hollow space. All of the graves were dug up, and Jan's fingers had pulled me underneath the rotten soil, burying me instead of all of my problems.

I needed to work. I needed to prep for the next event, I needed to triple-check every choice the teams below me had made, I needed to do outreach to ensure that the companies signed on still wanted to work with me despite our catastrophic failings recently.

But I also needed her, and that was the most horrific realization.

A little over three months was too quick to go from barely knowing someone, to needing them to function. And somehow, against my better judgment, I'd let it happen.

I was right back where I'd been two years ago.

When I finally got the energy to move, it wasn't because I'd told myself to or intentionally piloted my body. I just... went from sitting one second, to standing the next, and back to sitting again in the plush seat at my desk. The screen from my laptop lit the darkening space, and it was only then that I realized that somehow, in all of this, the sun had set between the skyscrapers.

I'd done nothing.

The moment I had the tiniest drop of clarity, I called Grace, asked her to stay with Lucas. I'd take the angry melt-down from him later about missing the new episode of our show tonight, I'd deal with the minor fall out and handle what I could. I just...couldn't go home. I couldn't face my son like this.

A knock on my door pulled me toward the surface, briefly, again.

Michael stepped through the door into the dim light of my office, a gray and black flannel overtop of his button-up shirt and dark jeans. So fucking unprofessional, but it was Michael, and at that exact moment, I couldn't have cared less.

"You're still here?" he asked.

In an instant, I slammed back into reality, and all of it hit me at once.

One shaky, broken breath in, and Michael was moving across the floor to me. "Shit, what's wrong?"

"Everything," I choked. "Everything."

———

It took everything in me to keep from replaying the words I'd spoken and the moment I'd walked away from Ava, over and over again, in my mind. But talking through the last three months with Michael as we sat in the dingy, rundown bar a block down from the Darkwater building, helped keep my mind somewhat distracted.

"Can I be honest, man?" Michael asked, his glass of beer dripping condensation down his arm. I nodded. "From the way you've described her and everything up until this point, telling her father doesn't sound like something she would do. Especially not to spite you."

I leaned back in my creaking chair, staring at the still glass of red wine in front of me. "She kept the pregnancy from me for three weeks."

"Yeah, she did. But those were the three weeks you'd been working yourself to the bone to deal with the fuckin' chaos that came from shutting down that event upstate," he continued. "I mean, you said it yourself that she told you she hadn't wanted to stress you out any further. She knew you had a kid to look after and knew you had a lot going on with work. I'm not surprised she was trying to wait for a good time for you."

The wine sloshed as I lifted it by the stem, tipping back a solid mouthful. It was cheap, barely developed. "She knows what I went through with Jan. It doesn't excuse it."

"And do you not think that what you went through with Jan might be exactly why she wanted to wait to tell you?" he asked, his brows raising and making the tufts of gray hair at his temples wiggle. "You didn't want to fall as hard as you have. She probably knew that and didn't want to freak you out on top of causing more stress."

I shook my head. As much as I wanted to believe that, it wasn't safe for me or my heart. "The fact remains that there's no one else who would have run to David and told him."

Michael narrowed his gaze at me. "You know that isn't true. Assuming you haven't been absurdly careful with all of this, your nanny could have."

I stilled.

"Ava's friend could have. That woman who cooks for you in the Hamptons could have. Have you looked into any of them? Have you considered any of it a possibility?"

"No," I relented.

"Did you ask David who had told him?"

I swallowed another sip of wine to calm the uncomfortableness in my throat. "No," I sighed.

Michael's lips pursed. "You assumed."

"Yes."

"Text him."

I snorted. "Absolutely not."

"He's your friend."

"Was." I winced at the memory of reiterating that word to Ava, remembering the look of abject horror on her face as it sunk in. "He was my friend. He is clearly not anymore."

"Just text him and ask him, man. It's not that hard," Michael grumbled.

Sighing, I slipped my phone from my inner breast pocket and navigated over to the last few messages I'd had with David.

Me: Can you please tell me if Ava was the one who told you what was happening?

I set my phone face up on the table between us, the messages still open, so Michael would know I'd done it.

"Good job, Ade," Michael grinned. "That's honestly..."

It vibrated, and a message popped up.

David: Why should I tell you?

Groaning in exhaustion from the situation, I picked up my phone and replied.

Me: Because I am still at a loss as to how this happened.

Me: I appreciate that you're upset about this. I am too. I'll honor your wishes. I just need to know if she told you.

Me: Please. Just give me that much, Dave.

Another minute, another vibration.

David: It wasn't Ava, but that changes nothing.

It...wasn't Ava? It wasn't Ava. It wasn't fucking Ava.

Dropping the phone onto the glass table, I stared at it with dread coursing through my goddamn veins. Michael's gaze flicked from it to me, reading it upside down and gauging my reaction.

"Told you," he said.

"I fucked up," I breathed. I set down my glass with shaking hands, feeling the temptation to slip away again, to go back into disassociation where it was safe and slightly comfortable. "Oh my Ggod, I fucked up."

"Deep breaths, man," Michael said, hitting the button on the side of my phone to turn off the screen. "You should look into who did it. I don't think pressing him more on the issue is going to help."

I tried to measure my breaths, tried to stay in the moment. "How?"

He shrugged. "I can help you find a private investigator."

"That's insane," I laughed, but it was hollow, broken. I'd fucked up. I'd fucked up horribly.

"It's not," he chuckled. "It's pretty common. I've hired them before on the company's dime."

"You've..." I stopped myself from questioning it further, steadying my breathing again. "Fine. Okay. We can look into it."

Chapter 35

Ava

Emily had been right. The first flurries of snow had come, and despite it not sticking, watching as the little, refracting crystals fluttered down from the sky had become my new pastime.

It seemed to be the only thing I was capable of concentrating on.

Hours passed as I sat in the window, eyes locked on each little flurry that drifted lazily down to the earth, swirling in the wind and meeting its fate on the roof of a car or the slightly too-warm sidewalk. Each one seemed to fall in slow motion, fragile and delicate and unknowing of its fate before it either melted or broke apart in the wind. If I were able to get myself together at least a little bit, I'd want to paint them—capture the way the light glinted off of them and turned each one into specks of silver as they reflected the cold exteriors of the skyscrapers around the West Village.

But that idea felt too far away to reach out and grab. Everything did.

In the moments where I couldn't watch the flurries or the moments where the weather died down and there was nothing left to focus on, I found it hard to keep myself from drifting back to every second, every choice I'd made when it came to Adrian. The anxiety that had been coursing through my system for weeks had died down, but not in the way I'd hoped—it took everything else with it. Everything happy, everything sad, everything angry, it was all...gone. I was left with a shell that didn't quite feel anything other than the smallest bit of intrigue over something I'd seen hundreds of times back home in Bostonthose stupid goddamn flurries.

I tried to sit down at my easel after four days had passed without being able to do anything at all. I couldn't decide what colors to use, so I went through the motions of putting a drop of each on my palette board, my body thinking for me and going through each of the steps. But when the time came to actually use my brain and decide what to do first, what paint to dip into first, what stroke to make first, I stalled out, stuck in my chair with a brush in my hand, my eyes glazed over and staring into the middle distance.

I just couldn't do it.

I tried to work, too—tried to sit down on the couch and open my laptop, tried to read the profiles of people Emily had set aside for me. Easy cases, she'd said. To take your mind off things. But all I could focus on was the little file on my desktop screen that had Adrian's full name on it. Page after scanned page of handwritten notes, downloaded profiles of women I'd thought could work, that stupid question that I kept going back to over and over again:

Ideal date? A night at an art museum, finished with a glass of wine on my sailboat.

I felt nauseous just thinking about it. The morning sickness had wound down significantly, but every time my mind drifted back to Adrian and all of those stupid choices, I wondered if it truly had calmed down or if I was just so numb I couldn't feel it until emotions crept back in like a viper.

Emily came over a handful of times in the week that followed my afternoon in Washington Square. She brought me homemade soup and groceries, meal-prepped for me so I wouldn't need to cook for myself, talked to me about how things were going with work to try to take my mind off things.

I just didn't have the energy in me to respond.

"Aves," she said softly, squatting down in front of where I sat curled up on the couch with layers of blankets over me. "You're not taking care of yourself."

"I'm fine." I pulled the blankets up a little higher, covering my arms.

"You're not," she insisted. "And it's okay to not be okay about this. But you're pregnant and you need to take care of yourself to take care of that little life."

I didn't respond. I knew she was right, of course, but I was perfectly happy to sit and stew in peace until I decided I was capable of taking care of myself again.

"Have you talked to your dad?"

I shook my head. The idea of talking to him about the Adrian situation was horrifying on its own, but adding in the pregnancy as well felt like the worst possible thing I could do.

"I think you should," she said gently. "Maybe there's more to this than what Adrian told you."

I couldn't help but wince at the sound of his name.

"For their sake," she pleaded, her eyes drifting to my stomach. "I think understanding would help you to move forward in whatever way that will look for you."

―――――

I didn't tell him I was coming.

Maybe I should have—maybe that would have made me less anxious about seeing him, maybe it would have made the words I wanted to say to him easier to practice in my mind. Maybe, just maybe, I wouldn't have thundered in like a raging storm, then.

But time was a funny thing and didn't like to be undone.

"Are you happy?"

Dad sat on his recliner, a glass of whiskey in his hand and some show about trucks getting stuck in the snow in Alaska playing too loudly on the absurdly large television. His bald head swung in my direction, wide eyes clashing with mine as I caught him fully off guard.

He kicked down the footrest as his gaze traveled lower, right to the bump I wasn't even trying to conceal. My paint-stained black shirt clung to it, and although my jacket obscured it slightly, I knew damn well he could see it. He couldn't stop seeing it. "Aves...?"

"Do you understand what you've done?"

He blinked rapidly, his body stiffening as he stood up. It was as if his mind couldn't quite catch up to the situation.

I didn't have the patience for him to be confused. I didn't have the patience for anything. "Fucking answer me, Dad," I snapped.

His mouth opened and closed like a goddamn fish. "You're...?"

"Pregnant?" I laughed, the sound coming out angry, hollow, vengeful. "Yeah. What gave it away?"

He shook his head in disbelief, his brows furrowing. "What the fuck is goin' on?"

"You threatened him," I said, kicking the door shut behind me. "You threatened him, and now I'm stuck in limbo because you couldn't wrap your goddamn head around the idea that maybe, just maybe, we weren't just having sex behind your back."

Vertigo hit as he took a step around the coffee table toward me, aiming the remote at the television to pause his precious, stupid show. "Jesus H. Christ, Aves, 'ya could have told..."

"No," I scolded him. The temptation to laugh at the absurdity of scolding my own father hit me as I gripped the back of the couch for stability, but I fought it. "You should have come to me first instead of Adrian. You know damn well you should have. But you attacked him, threatened him, without ever asking me how I felt about the situation. You didn't even consider me in this at all, did you?"

He cursed under his breath and averted his gaze, exhaling so loud through his nostrils I could hear it from ten feet away. "Is this," he motioned toward my stomach, "why you haven't been at the office?"

My eye twitched. "No, Dad," I said, keeping my voice as level as I could after my outburst. "I haven't been at the office because I've been so fucking depressed over this that I couldn't get out of my apartment."

His jaw tightened. "I didn't realize the extent of it."

"No," I laughed. "You didn't. He hates me now because he thinks I came to you on my own about this when we'd planned to talk to you together, and he won't talk to me because you threatened his entire livelihood if he tried."

I didn't have the guts to say that he was still upset with me for keeping the pregnancy from him, too. That wasn't something Dad needed to know, not right now.

We could have worked through that issue. I was sure of that. But this?

"I should've told him sooner that it wasn't you," he sighed. "I...apologize for not thinking it through."

It was my turn to blink at him in return.

I couldn't remember a single time in my life when Dad had apologized when he was in the wrong. He was always so headstrong in anything he did, any solutions he offered. This was...whiplash inducing.

I cleared my throat to stuff down the surprise. "How did you find out?"

He shook his head, grunting as he fished his phone out of the recliner. "I got an email of some photos," he said, almost cringing. He stepped around the back of the couch toward me, his arm outstretched with his phone screen lit up. "I only looked at the first one. And before 'ya ask, I've no fuckin' clue who sent 'em."

Hesitantly, I took his phone.

"I was just tryin' to protect 'ya," he sighed. "I thought he was using 'ya, kid. He told me he didn't want somethin' serious after Jan, and then when I got the photos, I was just terrified you'd have to deal with a scandal and heartbreak."

Oh my God.

The email address it came from was just a single string of numbers, and there wasn't a single word in the body of it. Just...photos.

I scrolled.

The first was one of me and Adrian on the balcony at

the first charity ball, when he'd followed me outside. My hands were in his hair, my body lifted and pushed against the side of the building, his hips slotted between mine. From the angle, it was clear what was happening, and the whole side of my rear was visible along with his fingers. It looked almost like it had been taken with some sort of long-lens camera—like a paparazzi shot. Surely, neither of us was well known enough to warrant paparazzi.

The second was shot through a foggy window, just two roughly human shapes on the other side of it with one head of black and gray hair and another of bright auburn, his body close to mine against what looked like a...fireplace. That was the Hamptons, on that last night. How the fuck...?

The third was us outside the bagel stand, a car halfway obscuring the photo. His hands were on my cheeks and his mouth was on mine. When he'd told me without telling me that he wanted a relationship.

The fourth showed me that this wasn't in order, but it was the most vulgar one by far, and I had to keep my roiling nausea at bay as best as I could as I realized how deep this invasion of privacy went. It was shot through the large window in his bedroom on his sailboat, with both of us completely bare. My back was arched against his chest, my rear against his hips, his hand around my fucking throat.

I was going to be sick.

I scrolled quickly past the final two: one of him kissing me on the street when I'd followed him to his date that he abandoned, and one of us stepping out of his car in the parking garage below his building, with me in only my buttoned up coat and my hair a mess.

I ran to the bathroom before Dad could say anything else, spilling my guts into the toilet. The phone sat next to me, still illuminated on that last one, taunting me, violating me.

I needed to find out who the fuck had done this, and I needed to tell Adrian. But even as I hurled up the home-made soup, even as I gagged and nothing came up, I wasn't sure if I could forgive him for not believing me.

It wasn't me. It would have never been me.

Chapter 36

Adrian

The moment the forwarded email landed in my inbox, all I could see was red.

It was forwarded from David's email address, but the note in the text body made it absolutely clear that he wasn't the one who decided to show me them.

Told you it wasn't me.

—Ava

I'd fucked up. I well and truly understood that. And although I wanted to grovel at her feet and apologize, I needed to focus on finding the person who had done this. Every image was too personal, too close to home, too sneaky to have been someone I knew trailing me.

And they went back to the first night.

This had to have been going on for longer than I'd had this secret.

With Michael's help, I hired a private investigator. Michael handled the majority of the communication except when it came to the email specifically—I couldn't stomach him seeing them, nor would I want another person violating our privacy like that. I didn't even want to imagine how she felt knowing these had been sent to her father.

In the week that passed, I kept myself from reaching out to her and kept my head down at work. I managed to focus for once, only because I had to, only because I knew that if I didn't, more questions would be raised sooner than later.

I spent more time with Lucas. I took him to the park, took him to the museum, took him anywhere he wanted to go. I let him skip school on the day I decided to work from home. I watched his basketball practice, I picked him up from school—and although it was likely far too hopeful on my end, I hadn't expected him to ask about her.

He asked me why Ava hadn't been around lately. He asked where she was and if she was okay. He asked if she could come over for dinner soon. He asked if we were still dating.

I didn't know how to answer a single one of his questions.

Lying was against our code, and yet I found myself lying every way I knew how to get him to stop bringing her up. Every time, it hurt me twice over—once for having to speak about her, and once for breaking a promise I had with Lucas. I'd tried navigating the conversation away from her, but his curiosity about her was too intense, too headstrong.

It only made me miss her more.

But as I sat there with him on the sofa, his exhausted little frame leaned up against me with a blanket over him, half asleep as we watched our favorite show, my cell phone rang.

As quickly as I could without jostling Lucas, I slipped it from the pocket of my pajama bottoms. Lucas stirred slightly, but his little snore cut through a second later as I read the name on my screen.

The private investigator.

"Hey," I said quietly into the phone. "Can you call me back in ten minutes? My son's zonked out on my lap."

"I know who sent the photos," Shaun said.

"Fuck," I breathed. "Okay."

"Dad, that's a bad word," Lucas grumbled sleepily, turning over in my lap. "You're not supposed to say that."

"I'm sorry, give me one moment," I said into the phone, being met with an exaggerated huff in response. I tucked the phone into my neck and spoke directly to Luc as I slowly slid out from under him. "I have to take a call, bud. I'll be right back."

"But our show," he groaned, his half-lidded, sleepy eyes looking directly up at me. He wasn't even watching it, but it broke my heart regardless.

"I know," I sighed. Leaning down over him, I pressed a kiss to his forehead. "It's really important. I'll be back before you know it."

I didn't wait for his protest. I took the stairs two at a time as I sprinted up to the studio, my heart pounding far too quickly, far too erratically. I shut the door behind me, locking it for good measure, and stared down the piano as I raised the phone to my ear again.

"Okay, go."

Shaun cleared his throat. "Right, as I was saying, Mr. Stone," he started, attitude thick in his voice. "The PI who was hired to trail you and take these is fuckin' sloppy. I won't bore you with the details, but once I was able to get into his files, it was fairly obvious."

"Is that...legal?" I asked.

I could hear the shrug in his voice. "His files weren't protected."

"That's not an answer..."

"The man who hired him is someone named Andrew O'Shaughnessy. I looked him up and it seems he's a member of the board at Stone & Co Global. I assume you know who he is."

A chill ran down my spine as my breath caught.

Andrew.

Of fucking course it was Andrew.

"I'll take your silence as a yes," Shaun continued. "From what I could gather, it looks like he was trying to dig up some kind of scandal he could present to the rest of the board. That's just from the emails he sent to this guy. I'll forward it all on to you."

Thank God I hadn't stayed on the couch with Lucas.

The temptation to smash my fist into the wall was so strong I had to physically hold my arm back by cupping it in my elbow, and although I hadn't consciously decided to move, I found myself in front of the sliding glass door that led out onto the pool deck.

"Thank you," I said as calmly as I could muster.

I hung up.

I stepped out onto the heated balcony flooring, shutting the door behind me, the below-freezing winds battering me from all angles at this height. But I didn't care.

I took a long, deep breath in.

And I screamed.

Surprising everyone but me, Andrew himself called for a board meeting the following morning.

Having signed over the authority for the private investigator to search Stone & Co's data, I'd been dropped with more information overnight. I'd spent the three hours I'd had between waking and arriving in my office putting everything together into a perfect package, combing through each email Shaun had found, and compiling it.

I waited until the scheduled start time to leave my desk and make my way down the hall. There wasn't a single part of me that wanted to be the first in the room—in fact, I was hoping to be the last, and as I pushed the door open, I found everyone had taken their seat around the table except Andrew. He stood at the front of the room. His laptop sat atop the podium, a cable poised to be plugged in.

"You're late," he said. "Fitting."

"Is it?" I plucked a mint from the bowl in the center of the table and popped it into my mouth. "Why?"

His desktop screen projected onto the wall behind him as he plugged the laptop in. "Because you might want to just keep standing for this. I have a feeling you'll walk out," he chuckled. I laughed right alongside him, and he leveled his gaze at me, his brows furrowing in slight confusion.

"Ah," I said around a mouthful of mint. "You going to show them all the photos your PI took of me fucking my girlfriend?"

His pale, freckled face turned ghostly white in an instant, his glasses just slightly too far down his nose.

"You know that's illegal, right?" I continued, shoving my hands into my pockets to keep from punching him square in the center of his jaw. "Especially the one on the boat. You pull that up right now and I can hit you with a revenge porn charge."

I could feel eyes on me from around the table, but I didn't care enough to look.

"So greedy," I chuckled. "Just couldn't keep yourself

from sending them to her father the moment you had them, huh? If you'd have just waited..."

"Adrian, ..."

"No, no, me first." I grinned at him wide enough to show him the mint between my teeth. "That was disgusting, you know that? Her dad had to look at that. Had to see his kid like that. Did I mention she's pregnant? That was a lovely bit of stress to put on a goddamn pregnant woman."

His throat worked as he ground his teeth. "I didn't know that."

"Unsurprising."

"Andrew, you had photos taken of Adrian's girlfriend? What on earth possessed you..."

"Shut the fuck up, Vicky," he snapped, ripping the cable out of his laptop so hard that the podium shook beneath it.

"Aw, no." I offered him a fake pout. "I thought you'd at least show us your emails to the ticketing agency telling them to rebook the same tickets for that conference upstate. What was it you said? We've reached out privately and given refunds to those affected, please open those tickets up for purchase again."

Silence. Utter, ringing silence descended over everyone, the only sound that of Andrew's breaths as he tried to steady them. "I have no idea what you're talking about."

I clicked my tongue as I set my laptop bag on the table. "I've got them all on my computer if you'd like me to show you."

"Is that true?" Vince, one of the quieter board members who really only spoke up if someone directly acknowledged him, asked.

"No," Andrew scoffed.

"Yep," I said. Slipping my laptop out and propping it open on the table, I pulled up the emails Shaun had forwarded me under Andrew's glare. A soft squeaking sounded out as I slid the computer along the table toward Vince, the little rubber bits scratching on the wood surface. "See for yourself."

I looked across the room at Andrew, watching as the paleness of his face turned rapidly to blotchy red spotting across his cheeks. I winked at him.

"If you really want to dig in deep," I added, leaning down toward Vince but keeping my gaze locked on Andrew, "I can tell you that he's had PIs trailing all of you, not just me. I'm a good enough person that I haven't looked at those images, but I'll bet he..."

"I resign." Andrew shut his laptop with a resounding clack.

I snorted. "Just like that?"

"Don't talk to me, Adrian," he snapped, shoving the cable into his back.

"Oh, come on," I goaded. "You can't be that easy to break."

Before I could get another word out, he stepped through the door, slamming it behind him.

Chapter 37

Ava

I stared at the glass door on the other side of the waiting room, watching it like a hawk as I sat uncomfortably in my chair.

As angry as I still was with him, I didn't want to do this alone.

Adrian had agreed to come, but I didn't know if he'd meant it. I'd given him a location, a day, and a time four days ago over text, and he'd said, *I'll be there*. But the clock was showing my appointment time, and in the haze of everything that had happened and my unwillingness to fully recover, I couldn't help but think the worst.

"Ava Riley?"

I turned my head to the woman standing at the door that led back to the exam rooms. She stood in blue scrubs, her brown hair braided back and nearly wrapped around the stethoscope that hung limply around her neck. She offered me a soft smile when I nodded to her.

The glass door at the front swung open as I pushed myself to my feet.

Adrian stepped in at three o'clock on the dot, his nose

pink, his gaze flitting between me and the woman waiting for me. "I'm here," he huffed, almost as if he were out of breath. He slid his gloves off and stuffed them in his pocket. "I'm sorry. There was traffic."

This is Manhattan, there's always traffic. I bit my tongue but gave him a tight nod in acknowledgment as I gathered my things and followed the woman through the door, Adrian right behind me.

I tried not to let it bother me that I hadn't seen him since that day in Washington Square three weeks ago. He'd called me exactly once since then, and I hadn't answered. He'd texted me a handful of times since I sent the email and each one had felt like an insult to injury. *I'm sorry. I fucked up. Can we talk?*

"So you're fifteen weeks, is that correct?" she asked, eyeing my stomach as she pulled the paper sheet over the bed.

"Yeah, approximately."

Adrian sunk into the chair to the right of the bed, his eyes trained on me. "She had to go into the hospital about four weeks or so ago and they confirmed she was eleven weeks at the time," he said.

"I thought you said this was your first ultrasound," the woman said, eyeing me jokingly as she patted the paper on the bed invitingly.

"It is. They didn't have an ultrasound tech on hand that day," I explained.

"Gotcha, gotcha," she grinned. "Have a seat and lay back for me. Dad, if you want to help her get her shirt up, that would be super useful."

I stared at her. Is she seriously insinuating...? "He's... he's not my dad..."

"She doesn't mean it like that," Adrian said softly,

reaching out a hand for me to leverage myself onto the bed. I glared at him, but took it, hoisting myself up and back into the not-so-comfortable bed. "She's referring to me as the dad."

The woman chuckled lightly as she pulled her wheeling stool over. On her chest, a name badge swung loosely that read OB Sadie Langdon. "I'm sorry, I should have been clearer. It's just what we say in reference to the father, and we usually call you Mom as well. I won't if you don't like it, Ava."

I swallowed as Adrian stood, holding out his hand again and lifting my back just slightly off the paper, enough to slide my shirt up to my bra. "It's fine," I said. "Just because he's older, you know, I thought you got confused."

He lowered me back before sinking into the chair again, his hand still holding onto mine. "Completely understandable. This is your first time," he said.

Sadie chuckled again as she squirted something clear onto what looked like a VR machine controller. "Not your first rodeo?"

"Second," Adrian grinned.

"Well, congratulations to both of you," she said, offering us a cheerful smile as she wheeled a little closer. "This might be a little cold."

Instinctually, I squeezed Adrian's hand when the chill of the lube pressed against my stomach. He squeezed right back.

"I'm assuming the hospital gave you some paperwork regarding prenatal care," she said, focusing her eyes on the screen with an intensity I hadn't expected.

"Yeah, I've been taking the vitamins and staying away from the foods it told me to." I tried to crane my neck to see the screen, but it was no use.

"I'll show you once I've got a clear view," she offered. "Don't worry."

It felt almost alien to lay there with the device roaming across my broadening stomach, Adrian's eyes flicking between me and the woman beside me. But the longer we sat and the more my anxiety grew, the more he watched me and me alone, his fingers squeezing mine reassuringly.

"Well," she grinned, pulling my attention back to her, "that'll explain why you're bigger than I thought you'd be at fifteen weeks."

I blinked at her. Bigger?

"We've got three heartbeats going."

My breath caught as she turned the screen toward me, holding her hand steady on my stomach. "Three heart-beats?" I breathed.

Adrian's hand squeezed so hard I worried my bones would break.

"Yours, and both of the babies," she explained. "Don't worry, there's not more than two."

"Twins?" Adrian breathed.

Sadie nodded, beaming at the both of us. "Twins. Both look great."

I tore my gaze from the screen when Adrian huffed out a little breath in surprise. His eyes went glassy as he looked from me to the monitor and back, the corners of his lips pulling up. He lifted our joined hands to his mouth, pressing a kiss to the back of mine.

For a moment, just the briefest second, I let myself not be angry with him long enough to feel the wave of shock and excitement and happiness that came from it.

"Twins, Aves," he laughed breathily. He sniffled, wiping his nose on his free hand and catching a stray tear that broke free with his thumb. "We made twins."

I chuckled along with him. "We did."

"Do you want to know the sexes?" Sadie asked, moving the stick around a little more and pulling my attention away from Adrian. "I need to add it to your file, but if you don't want to know I can keep it to myself."

"Yes," we said in unison.

We sat silently as she searched around more, taking photographs as she went and capturing better angles. The anticipation was killing me, and there in the lower right of the screen, I could see my heartbeat creeping up toward triple digits.

"All right, we've got a girl," she said, narrowing her eyes as she took another photograph.

"Lucas is going to lose his mind," Adrian chuckled.

"And...another girl!"

I tipped my head back onto the bed, not caring as the tears started to sprout. Twins. Two girls. This was unbelievable. This was everything.

"Twin girls," Adrian grinned. "Can you tell if they're fraternal? Identical?"

She shook her head. "Nope, you'll need DNA testing when they're born." The wand left my stomach a moment later and she wheeled back, grabbing a handful of paper towels before wiping down my stomach. "Everything looks great, though. I'd suggest taking things a little slower than the advice you've already been given would have said, but other than that, everyone's healthy and happy."

Adrian nodded his thanks and took over wiping me down for her. "Can we have a moment alone? Do you mind?"

"Absolutely not a problem," she grinned. "I'll go print off those photos for you, okay?"

The moment she slipped from the room and left us to

our own devices, though, reality came crashing back down like a cartoon piano. It was as if a switch flipped inside of me, erasing all of the glee and stamping it down into the ground.

Twins.

Exciting, thrilling, and...fucking horrifying. Not only was I going to be giving birth, but it would be to two babies, doubling the chances of complications, doubling the risk of hemorrhaging, doubling the work out the other end. And Adrian...

Adrian had fully expected me to be okay with raising them mostly alone, with his help and his money where needed, purely because he wrongfully assumed I was the one who had gone to my father about us.

Adrian expected me to get through the pregnancy without him.

Adrian expected me to handle giving the babies to him when it was his turn.

Adrian expected me to...

"Hey, hey, are you okay?"

Blinking, I realized that my breathing and my heart were too fast, my eyes were unfocused, and my free hand was shaking. Adrian sat on the edge of the bed beside my hip, one hand gripping mine and the other resting against my stomach from where he'd pulled my top back down. His brows were furrowed as he looked down at me, his mouth parted just slightly, and I could feel the worry in his gaze, could feel the way his eyes searched mine for signs of a problem.

"Aves," he said softly. "It's okay. I know it's overwhelming, but we can handle two."

I stared at him, barely hearing his words over the thudding of my heartbeat in my ears. He didn't get it, not at all, and the damage was so destructive here that I worried there was no path to recovery, no path to righting this. "Yeah," I said flatly, turning away to look out the window as I tried to steady my breathing. "Overwhelming."

He lifted his hand from my stomach, reaching forward between us and brushing a strand of hair from my face so gently that I wondered if he was worried I was made of glass. I flinched. "Look, I...I know you're probably scared, and honestly, I'm scared too. But I'm not going anywhere..."

"It's not about the goddamn twins, Adrian," I snapped, my voice beginning to tremble as I forced myself to look at him. This felt wrong, like I was marking a day that should have been celebrated as one to be forgotten, like I was ruining a moment we'd had. But I hadn't spoken to him in weeks and I felt as though I were backed into a corner with an impossible decision—be with a man who clearly couldn't trust me, or go through all of this without him by my side. "It's about you. It's about this. It's the fact that you didn't believe me when I needed you to the most. It's the fact that you thought I could do that to you."

He didn't move his hand from where it rested on my cheek, but I could see the rest of his body recoil, could see the flicker of shame that crossed his face. His throat moved as he searched for the words, his head falling just slightly as he exhaled. "I was wrong. I know that, and I'm genuinely so sorry," he said. "I should have trusted you. I..."

"But you didn't." I steeled my gaze. I was tired of sobbing, tired of breaking down, tired of feeling the things he'd put me through over this. Showing my anger was different, though, and storming Dad's apartment showed me that I could at least be somewhat level headed in my anger. "You didn't believe me. You were fully convinced that I was capable of hurting you like that. And I can understand, to a degree—you've been hurt, horribly, and that's awful and a lot to process, but Jesus fucking Christ, Ade, you were so up your own ass that you were happy to leave me to deal with this alone."

He closed his eyes and hung his head, waves of black hair with streaks of gray falling forward. "I never would have made you do it all alone," he said softly. "I'm sorry, I know I said that before but I can understand how you would have worried about that regardless."

He lifted his head again, looking me dead in the eyes as he squeezed my hand.

"I was an idiot. I'll shout that from the fuckin' rooftops if you want me to," he continued. "Please, just let me make it right. However that looks for you, I'm willing to..."

"I'm not sure if you can make it right," I said, and it hurt to admit, hurt to speak the words that gave life to what I was feeling. "How am I supposed to trust that you won't think the worst of me again? How am I supposed to carry on when I'm being held to a standard you've created in your mind that I couldn't possibly live up to? Things won't always be certain and as it stands right now, all I know is that when things get hard, you don't believe me."

His hand slipped back, my ear falling into the space between his thumb and forefinger. His chin tightened as his lower lip wobbled slightly, measured breaths raising his shoulders up and down. "All I can give you is my word until I can show it."

I opened my mouth to reply, but the sound was cut short, choked as another lump filled my throat. "I want to believe that," I said hoarsely. "I do. But something broke in all of this, Adrian, and I don't know if it can be fixed. I don't know if it can be put back together."

His face fell. Every line that marked his skin loosened in

a worried defeat, but a moment later they were back, determination setting in his gaze. "I'll fix it," he said. "I will figure out a way to fix this, Ava, because I am not going to give up on this. Not on us, not on the twins, not on you."

The ache in my chest spread outward as I sat there, caught in limbo somewhere between the love I still felt for him and the walls I'd been building to protect myself.

But then Sadie was coming back into the room with the photographs in hand, and whatever sense of realness we had at that moment faded away, slipping back into oblivion with the rest of it.

Chapter 38

Adrian

Much like his penthouse, David's office seemed so dark that it devoured everything in its presence.

Leaning against his desk and dressed in what could best be described as an almost pinstripe suit, he observed me as if I was someone new, as if I was something to balk at for simply striding in unannounced. But I came with a goal in mind and I wasn't going to let his irritated gaze and white-knuckled grasp on the sides of his desk keep me from that.

Because there, almost hidden in the shadow of him as she sat in his desk chair with her auburn hair swept up into a messy bun, was my reason for this. For everything.

Ava: I don't think he'll want to talk to you.

Ava: I've been in with him all morning sorting out stuff for my business and he isn't in the best of moods.

Ava: I don't understand why you want to try with him.

The last messages she sent me played over and over in my mind in her voice, circling, spinning. She met my gaze from across the room, her worried eyes tearing me apart just like her father but for far different reasons.

"You got a reason for bein' here besides staring at my kid?"

"Dad, stop," Ava groaned, her head tipping back into the seat. "We talked about this."

"I'm not bein' fighty, Aves, I'm just...askin' him a question," David grunted, but his eyes still shot daggers at me.

"I'm here for a few reasons," I explained. Letting my laptop bag slip from my shoulder, I deposited it on the side table, holding David's stare as I pulled out a few printed-off pieces of paper. "I figured you'd want to know why someone was taking indecent photographs of your daughter."

David's brows rose, and behind him, a silently curious Ava peeked around him.

My feet clacked against the dark wood flooring as I stepped across the office hesitantly, holding the papers outstretched. David practically ripped them from my hand.

"Dad," Ava hissed.

"I'm not gonna see somethin' I shouldn't in here, am I?" David asked, eyeing me warily before starting to scan the page. "Don't need that happenin' again."

"No, I've blacked everything out for both of you," I said.

"Dad, can I see..."

"Hold on, Aves," Dave grunted. He finished the first page before handing it back to Ava and starting on the second, and she took it gently from his grasp, her bump nearly knocking against the desk.

They both read in silence. I could hear the ticking of the clock on the wall behind me, each second passing painfully slowly as I stood and watched them. My hands turned clammy as a bead of sweat dripped down the back of my neck. Everything that had torn my life apart was in those pages. Proof that the scandal wasn't our fault. Proof that it had never been about Ava at all.

"A member of my board of directors hired a private investigator. He was trying to catch me out in a scandal," I explained, desperate to fill the suffocating silence.

"Ah, so he succeeded," David snorted.

I tried not to grind my teeth. "He succeeded in nothing but exposing your daughter in a way she shouldn't have been and getting me to pull the plug on that conference upstate. He knew I'd take the fall for it and was hoping this would be the cherry on top to get the board to unanimously kick me off."

David passed Ava another sheet of paper as he kept reading through. "So you're tellin' me that my pregnant daughter had to suffer 'cause you made an enemy on your fuckin' board?"

Ava glanced up at me from behind the desk, her face unreadable.

I cleared my throat. "He has since removed himself once this came to light, but unfortunately, yes. I apologize that this happened because of me and that Ava got wrapped up in this. It never should have touched her."

He passed the rest of the papers to Ava with a slow, deliberate motion, his fingers tightening on the edges briefly before letting her take them. He didn't say anything, just looked at me with that same wary, guarded expression I'd seen before.

Fuck.

Behind him, Ava tore through the pages, reading each one in its entirety.

I'd never handled silence well from David, but I was cracking under the mounting pressure that seemed to be going nowhere. Against my better judgment, I spoke again, purely to try and move the conversation along. "I'm sure Ava has already told you, but I wanted to make it clear that we intended to tell you together. We'd been trying to figure out the best way to do it."

"The best way to do it would have been to never fuckin' touch her in the first place," David grumbled.

"I'm not some porcelain doll, Dad," Ava said, her tone irritated as she went onto the next page.

"I know I broke your trust because of that. And I know that I can't expect to receive that back," I sighed, pushing a hand through my hair to get it out of my face. "I know I've made a mess of everything, for both of you. But we were trying to take things slow after the chaos that unfolded because of that event cancelation, and we'd decided together to tell you once the time was right."

Ava pursed her lips together as she looked toward me. Sitting there with one leg propped up on the chair, her knee bent up toward her chest, in a set of leggings and a paint-stained oversized band shirt that just barely gave a hint of her bump, I couldn't help but feel like everything was slipping away.

Because it was.

I'd fucked up horribly, massively, disgustingly—I hadn't trusted her. And the more I sat on the fact that she kept the pregnancy from me for weeks, the more I came around to her side on that, too. She'd put herself through literal hell on her own, sending herself so deep into it that she had panic attack after panic attack, purely to keep my level of stress one notch lower.

I should have trusted her. I should have trusted her from the beginning.

"We knew it would be a disaster either way," I said, my voice just slightly too hoarse for my liking. "There wasn't a part of either of us that thought you'd take it well, and that's fair. You have every right to be upset with me, David. Truly. I won't apologize for being with her, but I will for the way you found out. Your anger was and is entirely justified."

Ava set the papers down on the desk, her gaze flicking up to mine.

"Does he know?" I asked.

She shook her head. Not yet.

"Know what?" David grunted.

"Can I tell him?"

Ava looked between us, her lower lip catching on her front teeth. She nodded.

I hesitated for a second, the weight of what I was about to say settling in my chest. This wasn't how I'd imagined telling him, not under these strained circumstances. I'd hoped things would be lighter, but he was still standing there with his arms crossed, his body closed off entirely. "Twins," I said, gesturing toward Ava. "We're having twins."

I could hear Ava's shift in her breathing as she watched her father.

His reaction was subtle—there was barely a shift in his expression, but the flicker of surprise in his eyes was unmistakable. I pressed on regardless, hoping like hell I could get through to him enough to then get through to her. "Two girls, Dave. Granddaughters."

After what felt like hours spent in silence, he uncrossed his arms, his gaze dropping briefly as if the weight of that realization finally hit him. When his eyes met mine again, there was still wariness there, but something softer, too—a crack in the rigid frame he was putting on. His jaw worked as if he was holding back what he wanted to say. "Twin girls, eh?"

I nodded. "I understand that you don't want me anywhere near her," I continued, shoving down the nausea that boiled in my gut the moment he raised a single brow in my direction. "But I'm not going to leave her to the wolves or to fend for herself. I'll be there in whatever capacity she allows, be that a helping hand or a co-parent or a partner."

His mouth flattened before he opened it. "Ad—"

"I can handle your consequences," I continued. "I'll sell my apartment if I need to, sell my business, sell my boat. I'll sell my fuckin' wine collection. It doesn't matter. I would rather have Lucas and the girls and her than any of it."

I could see Ava from the corner of my eye, but without looking directly at her, she was too out of focus to gather anything other than the fact that she was looking directly at me. I could feel the burn of her gaze on my skin, and although the vulnerability I was lying at our feet was going to eat me alive, I let it fuel me instead.

"I would choose her with or without your blessing, if she wants that." I swallowed down through gritted teeth. "You, probably more than anyone, would understand why I hesitated to answer your question last time we spoke. But I can tell you now that I love her. And whether she returns that feeling or not, I'm not disappearing anytime soon."

David's eyes lingered on me for a long moment, the silence heavy but different now, almost contemplative. I couldn't bring myself to look at Ava, couldn't even track her in my peripheral anymore. It was too much.

He nodded once. A slow, reluctant gesture, but a gesture nonetheless. "I shouldn't have threatened 'ya," David said quietly.

That was the closest I was going to get to an apology, and I would gladly accept it.

"It's Ava's choice, then, with whatever she wants..."

David's voice cut off abruptly, and before I could process what was happening, I felt the soft warmth of arms wrapping around my neck, pulling me in. Ava stepped into me silently, burying her face in my shoulder, her nails digging into my jacket and the side of my neck. For a second, I couldn't move, couldn't breathe — too stunned by the feel of her against me, by the simple fact that she had chosen to close that distance between us, I didn't know how to react.

But the second I understood, I closed my arms around her gently, breathing her in, and for the first time in what felt like forever, the knot in my chest loosened.

"I'm so sorry," I whispered into her hair, my voice barely steady. "For everything, Aves. I'm sorry."

She only tightened her grip on me.

I looked beyond her, watched over her head as David's eyes clung to the two of us. That look of stone cracked just a little bit more, and the corner of his mouth twitched upward just enough for me to notice.

"If you're what she wants, Adrian, then 'ya can have my blessing," he said, a heaviness in his voice that I didn't quite recognize coming from him. "Just don't fuck it up and I'll support it."

Chapter 39

Ava

My apartment was a wreck, but I didn't care anymore.

I don't think either of us knew what to say the entire car ride from my dad's office to my apartment in the West Village. He'd invited me to spend a few nights with him as we'd descended in the elevator, offered me a spare bedroom if I didn't want to jump into things just yet. But he wanted me to stay around him and Lucas for a few days, wanted for us to tell him together—and I was on board for that. I just needed to grab some things from home, and he was more than willing to come along.

I didn't consider that he hadn't been over to my place at all until I unlocked the door and let him in.

I'd managed to clean up in the last week or so, so it wasn't nearly as bad as it could have been—but abandoned paint palettes were flung about on nearly every surface, the dishes needed doing, the couch was littered with work papers, and the canvas that sat on my easel only had a blue wash painted over it before I'd given up.

I wasn't necessarily self-conscious as he stepped inside

and looked around at the paintings that hung on the exposed brick and wood, but I found myself following his gaze, wondering what he thought of the things I'd made.

But then he was turning back to me as I shut the door, crossing the small bit of space he'd left for me, his eyes locked on mine as he descended. One hand found my waist, pulling me gently but firmly against him, the other on my cheek — and before I could even register what was happening, his lips were on mine.

I couldn't help but gasp against him from the abruptness of it. We hadn't spoken about what this would mean exactly, hadn't decided on a full course of action. But for a moment, as I sank into him, it didn't matter. His kiss wasn't hesitant or questioning—it was filled with everything we hadn't said, everything we'd been holding back for weeks. The desperation, the depression, the longing, the relief. It was enough for now.

My fingers slipped around the sides of his neck, holding him to me as I kissed him back. The air in my lungs felt like the first real breath I'd had in far too long, and God, I'd missed him. I'd missed him too much to function.

He pulled back just enough to rest his forehead against mine, and despite me straining my neck up toward him, he didn't bow to it. His hands didn't leave my body, though, and as he breathed against me, he kept me close with an almost unwillingness to let me go. "I'm sorry," he whispered, his eyes closing. "For all of it, Ava. I'm so sorry."

For the first time in what felt like forever, the ache in my chest eased, the weight of the last three weeks slowly lifting.

I believed it. He was here. And somehow, despite the chaos, we were going to be okay.

"It's okay," I said softly.

He pressed a kiss against my cheek, my nose, my top lip. "I missed you. Every fucking second, I missed you."

"I missed you too," I breathed. "And for what it's worth, I feel the same."

His eyes fluttered open, searching between mine, his mouth parting as his fingers dug into my skin.

Does he need clarification? "I love y—"

He kissed me again, harder this time, demanding enough to push me back into the wooden door. Just before my head collided with it, the hand on my cheek slipped around the back of my head, cushioning the impact as his tongue pressed between my lips, forcing mine apart.

The urgency in his body language doubled as he slipped between my teeth.

I tried to meet him where he was, but the intensity he brought was nearly unmatchable. I slipped my hands beneath the edges of his jacket and pushed them toward his shoulders, but mine was already pooling in my elbows with his hands beneath my oversized top.

I loosened his tie and unbuttoned his shirt, but my leggings were already halfway down my thighs and my jacket abandoned on the floor, the edges of my top firmly in his hands as he lifted it up and over my head.

I tried for his belt, but my bra was gone, my brand new maternity underwear the only thing still clinging to my body in the right place.

He kissed my jaw, my neck, my collarbones for quick little stints, but he couldn't keep himself long from my mouth. I kicked off my shoes as he kissed me again, his hand knotting in my bun and gripping onto it, pulling down and forcing my chin up. His lips trailed down over my chin, down the front of my neck, savoring me, devouring me.

"Get these off," he mumbled against my skin as he

hooked his fingers on the seam of my underwear, "or so help me God, I will tear them off of you, love."

"But...you're basically still dressed..."

His hands grabbed for mine abruptly and moved them to the sides of the fabric along my hipbones, his teeth sinking in just slightly on the top of my breast in warning. "Off, Ava."

I swallowed and pushed them down my thighs, letting them fall between my ankles before kicking them off along with the pooled nylon of my leggings. The moment they were gone, his arms hooked underneath my rear, lifting me gently and forcing my thighs around his hips.

"How are your nipples?" he asked, his voice gruff as he spun us around and took the few steps into the kitchen.

"Sensitive." I exhaled a squeak as he gently lowered me the half an inch it took for the counter to absorb my weight. "But not painful."

"Thank God."

His mouth closed around my right nipple as he leaned me back on the counter, one hand gripped around my waist and the other on the higher kitchen island behind me for stability. Between us, my little bump protruded, and seeing him there with his body on mine and not a care in the world regarding my own changing my body made my chest ache in the best way imaginable.

But then his tongue slid across the erect little bud of my nipple, and every inch of my skin caught on fire.

The glide of his hand across my flesh, the way his clothed hips pressed into the center of me, the way his mouth caressed one of my most sensitive parts—he destroyed and rebuilt me, tempted and abated me.

Finally, I worked his jacket low enough that he removed it himself. I pulled the sides of his shirt out from where they'd been tucked into his slacks, forcing them off his shoulders until the fabric pooled in his bent elbows, his tie hanging limply around his neck. Every muscle in his chest flexed as he kept himself hovering above me, every ripple of his abdominals standing out, and good god, he looked like some kind of Greek statue, like Achilles himself.

His mouth left my nipple despite my little cries of protest. Instead, he kissed lower, his lips trailing across my stomach and kissing the taut skin. His hips pulled back, too far from my reach to be able to do anything more with his slacks, and I whined again in demand of their return—but he was still going lower, lower, lower, dropping to his knees in front of the cabinet beneath the counter, his teeth sinking in gently to the soft flesh of my inner thighs.

From my position, I could only just barely see his eyes over the bump as his mouth found its mark.

"Oh my God." I struggled to keep my composure and forced my head not to loll backward onto the island as his tongue lashed out at my clit. His finger teased at my entrance, just barely dipping in and pulling back out, the featherlight touches driving me mad—and I could see the little smirk reaching his eyes, could hear his breathy chuckle as I pleaded with him for more.

"Greedy," he mumbled, the little vibration of the word from his mouth making me see stars. "I haven't touched you in weeks, love. Forgive me for wanting to savor it in my own time."

My breath hitched at his words, the world around me narrowing to a single point of pure, unadulterated pleasure as at least two fingers slid inside of me to the hilt, stretching me perfectly.

"You're lucky that I'm feeling generous today."

He pulled me an inch closer to the edge of the counter

while his movements with his tongue abruptly turned punishing, overwhelming, gluttonous. He sucked at the swelling bud of nerve endings, his teeth dragging along the sides gently, his fingers curling up inside of me before slipping all the way out and back in again.

I couldn't think.

Couldn't breathe.

Couldn't feel anything but this.

My release hit me sharply and without warning, turning me into a twitching, whimpering, sensitive mess —but he didn't relent. For once, he dragged me further, not letting up in the slightest, the broadest smirk across his face as I begged for a second's repose.

"Please, Adrian, it's too much."

"You're clenching," he laughed, hot breath coating my inner thighs. "Come again, Ava, and I'll give you a second to breathe."

"Please," I cried, but he was right, it was building again, rapidly. I shoved my fingers into his hair, tightened my grip at the root. A third finger slipped into me, a fourth, and oh my God, I was going to die here, right here on my fucking countertop, with a painting of some stupid flowers that I wasn't even that proud of hanging in my peripheral vision.

"I bet I can break you," he grinned, his eyes flicking up to mine. "How many times can I make you come before you're begging me to stop, hmm? Should we find out?"

He was rushing me to another release so quickly I couldn't keep up. "I hate you," I said, half-laughed and half-sobbed, gritting my teeth through the sensitivity as I hovered right at the edge of the cliff.

"I love you, too."

I broke again, just barely processing the words he said as he finally let up enough for me to try and catch my breath.

With his fingers still inside of me, lazily drawing in and out, he rose on shaky knees and pressed his lips to mine, the taste of me mixing between us in the haze of the comedown.

My hands wandered down his chest, down to where his hips rested against my thighs. The rigidity against his zipper made me smile —he was rock solid beneath, straining so hard that I could feel the seams pulling beneath my fingertips. There was zero chance he was done with me.

"Unless you want me to fuck here on the counter," he started, lifting his lips just an inch from mine, "then I suggest you tell me where your bedroom is."

I gulped and worked at the button of his slacks, his undone belt clanking against my hand. "Through there," I said hoarsely, nodding to the little hallway that broke off from my living room on the left. "It's a mess."

"Don't give a shit," he laughed. "I'd take you on a pile of trash right now."

We were moving again in an instant, my legs locked around him and him taking my weight. I could feel his heartbeat, calm and sure, as I pressed my bare body into his chest. Skin against skin, I played with the hair at the nape of his neck, kissed his hardened jawline.

With expert precision, he dodged the handfuls of clothes I'd left strewn on the ground in my bedroom, not paying a lick of attention to the assortment of empty cups and dirty laundry, not caring at all about my unmade bed or the bundles of papers on one side of it. He set me down gently on the sheets as if I were something fragile, but from the look in his eye and the bulge of his trousers, I knew he'd see me as anything but fragile soon enough.

"On your knees, love, facing away from me," he ordered, pushing his zipper and slacks down in one movement. He breathed a sigh of relief as his cock finally felt freedom, jutting out toward me with bulging veins and a glistening tip. My mouth watered, but I followed his demands, rolling over onto my front and propping my rear up for him, legs spread just enough to give him access and keep my stomach off the bed. "Good fucking girl."

Before I could protest, he was stepping around the side of my bed, one hand pulling open the little chest of drawers I used as a nightstand.

"Adrian..."

"It'll help," he said, lifting out a long velvet bag and opening one end of it before putting it back. He checked another, and then another, discarding each one back into the drawer. "Don't tell me you don't have a standard vibrator, Ava."

I swallowed. "Second drawer, purple box."

He pulled it open and plucked the box out, popping the top off before grinning like a Cheshire cat. "Oh, I'll ruin you with this," he laughed, tossing the little black wand onto the bed near my head. "Should be easier for you to reach using that with the bump."

Adrian's fingers wrapped around the little remote and pulled it out of its case before putting everything else away.

"Go ahead, love," he smirked. "Let me watch you squirm."

My face warmed intensely as I grabbed for the vibrator and pulled it beneath my body, gulping as I put it in the spot that I liked.

A second later, it roared to life on one of the highest settings, catching me so off guard that I gasped and flinched away from it. He rounded me again and propped himself up on his knees on the bed behind me, one hand reaching between my legs and forcing me to put the toy back on my clit.

I couldn't breathe.

I was already so sensitive from the other orgasms he'd given me already. It felt like an assault on the senses as he held it there, switching between one level higher and one lower, the unpredictability of it scrambling my brain.

"Fuck, you're dripping all over my hand," he laughed, flashing me a grin as I glared at him over my shoulder. "Don't you dare take it off."

His hand left mine, moving instead to his length, wiping the mess I'd made along it. I struggled to keep myself relaxed as something warm and rigid and big pressed against my entrance, but the second he went up two levels with the remote, it was all I could focus on—and not him splitting me in two as he pushed in a couple of inches.

"That's it, love," he groaned, the fingers of his hand digging into the thick flesh of my rear. "Open up for me."

I tried to breathe through the sensations, tried to keep myself from clenching around him and truly feeling his size. Inch by slow inch, he sunk in, taking me over, filling me, destroying me, devouring me—and for once in all of this, I wasn't afraid of what it would do to me moving forward, wasn't afraid that I'd never be able to escape the dreams of him or the want. He was claiming me, and I was perfectly happy with that.

Even if he was overwhelming me while he did it.

His hips met mine, and I couldn't help but squeeze, feeling every inch of him inside of me.

"Christ," he breathed. "You're too much."

I didn't want to wait until he thought I was adjusted. I wanted more, now, before the vibrator sent me over the goddamn edge again. I rolled forward, pulling my hips from him, shuddering at the sensation as he slid along that spot inside of me that made me see stars.

"Where the fuck do you think you're going?"

Steady, stern hands gripped me by my hips, pulling me back with a force I couldn't imagine matching, and he slammed in to the hilt. I fisted the sheets, stifling the little squeal that tried to escape my mouth with them.

He laughed, but the sound was dark, deep enough to send a chill up my spine. "Maybe I'm being too generous to you," he rasped, and the vibration against my clit slowly turned down, down, down, down until it must have sat at the lowest possible setting—barely enough to feel it. "Use your words to ask for what you want, Ava, unless you want things taken away."

"No, no, please," I begged, damp fingers searching frantically for the little buttons on the silicone. "Please turn it back up. Please."

The vibrations increased by the smallest amount.

"Adrian."

"Ava," he chuckled. "Ask for what you really want. Beg me."

I gulped as his cock twitched inside of me. "Please fuck me," I whimpered. "Please, Adrian. Please."

The vibrations built up again at the same moment that he started to move properly, his hips pressing in against mine.

It was everything.

He dropped the remote to one side and slid his hands along my back, my sides, my rear, each skate of his hands feeling like little fires erupting on my skin. He gripped my shoulder, dug his fingers in, used it as leverage to lift my upper half up off the mattress, coaxed me back until I was leaning against him, my head against his shoulder.

He buried himself in me, over and over and over again.

He kissed my shoulder, my neck, my ear, anywhere he could reach.

He held me with one hand on my hips, guiding both of us back into each other each time we came apart, and one hand around my front, wrapped around my throat.

He squeezed, and my head felt dizzy but in a way that I was excited by, not anxious about.

"Every fucking time," he said against my ear, his voice hoarse, "it's like finding heaven."

Another release shook my body, and in the haze of it, in the chaos of how unbelievably good it felt, I dropped the vibrator. A second later, it was back on in his hand, significantly reduced power just pulling me through it instead of overstimulating me. He was right—I was getting to a breaking point, a point where I might have to beg for it to stop.

"One more," he breathed. "You can handle one more."

"I can't," I whined, hooking my hand on the back of his neck as he released mine. Blood flooded my head, and in the fog of the rush, I didn't notice the power rebuilding in that stupid bit of silicone, didn't notice how quickly it built up that tension again.

"Attagirl," he chuckled. His hips bucked against me, stuttering and desperate. "God, love, I'm close. Please, one more, one more."

There was no controlling it at that point. I couldn't have decided either way—my body had a mind of its own, and Adrian's groans and pleas only sent me further and further toward another one. The pressure in me built higher, and higher, and higher.

"Fuck, please, Ava. Need...need you..."

His body gave out at the same time as mine, warmth flooding me from the inside and dripping down onto my sheets. My body broke, convulsed, slammed back into the ground after what felt like a lifetime up in the sky. Pleasure bloomed in every vein, in every corner of my body, and it was too much, too perfect, too heavenly to ever try to capture in words, in paint, in images.

"Breathe, love," he croaked, shaking me gently as our bodies stilled against each other.

Shit. Yeah.

I caught my breath as he held me, sweat dripping between our bodies, his arms around my front. I couldn't think straight, couldn't form a coherent thought that wasn't implanted. This was everything I'd been missing for weeks, everything I'd wanted for years.

The words came out without me even having to choose them.

"I love you," I said. Outside the window, little specks of snow began to fall, glittering in the sun like tiny, weightless diamonds, sending little rays of light blinking into my room. I wanted to paint them still, and to my utter surprise, it felt like I could.

"I love you, too," he breathed, kissing my cheek. "I love you, too."

Chapter 40

Adrian

The saltwater sloshed against the side of the boat, rocking it gently and sending the first hints of cooler air over us.

Laid out on a recliner at the far end of the deck and blocking the last views of the sun dipping below the horizon, Ava rested with a book in her hand, the red of her hair blazing brightly from the last rays of sunlight. Her black bikini and a little sash that tied at her waist were all that covered her, but as the wind hit again, she reached absent-mindedly for the towel behind her, feeling blindly with her hand until she could pull it over herself, not wanting to tear her gaze from the book for a second.

It was adorable, really, how she found herself so intensely absorbed by the images in her mind as she read instead of the view beside us. Mountains sprouted where the land met both the Tyrrhenian Sea and the Gulf of Salerno, with colorful houses and buildings and roads built into the sides of it. Streetlamps kicked on one by one, lighting it beautifully—and yet, she stared at her book.

I leaned back against the worn teak of the sailboat's deck, the soft creak of wood beneath me blending with the quiet lapping of the waves against the hull and the soft cry from the other side of the deck.

"Lucas," I said quietly, leaning down to my left and stroking the top of his head to get his attention. He looked up at me, tearing his gaze from his handheld games console. "Can you check on the girls for me?"

"Sure," he grinned, setting his screen to one side and pushing off his chair. He'd had a growth spurt recently, and I tried not to let it bother me that my ten-year-old was almost as tall as my shoulders. He was only a handful of inches shorter than Ava now.

I watched him as he walked across the deck in his bright yellow life vest, sticking out like a sore thumb against the deep brown of the deck and the darkening blue water. He squatted down in front of their swings, distracting both of them enough to calm the little cries from Leah. Or Lucy. It was hard to tell from a distance.

Letting my gaze drift back over to Ava as the sun finally blinked out, I fully expected to find her either still engrossed in her book or watching Lucas and the girls. Instead, I found a set of green eyes looking directly at me.

Hey, I mouthed.

Hi, she grinned.

I nodded my head away from both of us as a quiet request for her to come to me, laughed as she threw her head back and groaned in counterfeit exhaustion. She pushed herself upright and wrapped the towel around her shoulders, walked right past Lucas and placed a little kiss on the top of his head, before finally padding across to me.

Her skin had turned sunkissed in the month we'd spent

traveling around Europe, her freckles bolder, her eyes brighter. She was fucking beautiful—in all honesty, she was probably the most beautiful thing I'd seen, outshining every coastline, every work of art in every museum, every setting or rising sun.

And she was mine.

"I was reading," she grumbled, leaning her weight into me as I took her face in my hand.

"You were. And then you were looking at me," I chuckled. "Is it so awful of me to want a minute with my wife?"

Long lashes fluttered up at me as she stuck her lower lip out. "Yes," she deadpanned. "Criminal behavior, if you ask me."

I snorted. "Lock me up then."

"Oh, I'll absolutely be reporting you to INTERPOL."

"And rip our children away from their father? Monstrous." I pressed my lips to her cheek, her jaw, the soft spot beneath her ear, letting my nose trail along her skin. "At least I'll have something pretty to play with if I'll be on the run."

"You're such an ass," she said, a breathy chuckle turning into a little gasp as the tip of my nose ghosted across the spot on her neck that made her shiver.

"I love you, too."

I pulled her in with a hand around her waist, pressing her flush against me. The wind kicked up again, carrying the scent of salt and citrus from the shore, a reminder of the lemon groves nestled in the cliffs above. The temperature was dropping, and soon, we'd need to move somewhere warmer, somewhere sunnier. But for the next week at least, the Amalfi Coast was warm enough during the day to keep us a little longer.

"Their birthday is next week," I said softly, dragging her attention back to my eyes as I lifted my head from the crook of her neck. I'd been meaning to discuss her plans when it came to birthday celebrations, but every time she'd managed to distract me, managed to wipe the thought from my mind.

Her expression flattened sarcastically. "I know that."

"Did you want to fly back home?" I offered, tucking a stray bit of hair behind her ear as the wind whipped. One of the twins cried out again, and Lucas's voice carried as he soothed them. "Your dad might want to see them."

Her lips formed a hard line, and I dragged my thumb along her cheek, trying to smooth out the muscles. She sighed. "Can I be honest for a minute?"

"Of course you can."

"Guys, I think Lucy is hungry," Lucas called, his head popping up on the other side of the deck. "Want me to feed them both?"

"Yes, please," we said in unison.

Lucas lifted a single hand with his thumb up as he descended into the interior of the boat.

"Right, honesty hour," I chuckled, drawing her attention back to me as she tried to crane her neck to watch Lucas disappear. "Go."

Her mouth scrunched up on one side while she tucked herself back into my chest. "Yeah, sorry," she sighed. "I... don't think I want to go back to New York anytime soon."

My brows knit together as I studied her expression, trying to pick it apart in my mind. I bumped her nose with mine. "Why? We can't keep Lucas out of school once summer is over."

She shrugged. "It's just nothing in comparison to all of this." She nodded her head toward the cliffs and villages behind us. "We could homeschool Lucas, at least for a little bit."

A creeping laughter crawled up my throat. "I'm sorry," I chuckled. "But you were just nose-deep in a book five minutes ago and not paying a single lick of attention to our surroundings."

Her eyes rolled dramatically. "You know what I mean."

I pressed a kiss against her lips. "I do," I whispered. "We can look at homeschooling Lucas."

The grin that spread across her cheeks was as wide as the cliffs behind us.

"But that still doesn't give me any idea what you want to do for their birthday," I teased, pressing in a little further, forcing her back to bend as I kissed her again, and again, and again. Her stoicism broke, little fits of giggles breaking free, and there she was, pretty in the twilight and the reflections of the streetlamps in the water, pretty in my arms.

"I'll call him," she said through her fits. "We can see if he wants to fly out, okay?"

"Would you be happy with that?"

"Yes," she beamed. "I'd be happy with anything other than going home just yet, as long as I've got you and Lucas and the girls. Honestly."

Behind her, the stars were just beginning to blink into view in the velvety hues of twilight, the light of them reflecting just barely off the mostly calm water beneath. She looked up at me, those same stars twinkling in her eyes, shimmering and magnificent, and a sense of pure calm washed over me as I pressed my mouth to hers again, lingering against her lips. Out here with her, with our kids, under the fading light of day and the emerging glow of night, everything felt right—like this was exactly where I belonged, where we belonged, and for once, there was nothing missing.

"I'm not going anywhere, Aves," I grinned. "You couldn't get rid of me if you tried."

THE END

.

Made in the USA
Middletown, DE
25 August 2025

13007642R00176